Falling for the Firefighter

Angel's Peak

Ellie Masters

Master of Romantic Suspense

JEM Publishing

Dedication

This book is dedicated to my one and only—my amazing and wonderful husband.

Without your care and support, my writing would not have made it this far.

You pushed me when I needed to be pushed.

You supported me when I felt discouraged.

You believed in me when I didn't believe in myself.

If it weren't for you, this book never would have come to life.

SUGGESTED READING ORDER

START HERE

Rockstar Romance

The Angel Fire Rock Romance Series

EACH BOOK IN THIS SERIES CAN BE READ AS A STANDALONE
AND IS ABOUT A DIFFERENT COUPLE WITH AN HEA.

IT IS RECOMMENDED THEY ARE READ IN ORDER.

Heart's Insanity

Ashes to New

Heart's Desire

Heart's Collide

Hearts Divided

Hearts Entwined

Forest's FALL

Hearts The Last Beat

CONTINUE HERE...

Military Romance

Guardian Hostage Rescue Specialists

Rescuing Melissa

(Get a FREE copy of Rescuing Melissa

when you join Ellie's Newsletter)

Alpha Team

Rescuing Zoe

Rescuing Moira

Rescuing Eve

Rescuing Lily

Rescuing Jinx

Rescuing Maria

Bravo Team

Rescuing Angie

Rescuing Isabelle

Rescuing Carmen

Rescuing Rosalie

Rescuing Kaye

Cara's Protector

Rescuing Barbi

Charlie Team

Rescuing Rebel

Rescuing Stitch

Rescuing Mia

Jenna's Protector

Rescuing Sophia

Rescuing Malia

Rescuing Ally (Part 1)

Rescuing Ally (Part 2)

Delta Team

Rescuing Ember

Rescuing Aria

STANDALONES IN THE GUARDIAN HOSTAGE RESCUE SERIES YOU CAN READ ANYTIME

Military Romance

Saving Ariel

Saving Brie

Saving Cate

Saving Dani

Saving Jen

The LaRouge Triplets

Asher

Brody

Cage

Billionaire Romance
Billionaire Boys Club

Hawke

Richard

Contemporary Romance

Cocky Captain

Romantic Suspense

EACH BOOK IS A STANDALONE NOVEL.

The Starling

The Swan

~AND~

Science Fiction

Ellie Masters writing as L.A. Warren

Vendel Rising: a Science Fiction Serialized Novel

If you enjoyed this book by Ellie Masters, the LIGHTER SIDE of the Jet & Ellie writing duo, and aren't afraid of edgier writing, you might enjoy reading BDSM themed books written by Jet, the DARKER SIDE of the Masters' Writing Team.

The DARKER SIDE

Jet Masters is the darker side of the Jet & Ellie writing duo!

Romantic Suspense

Changing Roles Series:

THIS SERIES MUST BE READ IN ORDER.

Command Me

Control Me

Collar Me

Embracing FATE

Seizing FATE

Accepting FATE

HOT READS

A STANDALONE NOVEL.

Down the Rabbit Hole

Light BDSM Romance

The Ties that Bind

EACH BOOK IN THIS SERIES CAN BE READ AS A STANDALONE AND IS ABOUT A DIFFERENT COUPLE WITH AN HEA.

Alexa

Penny

Michelle

Ivy

TO MY READERS

This book is a work of fiction. It does not exist in the real world and should not be construed as reality. As in most romantic fiction, I've taken liberties. I've compressed the romance into a sliver of time. I've allowed these characters to develop strong bonds of trust over a matter of days.

This does not happen in real life where you, my amazing readers, live. Take more time in your romance and learn who you're giving a piece of your heart to. I urge you to move with caution. Always protect yourself.

Angel's Peak

Grab the First Book in The Guardian Hostage Rescue Specialists Series for Free

https://elliemasters.com/RescuingMelissa

Angel's Peak

Chapter 1

Collision Course

My boots pound against the sidewalk as I clutch an unwieldy stack of topographical maps to my chest. Each step sends them sliding precariously in my arms, threatening to spill onto Angel's Peak's still-damp morning streets. The spring air carries the scent of pine and possibility, but all I can focus on is the impending disaster of keeping twenty out-of-state hotshot firefighters waiting.

Especially their captain.

Captain Sullivan. The infamous "Smokeshow Sullivan" according to Eleanor, who briefed me over drinks at The PickAxe last night. Apparently, he's some kind of wilderness firefighting legend from California with a chest full of medals and an ego to match. Eleanor's friend Ruth googled him after Sheriff Donovan mentioned his crew was coming—former military, spotless record, and, according to Ruth's enthusiastic phone screen display, "criminally good-looking."

Three local departments apparently got into a bidding war for his team's summer contract.

Just what we need—another hero type who thinks a few wildfires make him an expert on our mountains.

"Arrogant, know-it-all flatlanders," I mutter, dodging a woman with a stroller outside the general store. "Coming in here thinking their fancy GPS systems can replace actual knowledge of the terrain."

Scout trots beside me, her German Shepherd alertness taking in everything while somehow managing to look judgmental about my tardiness. She gave me that same look when I overslept, as if she's been punctual her entire life and couldn't understand humans who weren't.

"Don't start with me," I tell her. "You're the one who chewed my alarm clock last month."

The maps shift dangerously in my grip. I stayed up until three in the morning updating trail markings and evacuation routes, determined to prove that my hand-drawn maps show details no satellite imagery could capture.

The morning fog obscured the sunrise I counted on to wake me, and now I'm paying the price.

I round the corner near Maggie's Diner, picking up speed. The scent of fresh coffee and huckleberry pancakes wafts through the air, making my empty stomach clench. No time for breakfast when you've overslept by forty-five minutes.

My phone buzzes in my pocket. Again. Probably Sheriff Donovan wondering where the hell I am with the emergency evacuation routes. I quicken my pace, mentally rehearsing my opening remarks to the visiting fire crew.

Welcome to Angel's Peak. I'm Josephine Mackenzie, wilderness safety coordinator. These maps detail...

Scout suddenly veers left, distracted by something I don't see. I'm too focused on my destination to correct her.

One second I'm rushing forward, the next I'm slammed backward by what feels like a brick wall with a heartbeat. My maps explode into the air like startled birds, fluttering down around me as I land hard on my back, the breath knocked completely from my lungs.

Hot liquid splashes across my chest and onto my precious maps. Coffee. The rich aroma mingles with something else—cedar, smoke, and warm male skin. My body registers the scent before my brain does, sending an unwelcome jolt of awareness through me.

For a moment, I can only stare up at the impossibly blue Colorado sky, stunned.

Then my vision fills with eyes nearly the same shade—piercing, intense, framed by dark lashes and even darker brows. A face hovers above mine, all sharp angles and strong lines. Devastatingly handsome in a rough-hewn way that has no business existing outside of ridiculous romance novels.

The man's body is half-sprawled over mine, one muscled thigh shoved between my legs, his broad chest inches from my face.

"Are you okay?" The voice matches the face—deep, authoritative, with a hint of gravel that scrapes along my nerve endings like a physical touch.

Reality crashes back. I'm flat on my back in the middle of Angel's Peak, my carefully crafted maps scattered like confetti, and some... some *tourist* is practically on top of me. And my body—traitor that it is—notices exactly how he feels against me before my mind catches up.

"Do I look okay?" I push against his chest, the solid wall of muscle beneath my palms sends another unwanted spark through my fingers. "Get off of me."

He shifts back immediately, but the movement drags his leg against mine, creating friction that makes my breath catch.

He notices—of course, he notices—a flicker of something hot and dangerous passing through those blue eyes.

I scramble backward, putting space between us as I push myself to my knees. Coffee drips from my shirt, the once-white fabric now clinging to my skin in a way that draws his eyes before he deliberately looks away.

I look in horror at the nearest map—my detailed rendering of Lookout Point Trail with all its hidden switchbacks and seasonal water sources. The coffee seeps into the paper, turning the blue waterproof ink into a muddy smear. Months of fieldwork are ruined.

"I apologize." He extends a hand. "Let me help you up."

I ignore his offer, rising on my own. "Great. Just great." I survey the disaster around us—maps scattered in a fifteen-foot radius, most damp with coffee, others being stepped on by curious onlookers. "Do you have any idea what you just did? I'm already late for a briefing, and now I have all these ruined maps—"

"I said I was sorry." His tone shifts slightly, a spark of amusement lighting his blue eyes as he tracks my agitated movements. "Though you were running full-speed around a blind corner."

He crouches down and collects the nearest maps, the movement pulling his shirt taut across broad shoulders. The fabric stretches over chiseled muscle as he reaches for a paper that's skittered beneath a bench. I force my eyes away, furious at myself for noticing.

"I know Angel's Peak like the back of my hand," I snap, dropping to my knees to rescue a map from a puddle. "I don't need to slow down on my own streets."

We reach for the same map simultaneously, fingers colliding. The contact sends electricity racing up my arm, and I jerk back as if burned. His eyes snap to mine, pupils dilating slightly.

He felt it too.

"Clearly." A smile tugs at the corner of his mouth as he examines one of my maps, the curve of his lips unfairly distracting. "Did you draw these yourself?"

The question catches me off guard. Most people don't notice the difference between my hand-drawn maps and mass-produced ones.

"Yes." I straighten a bit, despite myself. "I update them seasonally."

He studies the map with interest, strong fingers tracing the detailed contour lines of Widow's Peak. I shouldn't be watching his hands. Shouldn't be imagining how those fingers would feel tracing other curves.

"These are incredible. The detail is remarkable." His voice has dropped lower, almost intimate, as though we're having an entirely different conversation.

Something warm coils in my stomach at the appreciation in his tone, but I quickly squash it. I don't have time for flattery from handsome strangers, especially ones who've just knocked me on my ass and ruined my work.

"They'd be more impressive if they weren't scattered across the sidewalk." I snatch the map from his hands, our fingers brushing again. This time, the contact lingers for a heartbeat longer than necessary.

Our eyes lock, something electric and dangerous crackling in the air between us. The noise of the street fades as we stare at each other, neither willing to break the connection first.

Scout chooses that moment to bound between us, her muddy paws landing directly on the one map that somehow remained pristine throughout the collision.

"Scout! Off!" I yelp, but the damage is done. Paw prints now mark the trail to Angel Falls.

Instead of staying loyally by my side, my traitorous

German Shepherd immediately approaches the stranger, tail wagging as she nudges his hand with her nose.

"Good morning to you, too." He crouches, rubbing Scout's ears. My dog, who normally growls at strange men, melts under his touch, pressing against his leg like they're long-lost friends. "What's your name, beautiful?"

His voice on the word "beautiful" sends an unwelcome shiver down my spine.

"Scout." The word comes out huskier than I intend. I clear my throat. "And she's supposed to be guarding me, not fraternizing with the enemy."

"Is that what I am? The enemy?" His eyes meet mine over Scout's head, something dangerous and thrilling dancing in their depths. The question feels weighted with meaning beyond our sidewalk collision.

"You're a walking disaster who's making me even later than I already was." I stuff the maps back into some semblance of order, painfully aware of his gaze tracking my movements. "And now I have to present these ruined maps to... oh, never mind."

His eyes travel slowly up my body, lingering on the coffee stain spread across my chest before meeting my eyes. Heat blooms beneath my skin at his appraisal.

"These maps show exceptional skill, even with the... impromptu coffee staining." The pause before his last words suggests he might be talking about something else entirely.

I'm saved from responding by Scout's sudden alertness. Her ears perk forward, attention caught by something across the street. A squirrel, probably. At least she's remembering her job.

"I need to go." I clutch my reassembled stack of maps tighter, the warped paper crinkling under my grip. They're a mess now—soaked, smudged, months of work ruined in an instant. My jaw aches from clenching it. "Some of us have work to do."

He nods, stepping back just enough to give me space, though his eyes linger like he's not quite finished. "Can you point me toward the visitor center? I'm looking for information on local trail conditions."

God, he's got nerve. Strolls into town, wrecks my morning, then wants directions like I'm just another friendly local guide. My lips curve, but it's not a smile.

"Two blocks down, then take a left at the aspen grove. Can't miss it."

He will. It's the wrong direction—completely wrong. But let him wander in circles for a bit. Call it a teachable moment.

"And ask for Jo." I tilt my head, adding that final dig with sugar-laced precision. "They'll help you."

I'm Jo, and I'm definitely not helping him.

Something flickers in his expression—amusement? Recognition? But I'm already turning away, whistling for Scout to follow. I don't have time to play tour guide to attractive strangers, no matter how nicely they handle my maps or how betrayingly my dog responds to them.

Or how my body hums with awareness even as I walk away.

Ten minutes later, I push through the visitor center doors, flustered and frazzled. My maps are a disaster—coffee-stained, wrinkled, and in Scout's case, muddy paw-printed. My white shirt now features an impressive coffee tie-dye pattern that no amount of dabbing with paper towels can fix. Sheriff Donovan stands near the large central table, looking pointedly at his watch.

"Sorry I'm late," I mutter, arranging my maps on the conference table. "Had a collision with a tourist."

Eleanor Morgan, Hunter's grandmother and the town's unofficial matriarch, eyes me with knowing amusement. The morning light catches in her crown of silver braids as she pours coffee into mugs for the waiting hot-shot crew.

"Must have been some tourist to get you this flustered, Josephine," she observes, pushing a steaming mug in my direction. "Your cheeks are positively glowing."

I ignore the comment, focusing instead on arranging my materials. "Where's the hotshot crew? I thought they were supposed to be here at nine."

Sheriff Donovan checks his watch again. "Captain Sullivan should be here any—"

The door swings open behind me, and the temperature in the room seems to spike ten degrees.

"Apologies for my tardiness. Had a bit of trouble finding the place."

That voice—low, gravel-edged—sends liquid heat sliding straight down my spine. I turn slowly, already knowing.

Blue eyes lock on mine, recognition sparking like dry kindling. The room contracts, the air too thick to breathe.

It's him.

The sidewalk menace.

The map-wrecker.

The man I sent on a wild goose chase.

Only now he's in full uniform—flame-resistant yellow shirt rolled to the elbows, green tactical pants slung low on lean hips, and captain's bars gleaming at his collar like they own the damn room. The wet cotton and mischief from earlier have been replaced by dangerous control.

Authority.

Fire.

So much for him being a tourist.

My stomach plummets somewhere south of reason, taking several vital organs with it, as he steps forward with slow, deliberate confidence, extending his hand like this is a formal introduction and not the start of a war.

Captain Sullivan.

His lips curve into a slow smile that promises retribution as he steps forward, extending his hand formally.

"Captain Marcus Sullivan." His voice carries through the room, but his eyes never leave mine. "Everyone calls me Mac. Sorry I'm late. Took the scenic route," he murmurs, stepping closer. "Got turned around near a gorgeous little aspen grove. Sunlight streaming through the leaves, wind whispering through the branches..." His smile curves, slow and deliberate, like he knows exactly what he's doing. "Almost made me forget I was looking for someone."

His gaze drops to my mouth, lingers.

"Asked for Jo." The way he says it —low and loaded — sends a lick of heat straight through me. He leans in and whispers. "Fair warning..." His voice lowers to a dangerous purr, meant only for me. "I like the chase. You should know that upfront."

My fingers close around his reflexively. The moment our skin connects, that same electric current zings between us, stronger now, impossible to ignore.

His grip is firm, warm, and entirely too intentional. His thumb brushes over my pulse point, a deliberate caress that makes my breath catch.

He notices. Of course, he notices.

His pupils dilate as he holds my hand a heartbeat too long.

"Had to change after a little weather surprise. Got caught in a downpour. Soaked through." He lets the words linger, rich with implication. "Lucky I packed a spare set in the truck. Always prepared."

Scout, traitorous bastard, bounds over like Mac hung the damn moon. She presses against his legs and looks up at him adoringly.

Well, this should be interesting.

"Looking forward to working closely with you on those

evacuation routes, Ms. Mackenzie." His voice turns silk-edged steel, the emphasis on closely dragging heat through my veins. "And don't worry—I'm very good at navigating... even when someone intentionally sends me off-course."

He releases my hand, long after it's appropriate, but the damage is done. This is going to be a very long and perilous fire season... for me.

And he just struck the match.

Angel's Peak

Chapter 2

Professional Tension

I square my shoulders and force a neutral expression onto my face. The heat in my cheeks refuses to subside, along with the lingering awareness of how his hands felt gripping my arms during our collision. Every nerve ending in my body remains traitorously alert, as if he's still touching me.

"Let's begin the briefing, shall we?" I retrieve a fresh stack of maps from my bag—thank god I always bring backups—and spread them across the conference table. "I've prepared detailed evacuation routes for each sector of our jurisdiction."

Mac leans casually against the wall. Like he's got all the time in the world. He doesn't move, but his eyes never leave me, tracking every shift in my body like he's already memorized the way I breathe.

The lazy curve of his smile deepens as the door swings open behind me and his team filters in, boots scuffing, laughter low and familiar.

They enter in a loose, confident wave—nineteen men and women in flame-resistant yellow shirts and green tactical pants, exuding calm authority and casual competence. They fill the room with the controlled chaos of seasoned professionals, peeling off in small clusters, claiming wall space, or leaning against the edges of the table.

Mac doesn't sit. He remains standing. The position pulls his uniform taut across his shoulders, revealing the contours of muscle beneath. That infuriating half-smile plays at the corner of his mouth, promising trouble.

He watches me. Not the maps. Not the sheriff. Not his team.

Just me.

His gaze drags over my body like a slow touch, unapologetically focused. My coffee-stained shirt is dry now, but the pattern clings in a way that feels too revealing. I resist the urge to cross my arms or tug at the fabric.

Professional. Stay professional.

Sheriff Donovan clears his throat. "Captain Sullivan, would you like to introduce your team?"

"Of course." Mac straightens, the movement fluid and dangerous, like a panther unfolding just before a kill. My eyes betray me, following the way his uniform shifts with every subtle stretch of muscle.

He gestures toward the firefighters now settled in around the room. "Angel's Peak, meet California Hotshot Crew 37."

They nod, expressionless but alert, taking in every detail with the silent focus of people used to crisis. I catch a few raised eyebrows aimed at my coffee-stained shirt.

"Rodriguez, Martinez, Burke." Mac gestures to three firefighters near the windows. "Best sawyers in the business. Sanders, Williams, Nguyen—our medical specialists."

His voice fills the room, deep and assured, commanding

without trying. And I hate how much I feel it—low and warm, curling under my skin like smoke. Like it could wrap around my spine and tug.

I imagine that voice against my ear, darker now, whispering orders I'd actually obey. My skin flushes traitorously at the thought, heat pooling low, sharp, and aching.

No. Don't go there, Jo. Stay professional.

He continues through the crew, each name paired with a nod and their role in the team. They move with the instinctive rhythm of people who've faced down hell and walked out breathing.

"And Sergeant Parker." He gestures toward a tall woman with a silver braid and a sharp, knowing gaze. "My second-in-command and the person who keeps all of us alive when we're too stubborn to do it ourselves."

"Someone has to." Parker's weathered face cracks into a brief smile, her knowing eyes drifting between Mac and me. "Especially this one." Her gaze flicks from Mac to me, then back again, full of private amusement and something unspoken, like she's figured out a storm is brewing.

The tension in the room shifts—still professional, still contained—but there's a current now, undeniable and charged.

And Mac?

He's at the center of it.

Still watching me like I'm the next challenge he intends to conquer—the next mountain to chase down and claim.

I see the threat in his eyes.

The promise.

He likes the hunt? The chase?

Isn't that what he said?

The slow unraveling of resistance until there's nowhere left to run. Maybe that's why I hate him so much—because some cruel, secret part of me wants to be caught.

Wants to be dragged down, pinned beneath him, and forced to admit I care. That I feel every look, every word, every subtle threat he layers with a smile.

Okay, where the hell did that come from?

Let him blow off this mountain for all I care. Let him vanish into the smoke. I dismiss him with a shake of my head, then turn my attention to his team.

"Welcome to Angel's Peak." I gesture toward my maps, determined to regain control of the room. "I'm Josephine Mackenzie, wilderness safety coordinator. I'll be your primary local resource for terrain navigation and evacuation planning."

"Jo?" Mac's eyebrow quirks upward, my name on his lips a deliberate provocation. The room temperature rises several degrees. "You're Jo?"

"That's what I said."

He gives me a look—slow, dangerous. Like a predator recognizing its prey. His smile sharpens, dark amusement flickering beneath the surface.

His gaze holds mine, heat and promise simmering behind the professionalism. The warning is silent but unmistakable: Retribution is coming, and he's going to enjoy every second of it.

The crew exchanges glances, and I catch a few smirks.

Great. He's already talked about our collision. About how I sent him in circles.

"As I was saying," I continue firmly, "Angel's Peak presents unique firefighting challenges due to our elevation, complex wind patterns, and microclimate variations."

I launch into my briefing, pointing out key features on the maps—the ridge lines where downdrafts can suddenly change a fire's direction, the hidden springs that provide emergency water sources, the narrow game trails that can serve as escape routes when main paths are compromised.

To my surprise, the crew leans in with genuine interest. A

lanky firefighter—Ramirez—whistles softly at my detailed rendering of Widow's Peak.

"This is incredible detail. You've hiked all these areas personally?"

"Every inch." I tap the north ridge section, aware of Mac watching my hands, my face, and my mouth as I speak. "Twice yearly at minimum. Conditions change constantly in the high country."

"What about satellite imaging?" Mac pushes off the wall and approaches the table, his stride confident, predatory. The room seems to shrink with each step he takes. "Our tech team uses GPS overlays accurate to within three feet."

The challenge in his voice is unmistakable, as is the glint in his eyes. This isn't about maps. This is about territory—his versus mine, technology versus tradition.

"GPS can't tell you which trails will wash out after the spring thaw." I meet his gaze directly, refusing to be intimidated by his proximity as he stops across the table. "It can't identify which rock faces become unstable during August thunderstorms, and it certainly can't mark the seasonal water sources that don't appear on any official survey."

"Technology adapts. Updates happen hourly now." Mac leans over the table, bracing his weight on his palms. The position brings his face closer to mine, close enough that I can smell coffee and mint on his breath. "The margin for error decreases with each satellite pass."

"Unless those satellites are blinded by tree cover or confused by rock formations." I don't back away, even as my body responds to his nearness—pulse quickening, skin warming. "When was the last time your GPS warned you about the false ridge on Lookout Trail that's collapsed three hikers to their deaths?"

The crew's heads swivel between us like they're watching a tennis match. Mac's eyes darken, pupils expanding as our verbal sparring intensifies. I realize, too late, we're giving them quite a show.

"You're suggesting we disregard standard operational protocols in favor of—" he taps my hand-drawn map, his finger deliberately brushing against mine in a touch that lingers a beat too long, "—artistic interpretations?"

The simple contact sends an electric current up my arm. His eyes confirm he felt it too, and did it on purpose.

"I'm suggesting your protocols are designed for California chaparral, not Colorado alpine wilderness." I resist the urge to pull my hand away, refusing to give him the satisfaction. "And there's nothing artistic about accurate terrain mapping."

A firefighter with a buzz cut—Martinez?—chuckles. "She's got you there, Cap."

Mac shoots him a look that would wither a lesser man, but Martinez just grins wider.

"Told you she'd be a match for you," he mutters, just loud enough for me to hear.

My cheeks burn at the implication. Mac ignores the comment, but his jaw tightens.

"Ms. Mackenzie clearly knows her territory," Parker interjects, studying my maps with a professional eye that doesn't quite hide her amusement at our exchange. "Perhaps a practical demonstration would settle this debate?"

"Excellent idea." I flip to my map of Angel Creek Basin, grateful for the diversion. "See this tributary here? Your GPS will show it flowing northwest. Every official survey for the past eighty years shows the same thing."

I trace the blue line with my finger, hyperaware of Mac leaning closer. His presence at my side radiates heat that seems to seep through my clothes.

"But three years ago, a rockslide altered its course. It now flows northeast, creating a seasonal marsh here—" I tap the location, our shoulders nearly touching, "—that becomes impassable during spring runoff. It's not on any official map, but it could trap your crew if you relied solely on satellite data."

Mac studies the map, his brow furrowed. He's close enough that I could count his eyelashes if I were so inclined. Which I'm not. Obviously.

The silence stretches for five heartbeats before he straightens, his arm brushing mine in a touch that feels deliberate.

"Impressive." His tone remains neutral, but something in his eyes has changed. "Any other examples?"

"Dozens." I flip to another map, ignoring the pleased flutter in my stomach at having scored a point. "The old mining road on the west face. Satellite shows it as a viable access route, but the middle section collapsed last winter. Or the cave system near Thunder Ridge that provides emergency shelter during lightning storms."

With each example, Mac's team leans closer, their initial skepticism morphing into genuine interest. Rodriguez and Burke exchange looks, clearly reassessing their assumptions. Parker takes notes on a small pad, occasionally nodding.

"Your thoroughness is commendable." Mac's admission comes reluctantly, but his eyes never leave my maps—or is it me he's studying? "Though I maintain that a combination of technologies provides optimal safety."

"I never suggested abandoning technology." I cross my arms, mirroring his earlier stance. The movement pulls my coffee-stained shirt across my chest, drawing his gaze momentarily before he deliberately looks back at my face. "Just supplementing it with actual knowledge of the terrain."

Parker checks her watch. "Time for the morning check-in with base. Coffee break for fifteen?"

Mac nods, and the crew files out, not even attempting to hide their knowing glances and whispered comments. Only then do I realize how Mac and I have been leaning toward each other, barely six inches separating our faces.

I step back, my body oddly reluctant to break the connection. "That went well."

"Did it?" His voice holds a note of amusement. "I'd say it's just getting started."

I busy myself with reorganizing maps, struggling to regain my professional composure. "Your team seems competent."

"High praise indeed." He doesn't move from his position, watching me with unwavering attention. "Are you always this passionate about cartography, Mackenzie?"

"I'm passionate about keeping people alive." I don't look up, afraid of what he might see in my eyes. "These mountains don't forgive mistakes."

"That sounds like experience talking."

The unexpected gentleness in his voice makes me glance up. His expression has softened; the challenge replaced by something more complex. For a moment, we're just two people, the charged atmosphere between us settling into something almost comfortable.

Before I can respond, the door swings open and Scout bounds in, muddy paws leaving prints across the polished floor. She heads straight for Mac, completely bypassing me, and sits expectantly at his feet.

"Traitor," I mutter.

Mac crouches, scratching behind Scout's ears. The position brings his face level with my hips. I step to the side, disturbed by how my body responds to the proximity.

"Smart girl knows quality when she sees it." He looks up at me from his crouched position, a view that sends inappropriate heat coursing through me.

"What did you feed her when I wasn't looking?"

"Nothing yet." He straightens in one fluid motion, bringing him closer than before. The morning light catches the gold flecks in his blue eyes as he grins down at me. "I keep beef jerky in my pocket for emergencies."

"Firefighting emergencies or dog-bribing emergencies?"

"Same thing." He doesn't step back, forcing me to tilt my head to maintain eye contact. Scout remains pressed against his leg, the canine equivalent of taking sides. "These evacuation routes—I'd like to walk them personally."

The casual request carries weight. Fire captains typically delegate such tasks to their team. The implication hangs in the air between us—hours alone together on remote mountain trails.

"You don't trust my maps?" I raise an eyebrow, attempting nonchalance despite the sudden acceleration of my pulse.

"I trust verification." His expression turns serious, though his eyes still hold that dangerous spark. "If we need these routes in an emergency, I want them imprinted in my memory, not just on paper."

The logic is sound, but something tells me there's more to this request. Still, I can't refuse—not without seeming unprofessional or, worse, afraid of spending time alone with him.

"Fine." I close my map case with more force than necessary. "It'll take several days to cover the primary routes."

"I've got time." His voice drops lower, vibrating through the small space between us. "Unless you're too busy giving tourists creative directions around town?"

Heat flares in my cheeks at the reminder. "I can make room in my schedule."

"Good." The challenge returns to his eyes as he leans closer, close enough that I can feel his breath on my face. "I find hands-on experience far more educational than theoretical discussions."

The double entendre hangs in the air between us, impossible to ignore. I should be offended. Instead, something electric and dangerous sparks in my chest.

"Seven routes, Captain Sullivan." I refuse to step back, though every survival instinct screams at me to create distance. "Hope your hiking boots are broken in."

"Worried about keeping up with me, Mackenzie?" The question carries layers of meaning, none of them about hiking.

"Worried about having to carry you back down the mountain when your California lungs can't handle our altitude. And my name is Jo."

He laughs—a genuine sound that crinkles the corners of his eyes and vibrates through the air between us, somehow more intimate than his earlier provocations.

"Fair warning, *Mackenzie*..." He deliberately refuses to use my name. "I've summited Denali. Twice." His eyes track over my face, lingering on my mouth before returning to my eyes. "I have excellent... endurance."

Of course he does.

The crew filters back in, carrying coffee cups and pastry bags from Maggie's. They distribute them with the efficiency of people accustomed to sharing resources, and I'm surprised when Rodriguez hands me a steaming cup.

"Two sugars, no cream—right? Sheriff mentioned that's how you take it."

"Thanks." I accept the unexpected kindness, noticing several crew members watching the exchange with poorly disguised interest.

"So, Cap," Burke calls across the room, "Ms. Mackenzie convinced you about those trail markers yet?"

Mac takes a sip of his coffee, eyes never leaving mine over the rim of his cup. "We're still in negotiations."

"Negotiations, huh?" Martinez exchanges looks with Parker. "That's what they're calling it these days?"

A ripple of laughter moves through the crew. Mac silences it with a look, but not before I catch his own suppressed smile.

"Ms. Mackenzie has agreed to guide me through the evacuation routes personally," he announces, voice professional despite the speculation dancing in his eyes. "We'll verify the viability of each one."

"All seven routes?" Parker raises an eyebrow, her tone suggesting she understands exactly what's happening. "That's at least three days of hiking. Alone. In remote terrain."

"Thorough verification is essential for safety." Mac's tone doesn't invite further comment, but several crew members exchange knowing glances.

I focus on my coffee, pretending not to notice the undercurrents. Scout, still plastered to Mac's side, pants happily as if she's orchestrated this entire situation.

The rest of the briefing proceeds with professional focus, though I catch occasional smirks whenever Mac and I disagree, which is often. By noon, we've covered the immediate action plan for fire season preparation, and the crew disperses for equipment checks.

Mac stays behind, studying my map of Lookout Point Trail—the same one his coffee decorated earlier. He leans over it, strong fingers tracing the contours I've drawn with such care. The sight of his hands moving over my work sends an unwelcome shiver down my spine.

"This path here." He traces a thin red line I've marked, the pad of his finger dragging slowly across the paper like it's my skin. "It's not on any official trail map."

"Local knowledge." I step in beside him, closer than I should, but not close enough to flinch. The heat of his body rolls off him like sunbaked rock, all danger and gravity. I point to the junction, refusing to retreat. "It's a game trail. Links up to the main evac route. Saves twenty minutes."

His eyes never leave the map, but I feel the weight of him shift—attention sharpening, focus zeroing in. "Show me tomorrow."

"I need to mark the northern sector first—"

"And I need to know the most complicated terrain first-hand." His voice drops, firm and final.

When he turns toward me, it's a calculated move that closes the space between us. We're chest to chest. Breath to breath. His body doesn't touch mine, but it threatens to.

"Lookout Point sees the most foot traffic." He's close enough that I can feel his breath on my cheek. "If we're evacuating tourists, I want my boots on that trail."

He's not wrong. Doesn't mean I have to like it.

"Fine." I snap the map case closed and tuck it under my arm. "Meet me at the visitor center. 0800."

"I'll pick you up." He says it as if it's not a suggestion, but an order. He straightens, gathering his notes. His fingers brush mine as he takes a map I'm holding, the touch deliberate. "Where do you live?"

"That's not necessary." My voice tightens. Too breathy. Too revealing.

His gaze pins me, the corner of his mouth crooking with challenge. "One vehicle's more efficient, Mackenzie." Again with the name. His pupils darken, swallowing the blue. As for my name, he says it slow—drawling my last name like it's something he plans to sink his teeth into. "Unless you're uncomfortable being alone with me."

He's baiting me. Testing. Circling the perimeter of some invisible line I'm too stubborn to draw.

The unspoken dare slices through me like a live wire.

"I'm not uncomfortable," I bite out. "And my name is Jo."

The challenge hangs between us—professional on the surface, something else entirely underneath.

He takes a map from my hands, fingers brushing deliberately over mine. Slow. Possessive.

"Mackenzie," he repeats, soft but loaded. "You sent me on a wild goose chase this morning. Told me to ask for Jo, like some joke." His grin turns predatory. "I hope you're done with such antics."

He steps closer, close enough that I can feel the promise of what he isn't touching. The pressure of withheld contact. My body buzzes with the nearness of him, with the way his voice curls into places it doesn't belong.

"You want to lead me in circles, Mackenzie?" His voice is all smoke and heat. "Go ahead. But remember..." His breath grazes my ear. "I like the chase."

The words strike like a flint spark, igniting something reckless and hot beneath my ribs. I should walk away. I should remind him—and myself—that this is business.

There are boundaries. Structure.

Instead, I stare him down. "It's the cabin at the end of Spruce Lane."

He leans back enough to meet my eyes, satisfaction gleaming. "Sending me on another scenic route?"

"No." I meet his gaze steadily, refusing to back down. "That's where I live, but I'll drive."

"No. I'll pick you up." He moves like a man staking a claim. "And I'll drive. You don't set the pace here, Mackenzie. Not with me."

"I'm perfectly capable of driving myself and meeting you at the visitor center."

"I'll be at your place at 0800 hours. Don't keep me waiting." His proximity makes the simple statement feel like something else entirely.

My breath stutters. My pulse hammers. He's too close again, the air between us thick with challenge and something darker.

The intensity in his blue eyes suggests tomorrow will be about more than just verifying trails. Every nerve ending in my body lights up in anticipation and warning.

I should say no, and insist on meeting at the visitor center, surrounded by other people. I should create professional distance before this... whatever this is... escalates further.

"Don't be late," I say instead.

His grin turns slow and lethal while something ignites deep and dangerous in my chest, a slow-burning fuse leading to inevitable explosion.

"Wouldn't dream of it, *Mackenzie*." He reaches for a map I'm holding, fingers brushing mine—purposeful, possessive.

Angel's Peak

CHAPTER 3

INTO THE FIRE

IT'S THREE IN THE MORNING, AND I'M STARING AT MY cabin ceiling, watching moonlight cast pine-branch shadows across the wood beams.

Sleep refuses to come. Every time I close my eyes, I see Mac's face—that infuriating half-smile, the challenge in his blue eyes, the way he leaned over my maps like he was studying more than just terrain features.

"It's purely professional," I tell the empty room. "A simple trail verification with a visiting fire captain."

Scout lifts her head from her bed in the corner, her expression calling bullshit.

"Don't look at me like that." I roll onto my side, punching my pillow into submission. "You're the one who keeps abandoning me for him."

Her tail thumps against the floor once before she settles back down.

Professional. That's all this is. I'm simply showing evacuation routes to a firefighter who needs local knowledge. The fact that my skin buzzes whenever he stands too close is irrelevant.

By the time pink streaks appear on the horizon, I've convinced myself this day will be strictly business.

That conviction lasts until I stand before my closet at seven, agonizing over what to wear, as if it's a date instead of a work obligation.

"Ridiculous." I yank out my standard hiking gear—performance pants, a moisture-wicking Henley, and a lightweight jacket.

I swap the Henley for one that brings out the color of my eyes, then change back, disgusted with myself.

Scout watches from the doorway, head tilted.

"What?" I glare at her. "The blue one breathes better."

She blinks slowly, unconvinced.

"Fine." I grab my hair, twisting it into a practical braid instead of the loose waves I'd considered. "Better?"

Scout yawns dramatically.

"Some help you are." I lace my hiking boots with unnecessary force. "You'd probably suggest I wear a cocktail dress if it meant your new best friend would be impressed."

The knock at my door comes at exactly eight. Of course, he's punctual.

I open the door to find Mac in hiking gear that looks custom-tailored to his broad shoulders and narrow waist. His dark hair is slightly damp, curling at the edges like he just showered. The morning light catches the stubble along his jaw, highlighting cheekbones that belong on a sculptor's model rather than a firefighter.

This is going to be a long day.

"Morning, Mackenzie." He hands me a coffee cup, steam rising from the lid. "Two sugars, no cream."

"How did you—"

"Rodriguez mentioned it yesterday." He shrugs. "I've got a good memory for details."

Scout pushes past me to greet Mac, practically dancing with excitement.

"And good morning to you, too, girl." He crouches, rubbing her ears while she melts under his attention. "Ready for a hike?"

"She's supposed to be a working dog." I take a sip of coffee—perfect temperature, exactly how I like it. "Not a groupie."

"Dogs have excellent judgment." He straightens, taking in my cabin with curious eyes. "Nice place."

"Thanks." I grab my pack and map case, stepping onto the porch rather than inviting him inside. "We should get moving if we want to cover Lookout Point before the afternoon."

He follows me to his Forest Service-issued SUV, opening the back for Scout, who jumps in like she's been riding with him for years.

"Traitor," I mutter under my breath.

Mac's lips twitch. "Heard that."

The drive to the trailhead passes in silence, but it's not uncomfortable. Mac handles the mountain roads with easy confidence, one hand resting loosely on the wheel, the other cradling his coffee. I focus on the passing scenery rather than the way his forearm flexes with each turn.

At the trailhead, we synchronize our radios and check our packs. Mac's movements are efficient—a man who's done this hundreds of times. Scout circles us impatiently, eager to hit the trail.

"Lead the way." Mac gestures forward. "I'm here to learn."

The morning air carries the scent of pine and wildflowers as we start up the trail. I keep a deliberate three feet between us, pointing out features and trail markers. Mac asks intelligent questions, jotting down notes in a small, waterproof notebook.

"So this junction here." I stop where the main trail splits. "Official maps show both paths reconnecting a mile ahead."

Mac consults his GPS. "That's what the satellite data shows."

"Except this route—" I point to the right fork, "—washed out last spring. There's a fifteen-foot drop-off around that bend now."

"No warning signs posted." His brow furrows.

"Park service budget cuts." I shrug. "I've submitted the paperwork three times. Meanwhile, I update my maps and warn visitors at the center."

He crouches, studying the ground. "No obvious indications of danger."

"That's the problem with these mountains. They don't advertise their hazards." I move forward, leading him down the left fork. "Three tourists had to be rescued here last month. One with a broken ankle."

"Show me."

I guide him to the washed-out section, now carefully staying on hands and knees as we approach the edge. The drop-off appears suddenly—a jagged gouge in the earth where rushing snowmelt carved away the trail.

"Damn." He peers over the edge. "That's not a sprained ankle. That's a spinal injury waiting to happen."

"Exactly." I pull out my map, showing the marked hazard. "I document every trail change, regardless of whether official updates happen."

Mac looks from my map to the landscape, then back. His expression shifts from skeptical to impressed.

"Your attention to detail is... extraordinary."

"Just doing my job." I tuck the map away, ignoring the way his compliment warms my chest.

We continue along the trail, our conversation gradually shifting from professional assessment to more personal topics.

"How long have you been mapping these mountains,

Mackenzie?" His voice is lazy and smooth, as if he already knows the answer but wants to hear me say it.

Mackenzie.

Again.

I've corrected him a dozen times. Maybe more. He knows my name. I know he knows. That's precisely why he keeps saying it—poking at me, testing the perimeter, watching to see when I'll snap.

I won't.

Not today.

"Officially? Five years." I hop over a twisted root, jaw tight. "Unofficially, since I could walk."

I shove the tip of my trekking pole toward a narrow fissure in the granite. "See that? Spring bubbles up from between those rocks. Cleanest water on the south ridge."

He makes an appreciative sound low in his throat, crouching to study it, all muscle and casual grace.

Don't look at his arms.

Don't look at the stretch of his back under that snug shirt.

Do not, under any circumstances, imagine what he'd look like without it.

Too late.

A flash of stubbled jaw, dark hair tousled from the wind, and a body that screams Thunder From Down Under, he's walking kryptonite.

God. He even walks like he owns a stage. All slow swagger and sinful confidence, like he'd be just as comfortable holding a chainsaw as he would a woman against the wall.

Nope. No. Absolutely not. Do *not* think of him taking you against a wall. Thrusting hard. Hands bruising. Lips weaponized to undo me...

Shit. He's in my head.

Stay professional.

Mac rises to his full, infuriating height, glancing at me

with that trademark smirk—the one that says he sees right through the tight coil of control I'm clinging to.

"Your dad teach you how to read terrain that young?" he asks, tone deceptively casual.

I nod. Short. Sharp. Refusing to give him more than that.

He lets the silence stretch, eyes glittering beneath the brim of his cap.

Mackenzie.

He hasn't said it again, but the word hangs there, pulsing between us like static before a lightning strike.

I won't take the bait.

Won't correct him.

Won't give him the satisfaction of knowing he's getting under my skin.

Because he is.

Every inch of me feels flayed open beneath his gaze—and he knows it.

And the worst part?

Some traitorous part of me wants him to keep saying it.

Wants to hear what my name sounds like on his lips, rough and low in the dark as he unapologetically takes me.

No. Hell no.

Keep walking. Keep talking. Keep it together.

"Family business, then." Mac glances at me, completely oblivious to the thoughts racing through my head.

"Something like that." I glance back at him. "What about you? Firefighting in the blood?"

"Military first. Army Rangers." He ducks under a low-hanging branch. "Firefighting came after. Felt natural to keep running toward danger instead of away from it."

"Adrenaline junkie?"

His laughter echoes against the rock face. "More like purpose junkie. Need something that matters."

The conversation flows easily as the trail climbs. I learn he takes his coffee black, has a younger sister in medical school, and can name every native tree in California. He learns I've never been outside Colorado, prefer dogs to people, and make my own trail mix because store-bought never has enough chocolate.

By the time we reach the summit viewpoint, the careful professional distance has shrunk considerably.

"This is..." Mac turns in a slow arc, the wind teasing his hair as he takes in the jagged sweep of peaks and shadowed valleys bathed in late-afternoon gold. "Spectacular doesn't cover it."

"Worth the climb?" I ask, but my breath still stutters—not from the altitude.

From him.

He stands there like the mountain itself—solid, powerful, carved by elements I'll never tame. Wind tugs at the dark strands of his hair. His jaw flexes, a muscle ticking beneath sun-warmed stubble. And his eyes—God, those eyes—burn with a heat that melts straight through the alpine chill.

One corner of his mouth lifts, slow and deliberate, like he knows exactly what he's doing to me.

"Every step."

He lifts his water bottle, tilts it to his lips. His throat works as he swallows, slow and steady, and a single drop escapes, trailing down the column of his neck, carving a glistening path over sun-browned skin.

My mouth goes dry.

I should look away.

Too late.

The droplet disappears into the open neck of his shirt, and all I can think about is following it—tracing that trail with my fingers, then my tongue. Down his throat, across the broad plane of his chest. Over the sharp ridges of his abs—solid, sculpted, the kind of body built by fire and grit, not gyms.

And further still.

Heat blooms low, deep, dark, and slow, curling through me like smoke. My thighs press together. My breath shortens. Every inch of me tightens with want, aching, and alive.

I blink hard and snap my gaze to the horizon, but it's too late.

The hunger's already taken root.

You're here to assess evacuation routes, not fantasize about what lies beneath his belt.

But the image won't leave.

It lingers like heat lightning behind my eyes—searing, impossible to unsee.

And once it sparks, it spreads.

Fast. Wild. Unforgiving.

The fantasy unfurls before I can stop it—vivid, startling, unwanted... and god, so delicious.

Him. Towering over me. Broad, commanding, radiating heat like he's forged from fire.

That gravel voice drops an octave—low, feral.

No words of warning. No slow build. Just that look. That knowing.

Then a fist knots in my hair—tight—and he shoves his cock past my lips like I'm made to take it.

Like I exist for this. For him.

Not sweet. Not careful.

Savage.

Hips grinding slowly at first—testing me. Teasing me.

Then faster. Rougher.

Fucking my throat like he owns it. Like he's waited long enough and now he's taking what's his.

The stretch burns.

My eyes water.

I moan around the length of him, and he growls, hips jerking, pushing deeper until I'm gagging, drool slicking my chin, and he's panting curses into the air.

"Look at you," he'd snarl. *"Kneeling for me like you were born for this."*

My hands grip his thighs—hard muscle wrapped in denim—trying to anchor myself.

But he doesn't let up. Doesn't ease.

He fucks my mouth like he needs it, like this is his release and his religion.

My spit runs down my neck. My pulse hammers in my ears. My core throbs—needy and slick and completely untouched.

And when I reach for my jeans, desperate for friction, he yanks me off his cock with a filthy pop, breath ragged as he fists his length and rubs it across my lips.

"You don't get to touch yourself," he growls, voice like smoke and sin. *"Not until I say."*

Then he pushes back in—deeper, harder—fucking my mouth while I claw at my restraint.

Powerless.

Starving.

So fucking wet I'm shaking.

I blink suddenly, surprised by the intensity of the fantasy. My heart's hammering. My breath is sharp and ragged in the cool mountain air.

He stands there—real, solid, and completely unaware of the war raging inside me.

The ache clawing through me like wildfire.

The fantasy still pulsing at the base of my spine, slick between my thighs, the ghost of him still on my tongue.

God help me, I want it.

The command. That edge.

He wipes the corner of his mouth with the back of his hand, oblivious.

But if he looked at me right now—really looked—he'd see it.

He'd smell it on me.

And I don't know what terrifies me more—

That I want him to see...

Or that he already does.

"So these evacuation routes."

His voice—steady, professional, completely unaffected—slices through my lust-drenched haze.

He spreads my map across a flat slab of granite, crouching beside it like nothing's shifted. Like I wasn't just mentally on my knees, moaning around the hard weight of his cock.

"You've marked three alternates from the summit."

He taps one with a calloused finger, precise and focused.

The contrast hits like a slap.

Whiplash.

My mind scrambles to catch up—to tear itself away from the fantasy still burning like an ember behind my ribs.

But it's not gone.

Not even close.

Because I'm still throbbing.

Still soaked.

Still aching to give in to the raw power he doesn't even seem to realize he holds.

I drag in a breath, but it's shaky, thin—no match for the way he smells.

Like pine and smoke and heat.

Like danger dressed in denim and sweat and absolute control.

He doesn't look at me.

Doesn't glance up.

Just crouches there, legs spread, forearms braced on his thighs, the sun cutting sharp shadows across the muscles straining beneath his shirt.

Virility. That's the word that hits me next.

Not sexiness. Not attraction.

Virility.

Undiluted, masculine virility.

Like if he reached for me right now, I'd fold.

Collapse.

Submit.

I shift my weight, thighs pressing tight—because the pulse between them won't stop.

Won't be ignored.

"Yes," I manage, voice hoarse. "Three routes. Two eastward descents, one drops north—less exposed, but longer."

His eyes lift, finally.

And just like that, the air changes.

Like he feels it.

The tension. The heat.

His gaze holds mine for a beat too long.

Long enough for my breath to catch.

Long enough for everything inside me to scream, *Take me. Do it now.*

But he just nods, eyes unreadable.

"Good work."

Then he looks away—like he didn't just light me on fire and walk away from the blaze.

Like he's not the walking embodiment of everything I've spent my life resisting.

And still, I stand here—heart hammering, body betraying me—wanting it all over again.

Worse.

Rougher.

Real.

Focus!

"Different options for different scenarios." I point to each route. "This one's fastest but exposed—dangerous in lightning. This one's sheltered but steeper—risky in wet conditions. This one's longest but has water access and natural shelters."

"You favor the middle route." It's not a question.

"How can you tell?"

"The pencil marks are darker. You've traced it more times, considering it."

His observation unsettles me. Few people notice such details.

"It splits the difference between speed and safety." I tap the route. "Best compromise in most scenarios."

"I disagree." He traces the longest route with his finger. "Water access trumps speed in evacuation scenarios. Dehydration kills faster than most people realize."

"That route adds forty minutes to evacuation time."

"Forty minutes alive is better than twenty minutes dead."

"That's not how risk assessment works, and you know it." I cross my arms. "Longer exposure to danger increases mortality risk exponentially."

"Unless the danger is dehydration and heat exposure."

"On a mountain that's below freezing eight months of the year?"

The debate intensifies, each of us defending our position with increasing passion. We're no longer discussing hypothetical evacuations, but rather fundamental approaches to safety and risk.

"You can't apply desert firefighting protocols to alpine environments." I jab my finger at the map. "That's the kind of by-the-book thinking that gets people killed in specialized terrain."

"And stubborn adherence to tradition over evolving best practices is equally dangerous." Mac's voice rises to match mine. "Your father's methods might have worked twenty years ago, but—"

"Leave my father out of this."

"You brought him into it when you cited him as your qualification."

We're standing toe to toe now, the map forgotten between us. Scout whines softly from her spot under a nearby pine, sensing the tension.

"These mountains have rules that don't appear in your fancy training manuals." My voice rises despite my best intentions. "People who ignore local wisdom end up as statistics."

"People who refuse to adapt end up as cautionary tales." He steps closer, his height forcing me to tilt my head back to maintain eye contact. "Do you think you're the only one who cares about saving lives?"

"I think you're too busy proving your superiority to listen to someone who knows this terrain."

"And I think you're too busy defending your territory to consider that someone else might have valuable input."

"My territory?" I laugh, the sound sharp in the mountain air. "This isn't about territory. This is about you questioning every mark I make, every route I suggest, like I'm some amateur who wandered in off the street."

"I question because that's my job." His voice drops dangerously low. "Because when I lead my crew into a fire, their lives depend on my decisions. I don't make those decisions based on someone's hurt feelings."

"Hurt feelings?" My hands curl into fists. "You think this is about my feelings?"

"I think this is about you being so damn stubborn you can't admit when someone else might be right."

"And I think this is about you being so arrogant you can't imagine a world where your California protocols don't apply."

I open my mouth to respond when a distant rumble interrupts. We both look up to see dark clouds building over the western peaks, moving with alarming speed.

"Thunderstorm." Mac's eyes narrow. "Coming in fast."

Angel's Peak

Chapter 4

Shelter from the Storm

The mountain air shifts suddenly, temperature dropping as the first gust of wind hits us. In Colorado's high country, storms materialize with frightening speed, turning blue skies to violent tempests in minutes.

"We need shelter." I scan the surrounding terrain, my professional instincts temporarily overriding our argument. "We'll never make it back to the trailhead before that hits."

Mac checks his GPS. "Nearest ranger station?"

"Too far." I grab my pack, shoving the map inside. "There's one of Jackson Hart's emergency shelters half a mile north. We can make it if we run."

Without waiting for his response, I whistle for Scout and bolt down the north trail.

Branches whip at my arms. Rocks skid beneath my boots. Behind me, I hear him curse—low and sharp—before his footsteps follow, fast and relentless, eating up the distance I'm trying to put between us.

The wind kicks harder, howling through the trees. Pines bow under its force, their needle-laced limbs clawing at the sky.

Dust and debris swirl up around us, stinging my eyes, stealing my breath.

A low growl of thunder rolls over the ridgeline. Long. Ominous. Too close.

"Josephine—" His voice rips through the wind, but I don't look back.

We crest the ridge just as the first raindrops hit—heavy, cold, and sudden. Then the sky opens.

Sheets of water hammer down, drenching us in seconds. The storm doesn't build—it descends, fast and furious, like a living thing.

Lightning lights up the sky. Thunder cracks, sharp and violent.

Scout lets out a sharp bark, ears pinned as she runs ahead. Lightning flashes—too close, too bright—throwing the forest into stark black-and-white relief.

I stumble. Catch myself on a branch slick with rain.

Mac's hand shoots out, grabs my arm—firm, grounding. Heat from his palm burns through the chill, even as the storm rages around us.

"Shelter. Now." His words are clipped, commanding. No more arguing. No more distance. Just urgency.

I nod, breathless, soaked to the bone, the air crackling with electric tension.

Above us, the sky groans again—thunder rolling like the belly of something ancient and pissed off.

And behind us...

That storm isn't finished.

It's just getting started.

"There." I point to a small structure tucked against the rockface, almost invisible against the natural landscape.

We make the final sprint as hail begins to mix with the rain, stinging exposed skin. I fumble with the shelter's latch, fingers slippery with rain, until Mac reaches around me to help.

The door swings open, and we tumble inside, Scout shaking water everywhere as we secure the door against the howling wind.

Hart's emergency shelter is one room, maybe twelve by twelve feet. A small woodstove occupies one corner, a narrow bench along the opposite wall, and a small cot in the corner. Emergency supplies are stacked neatly on shelves.

The space feels even smaller with Mac's broad shoulders blocking most of the available light from the single window.

We stand dripping on the plank floor, suddenly aware of our proximity in the confined space. Water runs from Mac's dark hair down his face, catching in his eyelashes and trailing along his jaw. My clothes cling uncomfortably, soaked through in the brief dash.

The silence between us pulses with unfinished argument and something else—something electric and dangerous.

"Well." He pushes wet hair from his forehead. "That was exciting."

"Welcome to Colorado mountain weather." I move to the stove, desperate for something to do with my hands. "We should start a fire. Temperature drops fast during storms."

Mac moves to the supply shelf, finding matches and kindling while I arrange wood in the stove. We work silently, the tension between us thickening with each passing second. Scout settles on the floor, watching us with wary eyes.

The kindling catches, filling the small space with warm light and the comforting scent of pine smoke. A shiver racks my spine, sudden and sharp, my damp clothes clinging cold against my skin. I wrap my arms around myself, trying to trap what little heat I have as steam begins to rise from my sleeves.

"You should change." Mac nods toward my pack. "Hypothermia's a risk even in summer at this elevation."

"I'm fine." My voice comes out sharper than intended, the residual anger from our argument still simmering beneath the surface.

"You're shaking." His voice cuts through the crackle of firewood, low and unyielding—the same commanding edge that sparked our argument on the trail. "This isn't a suggestion, Mackenzie."

"Don't pull rank on me in my mountains."

"This isn't about rank." He steps closer, the firelight catching the sharp line of his jaw. "It's about basic survival. You of all people should know better."

"Now, who's questioning whose expertise?" The words come fast, sharp, but a violent shiver rips through me before I can hold it back, my arms hugging tighter around my damp clothes. *Dammit.*

"Fine." His jaw tightens.

He steps back—but not far enough. His fingers go to the hem of his soaked t-shirt, dragging it up in one slow motion. The fabric clings to every ridge of his chest before peeling free, water-dark and heavy. He drops it to the floor with a wet slap, standing bare-chested in front of the fire like something carved from sun-drenched stone.

I can't stop staring.

His chest is broad, thick with muscle, a dusting of dark hair catching the flicker of firelight. Defined pecs taper into an obscene, impossible six-pack—each line sharp enough to cut. And lower... a single drop of water tracks a lazy path down the deep groove of his abs, disappearing into the waistband of his pants.

My mouth goes dry.

He catches me looking and—of course—smirks. A dark, knowing thing that sends a pulse of heat straight between my legs.

"Something interesting, Mackenzie?" His voice roughens, amusement curled beneath it.

I jerk my gaze away, scowling. "Just making sure you weren't about to pass out from hypothermia."

He huffs a laugh, the sound low and infuriating. Then he hooks his fingers under his beltline, pausing there. Not unbuckling. Not yet. Just watching me.

"You can look if you want," he murmurs, tone all heat and steel. "But fair warning—if you don't want me watching you change, now's your last chance to turn around."

The fire crackles between us, but it's nothing compared to the burn crawling across my skin. Every breath feels too deep, too sharp. The shelter is suddenly too small. The air is too thick. And him, too much.

Too much confidence, too much heat, too much everything.

I don't move.

And neither does he.

Yet.

I huff, spin on my heel, and face the wall with more force than necessary. The timber planks are rough beneath my palms, the scent of pine smoke curling into my hair.

Behind me, the metallic click of his belt slices through the hush. Fabric drags slowly over skin, a whisper of sound thick with intent. Wet gear lands with a soft, final thump on the floorboards. Each noise punches low, deliberate, unhurried, designed to torment.

The silence that follows is louder than anything. He's not just changing. He's performing. And he knows damn well I'm listening to every second of it.

"You gonna change," he calls, voice maddeningly casual, "or stubbornly freeze out of spite?"

Teeth clenched, I dig into my pack and yank out a dry base layer, keeping my back to him. My hands tremble—not from cold anymore, but from the sheer effort of ignoring the heat rolling off his body like a goddamn furnace.

I strip off my wet shirt, the cold air biting at my skin. My bra clings damply, and I peel it away with a sharp inhale. Goosebumps rise instantly across my arms, my breasts, my spine. I reach for the thermal top, tugging it over my head as quickly as I can—but not quickly enough to stop the thought from hitting.

He's behind me. Half-naked. Dry. Watching.

Or not watching.

I have no idea which is worse.

Leggings next. They peel down slowly, wet fabric clinging like a second skin. I curse under my breath, kicking them off and stepping into warm, dry thermals with a muttered, "This is your fault," though it sounds more like a prayer than an accusation.

I grab my thick socks and yank them on with shaking fingers, then zip up my fleece halfway, forcing myself to inhale. *Breathe. Reset. Get your shit together.*

"You can turn around now," I mutter without looking.

"Thanks for the show," he says behind me, the smirk audible.

I spin to glare at him—and immediately regret it.

He sits on the edge of the bench in nothing but dry pants. He's shirtless. Smug. Sprawled like he owns the goddamn room.

His hair's damp, curling slightly at the ends, his forearms braced on his thighs. Relaxed. Infuriatingly male.

Unfazed by the storm—or my scowl.

"You watched?"

"Could've faced the wall," he says, not even pretending to apologize, "but then I'd have missed how hard you checked me out earlier. Fair's fair, Mackenzie."

My breath hitches. Heat flares across my cheeks.

"I wasn't—"

He lifts a brow. Waits. Lets the silence do the work.

I cross my arms over my chest, every nerve in my body sparking. "I *was not* checking you out."

"Sure," he drawls. "You just happened to stare at my chest like it held the coordinates to buried treasure."

I make a strangled sound and spin away from him again, practically vibrating with the effort not to launch something at his smug, insufferably beautiful face.

He chuckles behind me—low, deep, maddeningly amused.

"For the record," he adds, his voice dropping to a near whisper, "you looked for a hell of a long time."

I press my palm against the rough timber wall, willing myself not to turn back around. Not to give him the satisfaction of seeing how flustered I am. The image is already burned behind my eyes—the drop of water sliding down his abs, the smirk that knew exactly what it was doing to me.

And worse? The part of me that liked it.

I wanted to follow that drop with my tongue. I wanted to see just how far that lazy confidence would go.

What he'd do if I let him take control.

That dangerous fantasy returns, coiling hot in my belly— raw power, no hesitation, his hand in my hair while he used my mouth like it was his.

The thought alone has my thighs clenching. My pulse kicks into overdrive.

Nope.

Nope.

Absolutely, the hell not.

He's exactly the kind of man who would take what he wants and leave scorched earth behind.

And I am not the kind of woman who lets herself burn. *Well, for him...*

I grit my teeth, straighten, and pull the zipper on my fleece up to my chin like armor.

He's not saying another word. He doesn't have to.

His silence is louder than any tease.

"Looks like we're stuck here until it passes." Mac peers out the window at the driving rain. "Unless you have a magical shortcut that defies the weather."

"Even I don't mess with lightning." I settle on the bench, leaving space for him. "Should blow over within an hour or two."

He sits beside me, the narrow bench forcing our shoulders to touch despite my efforts to maintain distance between us. The contact sends an unwelcome jolt of awareness through my body.

"So about those evacuation routes—" He starts.

"Are we really going to continue that argument?" I interrupt.

"I wasn't aware it was an argument." His voice carries a dangerous edge. "I thought it was a professional discussion about safety."

"You called my methods outdated."

"I suggested they might benefit from contemporary input."

"Same thing."

"No, it isn't." He shifts to face me, his knee now pressing against mine. "Why are you so resistant to outside perspective, Mackenzie?"

"Why are you so determined to question methods that have worked for decades?"

"Because *it's always worked before* is the last thing people say before disaster strikes." His eyes flash. "Adaptation isn't criticism."

"You've been criticizing my approach since the moment you arrived."

"I've been challenging your assumptions. There's a difference."

"Not when it comes with that superior tone."

"Superior?" He looks genuinely startled. "That's what you think?"

"The hotshot captain from California with his fancy technology and impressive resume?" I stand, needing distance from his proximity. "Yes, you've made it abundantly clear you think your methods are superior."

He rises too, closing the distance I tried to create. "That's not—"

"It is." I back up until I hit the wall. "You waltz in here questioning maps I've spent years perfecting, dismissing local knowledge in favor of satellite data and standardized protocols that don't account for—"

"I'm questioning because I need to understand." He moves closer, voice dropping to a dangerous low. "Because people's lives depend on me making the right call, and I can't do that if I don't challenge every assumption and test every plan."

"There's challenging and then there's dismissing." My chest rises and falls hard, breath punching through clenched teeth. "You started with dismissal."

"And you started with hostility." He plants one hand on the wall beside my head, his body crowding mine without touching. His voice stays maddeningly even, low and firm like it's gospel. "From the moment we collided on that sidewalk, you decided I was the enemy."

"You ruined my maps."

"It was an accident." Calm. Controlled. Delivered like a final ruling from a bench I never asked to stand before.

We're nearly shouting now—or I am, at least. He's not. He's composed, voice moderated like he's got the whole damn playbook memorized while I'm still scrambling in the margins.

Our faces are inches apart. Breath mingles—his, slow and

steady. Mine, erratic. Furious. Too aware of the heat radiating between us. Too aware of him.

"Has anyone ever told you you're impossible?" His voice is a low growl, eyes locked on mine, jaw tight enough to crack.

"Has anyone ever told you you're insufferable?" We're toe to toe now, and my heart is pounding like a war drum in my chest.

"Stubborn." His gaze drops briefly—to my mouth—then drags back up, slow and deliberate.

"Arrogant." My chin lifts, daring him to get closer. My pulse is a wildfire in my throat.

"Defensive." He closes the last inch between us, breath hot against my rain-slick skin, tension snapping like live wire.

"Presumptuous."

The word barely makes it past my lips before his hand slams against the wall beside my head, caging me in. His chest rises, falls, heavy.

So does mine.

The air between us is thick, humid with the storm, charged with everything we haven't said.

Neither of us backs down.

Each word lands like a spark to tinder, narrowing the space between us until there's nothing left but breath and heat and defiance. I can count his lashes. See the nick just beneath his jawline. Smell the fire and damp earth clinging to his skin.

"You drive me crazy, Mackenzie." His voice drops to a dangerous growl.

"My name is Jo."

"Do you always need to correct me?" His voice drops, low and dangerous, my name rolling off his tongue like a warning and a promise all at once. "Challenge me?"

"No." But it's a lie, and we both hear it.

"You've been fighting me since day one. Every look. Every step. Every breath."

His other hand slams into the wall beside my head—hard. The sound echoes like a shot. "You think I haven't noticed?"

"This isn't a fight." My voice is breathless. Shaky.

"The hell it isn't." He leans in—just enough to make my knees threaten to give—but still doesn't touch. Not yet. Not quite.

His body radiates heat, lightning barely contained. His breath brushes my lips. The air between us pulses.

"You want to hate me," he growls, the words scraping across my skin like grit and fire. "But what you really want— what you've wanted since we met—is for me to rip that control out of your hands. Make you feel what it's like to be undone."

Silence coils, thick and breathless.

I don't answer. Can't. The tension is a vice around my throat. My heart thunders. My body trembles, no longer from cold but from the raw, aching hunger I've tried to deny since the moment we collided.

Then—

"Ah, fuck this. Don't even know why I'm pretending." It rips from him, raw and guttural, like something he's been choking back for far too long. "I'm done holding back."

His gaze drops to my mouth, then his mouth slams into mine.

Hard. Hot. Starving.

The kiss hits like a thunderclap—wild and brutal and consuming.

One hand spears into my hair, fisting tight. The other wraps around my waist, yanking me against him so fast it knocks the air from my lungs.

He doesn't coax. He conquers—tongue sweeping in, lips crashing down, owning me like it's his right. Like he's done waiting for permission.

And I don't resist.

I burn.

I moan, helpless and furious at the way my body melts for him, with how he knows exactly how to kiss me—hard enough to punish, soft enough to addict.

It's furious, full of everything we haven't said, every glare, every fight.

Tongue, teeth, tension.

My mind goes blank.

I kiss him back with the same savage need, tongues tangling, teeth clashing, the taste of him addictive and wild. I want more. I want everything.

My body arches like it's no longer mine. Like it's his now. Claimed.

He breaks away first, breathing hard, forehead pressed to mine.

"You think you can just... do that?" I manage, even as my hips sway toward him. "Kiss me?"

"You didn't tell me to stop." His breath is fire against my lips. "Didn't shove me away. Didn't even try."

"I didn't give you permission."

"I don't remember asking," he growls.

His grip tightens—my waist locked in his hands, held firm. Not cruel. Just certain. Possessive.

"This is happening," he snarls, voice ragged with restraint. "You don't get to pretend you don't want this."

"I don't—"

"If the next words out of your mouth are a lie, don't bother saying them." His hand fists my shirt at the small of my back, jerking me closer. "Because if you don't want this, say it now."

I should say it. Push him away.

I don't.

I should slam the brakes on whatever this is, but the breath catches sharp in my throat, and my spine curves helplessly into his hold, like my body already knows what I won't let myself say.

Heat pulses through me—shame, need, the terrible relief of being seen. My head tips back. Lips parted. Bare. Trembling.

But the words won't come. Not the right ones. Not the safe ones.

He waits. Still. Watching me unravel. Measuring how much further I'll fall.

His hand rises, threading into my hair.

"Say it," he growls. "Say what you want."

"I…" My voice cracks. I can't meet his eyes.

His grip tightens, and his eyes darken. "Not good enough."

A whimper catches in my throat.

"Try again."

I bite down, jaw tight, shame burning beneath my skin.

"You have to say it, Josephine." He leans in, mouth brushing my jaw. "Tell me the truth."

"Don't stop." My whole body trembles. The dam breaks. The admission rips out of me, raw and trembling.

His breath catches. Just a flicker.

And then—God—he smiles. Dark. Wicked. Victorious.

"There she is." His hand tightens on my hip. "At least, we're on the same page when it comes to this."

Angel's Peak

CHAPTER 5

GOOD GIRL

MAC'S MOUTH CRASHES TO MINE, RUTHLESS AND claiming. Bruising and hot, while the storm rages outside, forgotten. Nothing exists now but this—our bodies drawn tight with need, the press of his chest, the taste of his mouth, the certainty that we're both standing at the edge of something we can't take back.

He spins me, chest to wall, and pins me there—hard. His palm fisting in my hair, jerking my head back so his lips graze my ear.

"I'm gonna fuck you," he rasps. "It's going to be messy. Angry. And Hard. The way you've been begging for it since the second you ran into me."

"You ran into me," I snap, but my voice betrays me—breathless, shaking.

"No," he snarls. "You ran into me."

His hand yanks at the waistband of my pants, dragging them down rough and fast, panties with them, baring me in seconds. The cool air hits my skin, and I gasp—but then his fingers are there, sliding between my thighs, and all I can do is moan.

"Look at that," he mutters. "Soaked. You've been fighting me with your mouth, but begging with your body."

I want to deny it. Should. But I can't.

I hear the hurried sound of his zipper, the rustle of fabric as he frees himself. Then I feel him, thick and hot, nudging against my entrance.

"I'm going to give you exactly what you've been asking for, unless you say stop," he growls.

"Oh my god, just fuck me already."

His eyes flare when I say the words—*just fuck me already* —like I've finally surrendered the truth we've both known since the moment we collided.

"Finally," he growls, voice gone guttural. "I know what you need. Hard. Fast. Dirty. Raw. You need to be fucked, not coddled."

And then he gives it to me.

He slams into me with a single, brutal thrust that knocks the air from my lungs. I cry out—sharp, startled, wrecked—as he buries himself to the hilt.

"God—" It's not a prayer. It's a curse. A plea. A confession. "You feel good."

He thrusts and I scream—not from pain, but from the sheer shock of how good it feels to finally let go.

His grip is relentless—one hand on my hip, the other wrapped tight around my wrists behind my back, pinning me, holding me there while he pounds into me like he owns every inch.

"You like this," he snarls against my neck, voice shredded and breathless. "Need to be fucked until you forget how to fight me."

I moan, a raw, helpless sound. My body bucks into his thrusts, instinct overriding everything else—logic, shame, pride—none of it matters now.

"You pretend you don't want it. Act like you're in

control." His hand slides up my spine, fingers tangling in my hair to yank my head back. "But your body tells the truth."

He moves like he's angry. Like he owns me. Slamming into me over and over, breath hot on my neck, mouth dragging over my skin with growls and curses and promises I'm too far gone to process.

He bites down on my shoulder, not hard enough to break skin—but enough to mark. Enough to brand.

"You think I don't see it?" he pants. "You think I haven't noticed? You think I don't know what you need?"

My only answer is a broken cry as my body clenches around him.

He kisses me then, messy, consuming, biting at my lower lip as I fall apart beneath him.

My climax tears through me like a live wire. Blinding. Violent. My vision goes white, knees buckling, mouth open on a silent scream as I shatter in his grip.

He groans, curses, drives into me once, twice more—then stills, buried deep as he jerks with his release, growling into my neck like a man possessed.

His shudder rocks us both.

For a moment, we're still, pressed together, panting, and ruined. Then he leans in, lips brushing the shell of my ear.

And all I can think is—*God help me, I'd let him do it all over again.*

"I've thought about this since the second you ran into me," he breathes, voice thick and gravel-laced. "I wanted to fuck you then. All that attitude. All that bite. You don't know what you do to me, Josephine."

The name punches straight through my fog.

"My name is Jo," I mutter, breath still shaky.

His hand drags slowly along my ribs, thumb brushing under my breast with quiet ownership.

"Not for me. I've been inside of you, *Josephine*, and I'll call you what I damn well please," he growls, rough and close. "What I've earned. When you hear your name on my lips, you're going to remember this moment. The moment I claimed you."

His mouth finds the curve of my neck again, open and hot. "You fight like you want to be tamed. You come like you want to be wrecked. I'm going to do all of that and more, and Josephine...."

"Yes?"

"I'm just getting started."

Reality seeps back slowly. I become aware of Scout watching us with canine confusion, the dying fire in the stove, the fact that my pants are around my ankles, and Mac is still inside me, his breathing gradually returning to normal against my neck.

Carefully, reluctantly, we disentangle. I pull my pants up with trembling fingers, tug my shirt down with hands that won't stop shaking. The air feels colder without him.

Too quiet. Too real.

And I can't meet his eyes.

"We should check the weather." The words scrape from my throat, brittle and false.

His laughter catches me off guard—low, rough, almost amused. But there's nothing soft about it.

"You think we're going to check the fucking weather?" He reaches for my hand, his fingers warm as they intertwine with mine. "After sex like that?"

He tugs me toward him—gently, but there's no mistaking the intent. He spins me, makes me face him. And God, his eyes... all the fury and fire is still there, but now it's laced with something worse. Something better. Something dangerous.

"Mac—"

"Yes, Josephine." My name leaves his lips like a vow. His hands cradle my face, tender but unyielding, thumbs grazing my cheekbones like I'm something holy and breakable. Like I'm his.

I try to laugh, try to brush it off, back away—but the walls press close, the storm howls outside, and I've got nowhere left to run.

"That was a mistake. Just heat and adrenaline. It didn't mean—"

"Don't." His voice is a snarl, low and vibrating with control he's barely holding. "You don't get to dismiss this." His eyes darken. His grip tightens. Not enough to hurt—just enough to hold.

"Don't pretend what happened was accidental. Don't lie to me. Don't lie to yourself just because you came so hard you forgot your own damn name." His grip tightens. Just enough to anchor. Not to hurt.

My stomach flips. My knees go soft.

"You came apart around me like you'd been waiting your whole fucking life for it. If you want to talk about mistakes? That wasn't one. You're not above needing what I gave you? I know the truth. I felt it in the way your pussy clenched around my cock. Heard it in the way you begged under your breath."

He leans in, lips brushing mine without kissing.

"You don't get to run from this." His fingers tighten just enough to halt me, thumb brushing across my cheekbone like a promise. "I don't regret a goddamn thing," he says, voice low and steady. "And I don't regret taking you hard, the way you need it."

He leans in, lips brushing the corner of mine, not quite a kiss—more like a claim. His voice is low, steady. Dangerously calm.

I try to step back, but there's nowhere to go. Just walls. Just him. Just us.

His fingers trail up my side, slow and certain, slipping

beneath my shirt, rough palms grazing bare skin. Not tentative —testing. Measuring what I'll take. How far I'll let him go.

"I see you, Josephine." His words rasp against my throat. "I see the part of you that doesn't want soft or careful. You need to be handled. You need to be fucked like it matters. Like it consumes. You need a man who won't hold back."

His breath drags against my cheek, heat and promise. His lips brush the corner of mine, his voice low and certain, like a vow made in shadows.

"And I will. I'll show you what it means to be wanted without apology. Fucked like it's survival. Like I've waited my whole life for the permission your body gave me the second you stopped pretending you didn't crave this."

My breath catches, but I don't pull away.

"You want to be touched like a storm. Felt in the aftermath. You want to be shaken down to your bones and held there, right at the edge."

His other hand catches the back of my neck, fisting just enough to make me tilt my head, forcing my gaze to his.

"I'll take you there," he growls, eyes burning into mine. "Again and again. Until you can't look at me without remembering how it felt to let go. To let me take control. This isn't about lust. It's possession. And baby—" he leans in, voice a threat and a promise "—you're mine now."

His thumb brushes my lower lip. My knees nearly buckle. His other hand catches the back of my neck, fisting gently, tilting my head so our eyes meet—nowhere to run, no way to hide.

"And you'll let me because you need it. Because your body's already made the decision your pride's still arguing with." He drags his mouth down the line of my jaw, lips parting just enough for his teeth to scrape skin—deliberate, claiming.

"You can't outrun this. Not in this cabin. Not in this

storm. And not from me. We're just beginning. I'm going to fuck you again. And again. I'm going to fuck you until you can't look at me without remembering how it felt to surrender. To beg." His thumb brushes my lip, slow and taunting. "And don't pretend you're not going to beg."

His hand slides lower, palm flattening across my stomach, fingers dipping under the waistband of my pants.

"I'm not interested in weather updates. Or polite conversations. Not when I could be fucking you in every position this twelve-foot box will allow. On the table. Against the wall. With your legs over my shoulders or your face in the mattress—doesn't matter."

My knees tremble, but he's already there—holding, steadying, anchoring me in place like he knew I'd fall.

Outside, thunder crashes. The wind shrieks like it wants in. The storm doesn't terrify me—it's the way Mac sees me.

The way he knows.

God help me, he knows.

His palm flattens against my stomach, sliding lower, fingers slipping beneath the waistband of my pants again—slow this time, torturous, possessive.

"You can tell me to stop," he murmurs at my throat, lips grazing my pulse. "But if you don't—if you let me keep touching you—I'm going to fuck you again."

My breath catches.

My thighs part.

I don't say stop.

And he doesn't.

Not even close.

Because once isn't enough. Not after the way I came for him. Not after the way I broke open.

This next kiss is nothing like the first. Where that was fury and fire, this is slow, deliberate heat. His lips move against mine with intention, coaxing rather than claiming.

My hands find his chest, feeling his heartbeat beneath my palms.

I take my time exploring newly revealed skin with curious fingers and appreciative murmurs.

What follows is a revelation—hours of discovery and pleasure that melt the remaining ice between us. The storm outside fades to nothing as we create our own weather system of sighs, whispers, and breathless pleas.

My vision blurs. My body pulses with aftershocks, twitching beneath him as he groans low, dark, and satisfied—before following me into that same abyss.

"From the second you glared up at me on that sidewalk, I imagined this," he growls. "Shoving my cock so deep you forget your own name. Making you beg like you're doing now."

His mouth finds the back of my neck, breath hot against sweat-damp skin.

Neither of us moves for a long moment. Thunder rolls outside, but it's a distant thing now—muted by the sound of our shared silence.

Hours blur together.

At one point, he pulls me into his lap and wraps his arms around me. His lips trail reverent kisses across my shoulder. He lifts my hand to his lips, pressing a kiss to the inside of my wrist. I shiver—not from cold, but from the gentleness threading through the aftermath.

Later—much later—we lie tangled on our discarded clothes, my head on his chest, my leg thrown over his, skin slick with sweat, marked by teeth and bruising grip.

The fire has dimmed to embers, but he hasn't let me go— not for a second.

His fingers drag slow patterns across my shoulder, like he's tracing something only he can see.

"So," he murmurs, voice rough, lips brushing my temple. "About those evacuation routes…"

A breathless laugh escapes me—unexpected, too light after the storm we just unleashed. "Are you seriously thinking about maps right now?"

"No." His arm tightens around me. "I'm thinking about all the places I haven't fucked you yet."

Heat curls in my stomach. I shift against him, pulse quickening as his hand trails lower, skimming my waist.

"We'll need to explore," he adds, voice darker now. "Thoroughly. Every trail. Every overlook. Maybe somewhere quiet and secluded. Somewhere I can make you come loud enough, it echoes through the mountains."

My breath hitches. He notices—of course he does.

"Something just lit up behind your eyes." His voice is darker now, amused. "What was that thought, Josephine?"

"Nothing," I murmur.

"That wasn't *nothing*." His mouth hovers at my jaw, lips brushing the shell of my ear. "You got quiet. Your thighs tightened. What did you imagine just now?"

I bite my lip.

He doesn't let it go. One hand slides between my legs, not stroking, just there—heat and threat and promise.

My throat tightens. I swallow, but it doesn't go away.

"You're going to tell me."

He shifts, rolling us so I'm beneath him again, his body all heat and weight and restraint. One hand cradles the side of my face, thumb brushing my cheek like a benediction. His gaze doesn't waver.

"Tell me." His tone is silk and steel. "Or I'll make you come and then make you confess. Your choice."

My voice breaks on the first word. "It's stupid."

"I like stupid," he growls. "Especially when it ends with you on your knees."

I shiver. His fingers flex.

"There it is," he whispers. "That little tremble. Shame and hunger, wrapped up tight. You on your knees? Is that what it is?"

I close my eyes. "That first day. The sidewalk."

He stills.

"You grabbed my arm. Got in my face. And I couldn't stop imagining you—"

"Say it."

"—shoving me down. Making me open my mouth and take you. Rough. Angry. No questions. Just—control."

"Fuck." His breath hisses between his teeth. "You've thought about me using you," he finishes, voice like gravel.

"Yes."

"No asking. Just gripping your hair, unzipping my pants, and shoving my cock past your lips."

"Yes." My thighs part without thinking.

"Jesus, Josephine," he growls. "You could've told me."

"I couldn't."

"Why?" He leans down, dragging his teeth along my jaw. "Afraid I wouldn't want it?"

"Afraid you'd think less of me."

He grabs my chin, forces my eyes to his.

"I've seen you from day one. You want it hard. Dirty. Forced without force. You want to kneel. To serve."

I swallow, but it's useless. My body's already answered.

"You'll get that," he says, deadly soft. "Out there. On the trail. You'll hike ahead, and I'll follow. When I decide it's time, I'll put you on your knees and fuck that filthy little fantasy into your throat."

His hand slides lower, cupping between my legs.

He smiles, slow and wicked. "Start praying for clear skies, sweetheart. Because once the storm breaks, I'm taking you outside and making that mouth mine."

God help me, I want every filthy piece of it.

Reality seeps back slowly. I become aware of Scout watching us with resigned acceptance from her corner, the dying fire in the stove, the fact that we're completely naked and entwined on a narrow cot in Jackson Hart's emergency shelter.

Eventually, reluctantly, we dress. Every movement feels charged, meaningful in ways it wasn't before. I catch him watching me when he thinks I'm not looking, his expression a mix of wonder and something more profound I'm not ready to name.

Once the rain stops, we step outside. Sunlight breaks through dissipating clouds, turning raindrops on pine needles into diamonds. The fresh-washed mountain air fills my lungs, but does nothing to clear the fog in my brain.

We walk back in silence, the usual comfortable banter impossible after what just happened. The trail seems both longer and shorter than before, time stretching strangely in the aftermath of that kiss.

At the trailhead, Mac unlocks the SUV, holding the door for Scout, who jumps in with subdued energy, tail low but alert, sensing the shift between us like a storm about to break.

Mac doesn't look at me as he circles to the driver's side. Doesn't ask if I'm ready, okay, or if I need a minute. He just gets behind the wheel, starts the engine, and waits—expecting me to fall in line.

I do.

The drive back to my cabin passes in silence, but the air between us hums. Every nerve in my body is aware of him—his hand steady on the gearshift, the muscle ticking in his jaw, the low rumble of his breath syncing with the hum of the engine. He doesn't fidget. Doesn't glance over. He simply exists with complete focus, radiating calm, coiled control. And

God help me, it stirs something low in my belly I thought I'd buried years ago.

What do you say after kissing someone like the world was ending? After letting him take you apart like it was his right?

When we reach my cabin, he puts the vehicle in park and kills the engine without a word.

Silence stretches. Tension thickens.

Then he speaks. One word.

"Josephine."

The way he says it—low, sure, already claiming me—sends a tremor through my chest. Not a question. A summons.

"What?" I turn my head slowly.

His gaze meets mine, dark and steady. He doesn't blink.

"Ask me to come inside."

Not *Can I come in?* Not *Do you want me to stay?* A command, disguised as a request. Softened at the edges, but still a command.

I should say no.

I should tell him this was a mistake, draw the boundary I already bulldozed.

Instead, I swallow hard, pulse fluttering at my throat. "Please come in."

His smile is slow. Dangerous.

"Good girl."

Two words. That's all. But they land like a brand, low and deep and molten.

I follow him into the cabin without another word.

Angel's Peak

Chapter 6

Six Trails

The cabin door clicks shut behind us, and everything else falls away.

The only sound is our breathing, the only light the golden afternoon sun filtering through pine-framed windows. The charged silence between us crackles like static before a lightning strike.

He doesn't speak. Doesn't ask. He steps in close and grabs the hem of my shirt, pulling it over my head. His mouth is on mine before the shirt hits the floor.

There's no space for doubt. No room for fear. Just the scent of pine and sweat and man, the taste of coffee and desire on his tongue.

He lifts me onto the kitchen counter, hips pressing between my thighs, granite cool against my heated skin. The scrape of stubble on my throat, the rough glide of his palms down my ribs. His touch leaves fire in its wake, turning bones to liquid, resistance to need.

"You love this, don't you? You need this," he murmurs against my throat, voice rough like mountain stone, already knowing the answer.

"Yes." I drag him closer, fingers digging into the solid muscle of his shoulders, anchoring myself to the only steady thing in a spinning world.

He takes it as permission.

We fuck in the kitchen, fast and filthy. My back against the cabinet doors, legs wrapped around his waist, every thrust punctuated by the rattle of dishes and my gasping breaths. He fucks me in the shower, where steam fogs the mirrors and hot water cascades over us. I bite his shoulder to keep from screaming as he pins me to the slick tile.

We fuck in bed, where he slows down just enough to make me beg, over and over, until my muscles ache and my mind goes quiet from too much pleasure. And when I fall asleep curled against him, his heartbeat steady beneath my ear, it's not comfort I feel.

It's possession.

The next morning, the rain lightens to a pale mist. The world outside my cabin windows shimmers with droplets that cling to pine needles and spider webs, turning the forest into a crystal cathedral. The storm broke, but whatever passed between us hasn't.

We pack in silence for more trail exploration, but something's shifted. He moves with certainty now, no longer a visitor but someone claiming space.

Takes the lead without speaking.

His hands occasionally brush against mine, casual touches that feel deliberate and proprietary.

On the trail, I follow. His long strides eat the miles, boots crushing wet leaves that release the scent of earth and decay. Water drips from branches overhead, occasionally landing cool against my heated skin.

He doesn't glance back, but he knows I'm there.

Every time I stumble on a slick stone or a hidden root, his hand is already out.

Steady. Ready.

The warmth of his palm against mine feels like more than mere assistance.

We reach the ridge overlook mid-morning. The mist has burned away, revealing valleys unfurled below us like a crumpled green blanket, distant peaks piercing a sky washed clean by yesterday's storm.

I unclip the topo map from my belt, the paper crisp between my fingers.

"We're off by a quarter mile from the firebreak projection." I hold out the drawing, my lines precise in blue and red. "The runoff pool's farther west than your GPS thinks."

Mac pulls out his device, the sleek technology incongruous against the ancient landscape. He frowns, sunlight catching the gold flecks in his eyes, then meets my gaze.

"My GPS says otherwise."

I jab the map, paper crinkling under my finger. "And I live here. My lines are drawn from memory and what the ground says. You want to override that?"

He steps into my space, close enough that I can smell yesterday's desire on his skin. Takes the map, folds it carefully with those strong fingers that mapped my body hours before, then slides it back into my pack. The casual intimacy of the gesture leaves me breathless.

"No," he says, voice like gravel over velvet. "I want both. Redundancy saves lives."

I blink. That wasn't what I expected. Not the easy capitulation, not the acknowledgment of both our strengths.

But before I can reply, he grabs my hand, pulls me into the trees behind the overlook where shadows dance across damp pine needles, and kisses me like he needs it to breathe. Like we're still in my cabin, not standing out in the open on public land. His mouth tastes of coffee and certainty.

He palms my breast through my jacket, mouth dragging

along my jaw, stubble rasping against sensitive skin. I gasp, and heat floods my veins.

"That sound. I'll never get enough of it." He doesn't linger. Doesn't soften. Just turns and strides back onto the trail, leaving me trembling in the dappled light like he didn't just set me on fire.

I catch up to him breathless, heart hammering from more than the incline. He walks like nothing happened, like he didn't just kiss me breathless in the trees. Like my nipples aren't still peaked and aching, jacket zipped tight against the evidence.

He doesn't look back. Just tosses over his shoulder, "Keep up."

I do. Barely.

The next half-mile is steep, rocky, and shaded by sun-dappled trees. Pines crowd the trail in places, casting shadows over everything. My thighs burn. My breath fogs. But it's nothing compared to the ache between my legs. The weight of that kiss. Of the promise in his hands. Of what I told him in the dark.

When the trail bends around a granite outcrop, he stops.

Dead.

I stumble to a halt behind him, nearly crashing into his back. "What—?"

He turns. Eyes dark. Sure.

No smile. Just heat.

Predatory.

I freeze mid-step, my breath catching, something in my chest folding in on itself. His gaze tracks me like a target. Like I've already said, yes, even though my lips haven't moved.

He steps closer, gaze locked to mine, until there's no space left between us.

"You said you imagined me. That first day. Shoving you to your knees."

A breath stutters out of me.

My stomach tightens. My pulse goes wild.

I can't look away.

His fingers curl into my collar, tugging me close, our boots crunching against pine needles. Trees sway in the wind, but everything else stops.

Then he drops his pack, unbuckles his belt, eyes never leaving mine. Then he pulls his cock free.

Thick, hot, already leaking.

"On your knees."

My breath leaves me in a rush. Heat floods every cell.

"You're going to look so fucking pretty with your mouth full," he rasps. "Just like you imagined. Just like you begged for."

I drop. Right there, on damp pine needles, knees sinking into the soft ground.

I kneel.

Willing.

Shaking.

His eyes gleam. "That's what I thought."

He strokes himself once, slow, thick, and hard, standing over me like a god I just gave permission to ruin me.

"Open."

My lips part. My mouth waters.

He doesn't ease in—he pushes. Deep. Claiming. Groaning as his cock slides past my lips, forcing my jaw wide, his hand tangling in my hair to keep me still.

"Fuck," he hisses. "That's it. That's my girl."

My lips seal around him. My moan is immediate, involuntary.

He grips my hair tightly, starts to thrust, his movements controlled and measured, then deeper. My throat works to take him, spit trailing from the corners of my mouth, eyes watering as he pushes further.

"You wanted this." He's panting now, hips moving with brutal rhythm. "Thought about me using your mouth like this. Not gentle. Not asking. Just taking."

Tears streak down my cheeks, and I love it. I fucking love it.

His breath shortens. His grip tightens. Every thrust is possession.

"Look at you," he growls, watching me come undone. "On your knees for me. Taking every inch."

I hum around him, eyes locked to his, the sound filthy and desperate. Saliva spills from the corners of my mouth. He moves harder, deeper, fucking my mouth like he owns it.

"You've been aching for this. Dreaming about me using you like this. Ever since you crashed into me and looked up like you wanted to bite."

His hips rock forward. My throat tightens. He drags back, then slams in again.

"Look at you now. Letting me fuck your throat like it's mine."

Tears blur my vision. I don't stop.

Can't stop.

Every stroke is a reminder—this is him. Not some faceless stranger in a fantasy. Him. The man who saw me, who knew. Who isn't afraid of holding back.

He growls low, sharp. His grip tightens in my hair.

"Fuck—I'm gonna come down that pretty throat."

I hum for him. Sink deeper.

He shudders. Comes hard.

Groaning my name like a confession and a curse. His release hits the back of my throat, and I swallow it all.

He doesn't let me go right away. Just holds me there, softening slowly between my lips while his thumb brushes the corner of my mouth. Finally, he pulls back, tucking himself away with shaking hands, eyes dark and satisfied.

I'm ruined.

He stares down at me like I just handed him every secret I've ever had.

Mouth swollen. Knees scraped. Chest heaving.

He crouches in front of me, thumb sweeping over my lip like he's marking me all over again.

Then he offers a hand. Helps me stand. Then he brushes a kiss against my ear.

"On the way down, I'll bend you over that boulder and fuck you like you were made for it."

Mac keeps his promise on the way down.

ON THE THIRD DAY, WE ATTACK A ROUGHER PORTION of the trail. The terrain is steep. Mud clings to our boots, and pine needles stick to damp packs.

The air thins, making each breath sharper, more deliberate. Mountains rise around us like sleeping giants, indifferent to our passage.

I point toward a fork where two narrow trails diverge around a massive boulder. "We'll cut left, loop back past Grizzly Rock."

He hesitates, the sun casting his face in sharp relief, highlighting the stubborn set of his jaw. "That trail's marked impassable on the map."

"Because no one's walked it since the '98 burn." I meet his gaze, refusing to look away. "I have. Recently."

His eyes search mine, no longer challenging but assessing, weighing not just my words but the confidence behind them. Then he nods, the gesture a concession and acknowledgment wrapped in one.

"Lead the way."

The trust in those three words settles in my chest, heavier

than it should be.

By noon, we're off track according to GPS. The forest has reclaimed this path, wildflowers pushing through charred stumps, life persisting despite devastation. But the route opens onto a quiet glade, high and wide and ringed with granite that gleams silver in the midday sun.

A perfect natural shelter, invisible to technology but known to those who read the land itself.

We wander across the glade to the sheer granite walls.

He drops his pack. Pulls mine off me in one clean motion, the sudden lightness making me sway toward him.

"I've been thinking about this all day," he says, voice deeper now, commanding. "How I want to fuck you."

He pins me against the rock wall, his thigh sliding between mine, stone cold through my clothes, while his body radiates heat. "Have you?"

"Yes."

He grips my wrists, holds them above my head against rough stone. The position makes me arch and press against him in a silent plea.

He fucks me like he doesn't care who hears—fast, aggressive, relentless. The rock cold at my back, his mouth hot at my throat, the contrast as dizzying as the altitude. Beneath us, the valley stretches to the horizon, witness to my claiming.

I come undone with my eyes locked on his, the vast open sky reflecting in blue irises turned stormy with desire.

And he doesn't look away. Doesn't blink. Doesn't let me hide from what's happening between us

---

Back at the cabin, I barely close the door before he grabs me, wood thudding as my back hits it. The sound echoes through the small space, followed by the rasp of his breathing.

No words. No warning.

Just raw, unbearable need.

He spins me to face the wall, tears my leggings down, and thrusts inside me like he can't wait. Like he's been holding back all damn day. The wood is rough against my palms, my cheek, contrasting with the smooth heat of him stretching me, filling me.

One hand fists in my hair, pulling just enough to make my back arch, my body yield. The other spreads across my stomach, fingers splayed wide, holding me in place. His palm is calloused, his skin rough from years of fighting fires and saving lives.

"I can't get enough of you," he groans, fucking me through the words like he needs them to come harder, like my surrender feeds something primal in him. His rhythm turns brutal, perfect, pushing me past thought into pure sensation.

On the fourth day, I take him on a route that is significantly longer than the previous ones. We hike all day through terrain that shifts from dense forest to alpine meadow.

Summer wildflowers nod in the breeze, painting the slopes in splashes of purple lupine and golden paintbrush. I lead through brush-choked switchbacks, correcting his GPS again and again as we climb. He doesn't argue this time, nods and adjusts, marking waypoints where our knowledge differs.

But when we stop to rest beside a tumbling stream, water chattering over ancient stones, he doesn't let me sit on the fallen log I've chosen.

Instead, he grips my jaw with gentle fingers. Kisses me deep, tasting of trail mix and desire. Then pushes me to my knees, the motion a silent command.

My breath catches in my throat as I look up at him, sunlight haloing his dark hair, turning him into something almost mythic against the mountain sky.

He pauses. Watching. Checking.

His eyes have softened since that first day, not less intense but more attentive, reading my responses beyond words.

I nod. Just once. Permission and plea wrapped in a single gesture.

"Open that mouth, my Josephine. Please me." His voice drops to that register that makes my skin tighten, my core clench.

The moss is damp beneath my knees; the earth yields as I sink into it. He cups the back of my head, guides me, his touch both firm and careful. Takes what he wants. Gives me exactly what I need. The stream's music covers my sounds, his groans, creating a private world despite the open mountainside.

When he finishes, he pulls me up, kisses me like I just gave him air after drowning, and we hike on like nothing happened.

But everything has.

With each trail, each encounter, boundaries blur—professional, personal, and physical.

By the last trail, we don't pretend anymore.

The final route takes us to the highest point, where trees surrender to rock and sky. The wind whips my hair, carrying the scent of snow from distant peaks. Below us, Angel's Peak looks like a toy town, vulnerable to the whims of nature.

We argue over the final evacuation sector. He wants a GPS overlay for the emergency services. I want the hand-marked elevation guide that shows which slopes become unstable after heavy rainfall.

We don't agree. However, the argument lacks the intensity of our first confrontations, having evolved into something collaborative despite our differing approaches.

When we get back to the cabin, he fucks me over the table, my hands splayed across maps I drew, routes I marked, all pressed into my skin as he claims me.

When I come, shuddering against smooth paper and rough wood, he presses his forehead to mine and murmurs, "I've never fallen this hard, this fast."

And just like that, I forget how to breathe. Because it's no longer about maps. Not about routes and protocols and whose knowledge matters more.

Six routes. Five days.

Countless arguments. Countless orgasms.

He pushes. I resist.

He takes. I give.

The rhythm of it becomes its own language. My yielding is a choice. His dominance isn't control but an offering—showing me what he sees, what he wants, what he believes I need.

And somewhere in all the friction, we find a harmony I never expected. My knowledge of the mountains, his tactical expertise. My caution, his confidence. His command. My surrender.

Not *just* sex. Not *just* work.

It's *something* else.

Something I'm scared to name.

Because he still won't call me Jo—that casual nickname everyone else uses.

And I'm starting to like the way he says *Josephine* too damn much. The way the syllables roll off his tongue like a caress, like he's tasting something precious.

Like he's claiming not just my body, but the person I've always been. The woman waiting for a man like him to take what I need to give.

Angel's Peak

CHAPTER 7

BURIED EMBERS

MAC'S ARM LIES HEAVY ACROSS MY WAIST, HIS breathing deep and even against my neck. I've been awake for an hour, watching shadows retreat from the corners, wondering how my life transformed so completely in just six days.

Six days. Six trails. And whatever this is between us.

I ease from beneath his arm, holding my breath when he stirs. His face in sleep lacks the intensity that normally charges his features—softer somehow, vulnerable in a way he'd never allow while conscious. For a moment, I almost reach out to trace the line of his jaw, the curve of his lower lip. Instead, I slip from the bed and pad silently to the bathroom.

In the shower, hot water pounds against my shoulders, washing away the physical evidence of last night but doing nothing for the memories etched into my skin.

Every muscle carries the pleasant ache of being thoroughly used. My wrists bear faint marks from his grip, my inner thighs the shadow of beard burn. I should be horrified by how quickly I've surrendered to this—to him—but all I feel is the low hum of satisfaction and the disturbing absence of regret.

This isn't me. I don't do this—fall into bed with arrogant men who call me by a name I don't use, who take control like it's their right, who somehow find the hidden switch that transforms my usual independence into willing submission.

I step from the shower and wipe the steam from the mirror. My reflection stares back, unchanged yet unrecognizable. Same eyes, same face, but something's different in the way I carry myself. Like my body knows a secret my mind isn't ready to acknowledge.

"Stop overthinking," I mutter to my reflection, wrapping a towel around my torso. "It's just sex."

Except it isn't, and lying to myself has never been a particular skill of mine.

When I emerge, the bed is empty, sheets thrown back. The scent of coffee reaches me, mingling with domestic sounds from my kitchen. Mac's at my counter, moving through my space with an ease that suggests he belongs here. The presumption should irritate me.

It doesn't.

He belongs. Definitely belongs. Just as I belong to him now.

"Morning." Mac's voice is morning-rough, a lazy drawl that sends an involuntary shiver down my spine. He stands shirtless in my kitchen, wearing only his tactical pants, feet bare against the hardwood. His hair is sleep-mussed, with stubble darker than it was yesterday.

"You made coffee." I adjust my towel, suddenly self-conscious in a way I wasn't when he had me bent over the kitchen table last night.

"Figured you'd need it." He slides a mug across the counter. Two sugars, no cream. Perfect. "You were restless last night."

I take the mug, careful that our fingers don't touch. "I don't sleep well with someone else in my bed."

The lie comes easily, but his raised eyebrow tells me he sees right through it. I've spent five nights sleeping soundly in his arms. Until last night, when the reality of what we've been doing, what we've become to each other, finally caught up with me.

"We should talk," he says, leaning against the counter.

"About what?" I blow on my coffee, avoiding his eyes.

"Don't play dumb, Josephine. It doesn't suit you."

There it is. That name again. The one that sounds like possession on his lips.

"I need to get to the visitor center." I move toward the bedroom. "There's a group of hikers coming through this morning, and I promised Eleanor—"

His hand catches my wrist as I pass, not roughly, but with enough intention to stop me in my tracks. The simple contact sends electricity skittering up my arm.

"We've verified all seven routes." His thumb brushes over my pulse point, a casual intimacy that feels anything but casual. "What happens now?"

What happens now?

I don't know.

The question hangs between us, weighted with implications neither of us has voiced. We've spent five days fucking on mountainsides and in my bed, learning each other's bodies with single-minded thoroughness, but we've carefully avoided discussing what comes after the routes are verified.

"You go back to firefighting." I pull away, retreating to the bedroom. "I go back to my maps."

I dress quickly, choosing clothes like armor—functional hiking pants, a long-sleeved thermal shirt, despite the summer heat. When I return to the kitchen, Mac has pulled on his shirt and boots. His expression has shifted from morning softness to something more guarded.

"Is that what you want?" He studies me with an intensity that makes me want to squirm.

"It's what makes sense." I busy myself preparing a travel mug of coffee, needing the distraction. "We have jobs to do."

"Right." Mac drains his mug and sets it in the sink with deliberate care. "Jobs."

The silence stretches between us, taut with unspoken words. For a moment, I think he might push—might demand the conversation I'm so desperately avoiding. Instead, he grabs his jacket from the hook by the door.

"I've got crew evaluations this morning. I'll be at the station if anything comes up."

And just like that, he's gone, the door clicking softly behind him. Something that feels suspiciously like disappointment settles in my chest. I push it away, whistling for Scout, who emerges reluctantly from the bedroom, looking as disappointed in me as I feel in myself.

"Don't you start," I tell her, clipping on her leash. "It's for the best."

She doesn't look convinced.

The visitor center is quiet when I arrive—too early for tourists, too late for the pre-dawn hikers. I settle at my desk, spreading out the maps Mac and I verified. Despite everything, our work was thorough. Each route has been walked, assessed, and updated with both my notations and his GPS coordinates. A true collaboration, despite our different approaches.

I lose myself in the familiar rhythm of mapmaking, transferring field notes to master copies, and updating trail conditions with fresh colored ink. The work has always centered me, given me purpose. Today it feels hollow, mechanical.

My phone buzzes with a text from Eleanor: *Did you hear about the fires?*

I frown, typing back: *What fires?*

Her response comes quickly: *Three new spot fires reported*

overnight. All in remote areas. Sheriff's concerned. Deliberate, they think.

My stomach tightens. Early-season fires aren't unusual in Colorado, but deliberate ones are. And three in remote locations suggests something more sinister than careless campers.

Before I can respond, the visitor center door swings open. Mac strides in, looking every inch the captain in his yellow uniform shirt and green tactical pants. The casual intimacy of this morning has vanished, replaced by focused professionalism that makes him even more magnetic. Parker follows behind him, carrying a rolled map tube.

"Ms. Mackenzie." His tone is all business, but his eyes tell a different story. "Got a minute?"

"Captain Sullivan." I match his formality, aware of Parker's presence and the subtle shift in dynamics. "What can I do for you?"

Parker unrolls a satellite map across my desk, securing the corners with paperweights. Red X marks dot the terrain in a distinctive pattern.

"Three new fires," Mac explains, pointing to each X. "All started within a four-hour window last night. All in remote locations without trail access."

I study the map, recognition dawning. "These are all in the northwest sector. Near the old mining claims."

"That mean something to you?" Mac watches my face with the intensity I've come to expect.

"Maybe." I pull out my own map of the area. "This sector has been abandoned since the Silver Creek Mine shut down in the 90s. No official trails, minimal access. You'd need serious backcountry skills to reach these spots."

"And intimate knowledge of the terrain," Parker adds, eyes sharp.

I trace the pattern with my finger. "These aren't random. They form a perimeter around this valley." I tap the center of the triangle created by the fire locations. "Old prospector territory. Dozens of abandoned claims."

"Any idea why someone would target that area?" Mac leans closer, his arm brushing mine as he studies the map.

The contact, however brief, sends warmth cascading through me. I step back slightly, needing distance to think clearly.

"Not immediately, no. It's remote, rarely visited. No valuable structures or resources." I frown at the pattern. "But the placement feels deliberate. There's been no lightning in the area to account for one fire, let alone three."

"That's our assessment, too." Mac straightens, all captain now. "Fortunately, they were quick to put out the fires, and they're no longer a threat, but we're concerned about reoccurrences."

"You think whoever set those will set more?"

"Can't risk ruling it out, which is why I want to position observation teams at strategic points surrounding this valley. Eyes on all potential access routes, monitoring for further activity."

"Sheriff Donovan can help with that. Or Jackson Hart. He's a local guide who knows those mountains almost as well as I do."

"Sheriff's coordinating with state authorities." Mac's eyes lock with mine. "Jackson's already out with clients and unavailable. We need someone who knows the unofficial routes. The game trails, the old mining paths—the ones that don't appear on any official map."

Understanding dawns. "You need a guide."

"We need you," he says.

"No." Ice slides through my veins, my heart rate spiking.

"Josephine—"

"I said no." My voice comes out harder than intended. "I don't guide people. Not anymore."

Parker glances between us, sensing the sudden tension. "I'll check in with Rodriguez on the equipment status," she says, tactfully retreating to the far end of the visitor center.

Mac waits until she's out of earshot.

"You guided me."

"That was different." I cross my arms, hating how defensive I sound. "You're a professional, and those were established evacuation routes. This is—"

"This is what you do." His voice softens. "You know these mountains. My team needs that knowledge."

"I make maps." I turn away, rearranging papers on my desk with shaking hands. "I don't take people into the backcountry."

"Why not?"

The simple question slices through my defenses. I could lie, make up some excuse about being too busy, but he'd see through it immediately. Something about Mac has always made it impossible to hide.

"Three years ago," I say finally, my back still to him. "I was leading a guided hike. Family of four—parents, two children. The youngest, Sarah, was eight." I swallow past the tightness in my throat. "She wanted to see mountain goats."

I feel rather than see Mac move closer, his presence solid behind me.

"The trail wasn't dangerous. I'd led a hundred groups down it without incident. Safe. Familiar. I knew every root, every turn." My fingers tighten around the pencil, the wood creaking. "But that spring, the snowmelt hit early. Hard. Underneath the trail, near Crystal Falls, the runoff carved it out. Left the top looking solid."

The pencil snaps in half.

"It wasn't."

He doesn't speak. Just listens.

"Sarah was excited. It was her first time seeing a real waterfall. She ran ahead—laughing, calling back to me—and before I could stop her..." My breath shudders out. "The ground vanished beneath her feet."

I can still hear the sound—earth crumbling, that horrible second of silence before the scream.

"She fell fifty feet. Straight down onto jagged rock." I force the words through the knot in my throat. "Her arm snapped. Her skull cracked so loudly I thought she was already gone. Fifty-two stitches to close her face. But the worst part—the part that never heals—was her back."

I finally lift my gaze to his.

"The fall shattered her spine. She'll never walk again. Eight years old, and I'm the reason she'll spend the rest of her life in a chair."

"Jo—"

"I was her guide. Her protector. And I missed it. I should've seen the undercut. I should've stopped her. I should've—" My voice breaks. "She trusted me, and I failed her. That's the truth. And I live with it every time I close my eyes."

The admission hangs in the air between us. Mac's expression shifts from gentle concern to understanding. He steps closer, into my space.

"Accidents happen," he says quietly. "Even to the most experienced guides."

"Not to me." I meet his eyes, needing him to understand. "Not before that. Not after. I don't guide anymore. I make maps."

He studies me for a long moment, blue eyes searching mine. Then he does something unexpected. He shares a piece of himself.

"Two years ago, I made a call during a canyon fire." His voice is low, steady. "Split my team to cover more ground. Standard procedure, one I'd executed dozens of times before."

Something in his tone makes my heart constrict.

"Wind shifted. Fire jumped the line." His jaw tightens. "Lost radio contact with the second team for seventeen minutes. Longest seventeen minutes of my life."

I see the shadow pass behind his eyes, the ghost of whatever happened in those seventeen minutes.

"They made it out." His voice roughens. "But it was close. Too close."

He doesn't elaborate, but I understand what he's doing. Offering me a glimpse of his own fallibility, his own burden of command. A bridge between us built of shared responsibility.

"I'm not asking you to guide tourists on sightseeing trips," he says. "I'm asking you to help seasoned firefighters protect the mountains you love."

His hand reaches up and brushes a strand of hair from my face. The simple touch undoes me more than any passionate kiss.

"My team knows what they're doing," he continues. "They're the best. However, they are unfamiliar with this terrain. You know it."

I stare at the map, at the red X marks forming their ominous triangle. If the fires are deliberate, they're just the beginning. Someone is out there with a plan, using the mountains I love as their weapon.

"I can't be responsible for people's safety." The words come out small, revealing more vulnerability than I intend.

"You already are." Mac's voice gentles. "Every map you draw, every trail warning you post, every evacuation route you plan—you're already taking responsibility."

His logic finds purchase in the cracks of my resistance, taking root in an uncomfortable truth.

"It's different when they're right there beside you," I whisper, finally meeting his eyes. "When their lives depend on your split-second decisions."

Understanding dawns in his expression. "Is that what happened with Sarah? A split-second decision?"

"I hesitated." The admission costs me. "Just for a moment. Saw the danger too late. Called out too late."

"And you've been punishing yourself ever since."

It's not a question, but I answer anyway.

"Wouldn't you?"

Something flickers in his eyes—recognition, perhaps. Or a shadow of his own guilt.

"Every day," he says quietly.

The simple acknowledgment hits harder than any argument could. For a moment, we stand there, two people carrying the weight of responsibility, of choices made and consequences faced.

"I need your help, Josephine." No demands. No manipulation. Just the truth. "Lives could depend on it."

I close my eyes, weighing risk against responsibility. When I open them, my decision is made.

"I'll help position your observation teams, but I'll set the routes. The pace. The safety protocols. No arguments."

Relief softens his features. "Agreed."

"And no civilians." I need this boundary to be firm and clear. "Just your crew. I'm not guiding tourists again."

"Just my team." He nods. "They follow orders and know their jobs."

Something almost like excitement flutters beneath my fear —the long-dormant part of me that loved guiding, that thrived on sharing my mountains with others. I squash it ruthlessly. This is about duty, not pleasure. About responsibility, not redemption.

"When do we start?" I ask, already mentally cataloging the gear we'll need.

"Tomorrow at dawn." Mac's expression turns professional again, but something warmer lingers in his eyes. "I'll brief the team this afternoon. We'll need observation points with good visibility but natural cover, access to emergency evacuation routes, and minimal fire risk."

I nod, already mapping possibilities in my head. "I know some places. Old hunting blinds, abandoned fire towers. I'll mark them tonight."

Mac moves back to the map, his focus shifting to the tactical planning that comes so naturally to him. For the next hour, we work side by side, plotting positions and routes, discussing team compositions and supply needs.

The earlier tension doesn't disappear, but it transforms into something more productive—a partnership born of mutual respect and shared purpose.

When Parker returns, we've outlined a comprehensive strategy. Six two-person teams positioned around the perimeter, with Mac and me mobile between positions. Three-day rotation, with daily supply runs and communication checks.

"Looks solid." Parker studies our plan with approving eyes. "I'll coordinate the equipment prep."

"We move at 0500," Mac tells her. "Ms. Mackenzie will be our primary guide for positioning."

If Parker is surprised by my involvement, she doesn't show it. She nods, professional respect in her eyes.

"I'll inform the team." She gathers her notes and heads for the door, leaving Mac and me alone again.

The moment the door closes, Mac turns. The map still lies between us, but the air shifts, tighter now. Charged.

"I'm coming over tonight."

I blink. "Excuse me?"

His gaze doesn't waver. "You heard me."

I duck my head, suddenly fascinated by the corner of the map. "Mac... it's not necessary. This past week was amazing, but—"

"There's no way you're shutting the door on this," he cuts

in, voice low but absolute. "Don't pretend the past week meant nothing."

"It was just sex." I lift my chin, defiant. Lying. Both of us know it.

"Don't insult us both."

Silence pulses between us. My heart kicks against my ribs like it wants to escape the room. His body's still, but the air around him feels molten. Ready to ignite.

"We agreed to keep the personal separate," I say. "Focus on the job."

"No. You said that. I let you say it because you were scared. Still are." He leans down until his mouth hovers beside my ear. "But I've had my cock inside you, Josephine. Felt you clench around me like you couldn't get enough. Watched you beg me not to stop. You think I'm the kind of man who fucks and walks away?"

Heat surges up my throat. My fingers tighten around the pencil again—this time, I don't snap it. But I want to.

"I don't know who you've had in your bed before," he says, stepping around the table, slow and steady like he's stalking prey, "but I'm not the kind of man who fucks and walks away. Especially not from a woman like you."

I hold my ground. Barely.

His thumb brushes the corner of my mouth, a touch so reverent it steals my breath. "You and I... we don't just fit. We burn. Same fire. Same fucking spark."

He exhales slowly, gaze locked on mine like he's reading every fractured piece. "I've never met a woman who gives like you. Who fights like she's made of armor, but surrenders like it's a gift."

My pulse stutters, betrays me.

"This isn't over," he murmurs, his mouth brushing my temple, voice rough velvet. "Not by a long shot. I'm coming over tonight. And we're going to talk. Quiet. Honest. No interruptions. You're mine, and I'm going to show you what that means."

A promise, not a threat. But it still leaves me trembling.

Then he turns—no hesitation, no backward glance—and walks out like he just rewrote the rules.

And all I can do is stand there, every nerve lit, every wall cracked wide open... already burning for what comes next.

Angel's Peak

Chapter 8

Smoke Signals

Last night plays on repeat behind my eyes—the low rasp of Mac's voice in the dark, the way his words didn't just settle under my skin, they branded me.

"You're mine, Josephine. Not just in bed. Not just in heat. I see you—all of you. And I'm not going anywhere."

It wasn't a demand. It was a vow. One he sealed with slow, devastating possession. The kind of sex that rewires a woman.

Feral, filthy, reverent.

He worshipped me with his mouth, his hands, his body—then ruined me completely until all I could do was scream his name into the mattress and beg for more.

He didn't just fuck me.

He claimed me.

And I let him.

Now, dawn breaks in shades of amber and rose as Mac's team assembles at the trailhead. The air carries the scent of pine and possibility, dew clinging to every surface like tiny prisms. Under different circumstances, I might pause to appreciate the beauty.

Today, there's no room for awe.

My focus narrows—hazard points, terrain changes, emergency egress routes, weather fronts closing in.

Everything that could go wrong.

Because out here, one misstep costs everything. And after last night... I have too much to lose.

I shift my pack higher on my shoulders, scan the perimeter, and force my breath to slow.

If any of them knew.

If they had the slightest idea what Mac did to me this morning—how he woke me with a grip in my hair and a command on his tongue.

Heat flares across my cheeks, my thighs clenching involuntarily.

I'm his.

And Mac? He's going to make damn sure I never forget it.

He stands at the center of his crew, issuing final instructions. He's transformed overnight from the man in my bed to Captain Sullivan, all crisp authority and tactical precision. His team forms a semi-circle around him—twelve firefighters in yellow and green, loaded with observation equipment and survival gear. The other half of his crew remains on standby at the station, ready to respond if the arsonist strikes again.

"Our priority is intelligence gathering," Mac tells them, voice carrying in the morning stillness. "We're looking for evidence of human activity, unusual patterns, anything that might help identify who's behind these fires."

I hang back, checking my pack for the third time. Water purification tablets, emergency blanket, first aid kit, compass, topographical maps—everything in its place, just as I've packed a hundred times before. Yet my hands won't stop their methodical inventory, driven by anxiety I can't quite suppress.

Scout sits beside me, her intelligent brown eyes tracking my nervous movements. She tilts her head as I check the same pocket for the fourth time, then nudges my hand with her wet nose—a gentle reminder that my anxiety is showing. I scratch behind her ears, finding comfort in her steady presence.

"At least one of us knows what we're doing," I murmur to her. She wags her tail once, confident and ready, the way she always is before we head into the mountains.

"Ms. Mackenzie will be our guide." Mac gestures toward me, and twelve pairs of eyes shift in my direction. "She knows these mountains, the terrain, the pitfalls and dangers. When she speaks, you listen. Clear?"

A chorus of affirmations ripples through the group. I straighten my shoulders, feeling the weight of their trust settle uncomfortably across my back.

"We'll divide into six teams of two," Mac continues, unfolding the map we prepared yesterday. "Each team will establish an observation post at these designated coordinates. Ms. Mackenzie and I will guide you to your positions, then maintain mobile patrol between posts."

Rodriguez raises a hand. "What kind of terrain are we looking at, Cap?"

Mac defers with a nod in my direction. "Ms. Mackenzie?"

I step forward, pushing down the flutter of nerves in my stomach. "Mostly old mining territory. Steep slopes, loose shale in places. Several unmarked caves and abandoned prospector camps. The western ridge is unstable after last spring's landslide." I trace the area on the map. "Navigation is tricky—GPS signals bounce off rock faces, creating false readings. Follow the markers I've indicated, not your devices."

Parker studies the map, brow furrowed. "What about water sources?"

"Three reliable springs marked here, here, and here." I point to the blue X's on the map. "The northeastern stream runs high with snowmelt, but it's contaminated with old mining runoff. Don't drink from it, even with filtration."

The questions continue—terrain hazards, wildlife activity,

and emergency extraction points. I answer each with growing confidence, my anxiety receding as I slip into the familiar role of mountain expert. This part I've always been good at— reading the land, understanding its moods and dangers.

Scout moves to my side as I speak, her presence grounding me. She's been my partner on every trail survey; her nose detects wildlife signs before I spot them, and her ears alert me to changes in weather patterns through sounds I can't hear.

The crew notices her immediately—the way she positions herself, alert but calm, scanning the terrain with professional focus.

"Your dog always work with you?" Williams asks with genuine curiosity.

"Scout's saved more hikers than I have," I reply, one hand resting on her head. "She can track scent trails through terrain that would take me hours to navigate, and she knows the difference between normal wildlife activity and something wrong."

It's the human element that terrifies me.

"Move out in five," Mac announces, folding the map. The teams break formation to perform last-minute equipment checks.

Mac approaches, stopping close enough that only I can hear him. "You okay?"

His concern shouldn't warm me, but it does. "Fine."

"You've checked your pack four times."

"Three," I correct automatically, then bite my lip at his knowing look. "Just being thorough."

His eyes soften a fraction. "You don't have to do this."

"Yes, I do." I adjust my pack straps, avoiding his gaze. "Just don't expect me to be happy about it."

"Noted." A hint of amusement colors his voice. "For what it's worth, they're impressed. Not everyone can silence a hotshot crew with mountain trivia."

"It's not trivia when it might save their lives." The words come out sharper than intended.

His expression shifts, something unreadable flickering across his features. "No. It isn't."

Before I can decipher his reaction, Parker approaches with a radio check request, and the moment passes.

We lead the first team—Martinez and Williams—up the eastern slope toward Thunder Ridge. The trail starts easily enough, following an old logging road before branching onto a game path I've mapped but rarely traveled. Martinez moves with surprising grace for his size, while Williams maintains a running commentary on the flora we pass.

"These are different from the ones in California," she says, pausing to examine a cluster of blue columbines. "Our wildflowers don't handle altitude well."

"State flower," I tell her. "They only bloom above 7,000 feet."

"Beautiful," she murmurs, then jogs to catch up.

Mac takes point, setting a steady pace that respects the terrain without wasting time. I bring up the rear, eyes constantly scanning for signs of danger—loose rocks, unstable ground, wildlife movement. Every snapped twig makes me flinch. Every rustle in the underbrush spikes my pulse.

Scout ranges ahead of me, staying within sight but using her superior senses to scout the trail. Her ears swivel constantly, cataloging sounds beyond human perception.

When she pauses and looks back at me with a soft whine, I know she's picked up something—a scent or sound that doesn't belong. I signal Mac, who holds up a hand to halt the team while Scout investigates a cluster of boulders off the main trail.

She returns with nothing more threatening than the lingering scent of elk, but her diligence reminds me why I trust her instincts more than my paranoia.

"Relax, Mackenzie." Mac drops back to walk beside me while his team navigates a narrow stretch ahead. "You're hyper-vigilant."

Out here, he calls me *Mackenzie*. Everyone in his crew uses each other's last names when on the job. In person, when it's just us, he switches to *Josephine*, the only person who calls me that. Makes it all the more special.

"That's my job." I step carefully around a jutting rock. "Someone has to be."

"Not to this degree." His voice drops lower. "You're going to burn out before we reach the first position."

"I'm fine."

"You've checked every foothold Martinez and Williams have used. Tested branches they've already tested. Recalculated distances I've already confirmed." His observation is too accurate for comfort. "Trust the process, Josephine."

"I trust facts, not processes." I scan the ridge line above us. "Processes fail. People make mistakes."

"Some mistakes can't be anticipated."

I glance at him sharply, but his expression reveals nothing beyond professional concern.

"All mistakes can be prevented with proper preparation." The words come out like a mantra, one I've repeated to myself a thousand times since Sarah's fall.

Mac studies me for a long moment, then simply says, "No. They can't."

Before I can argue, he moves ahead to rejoin his team, leaving me with an unsettled feeling that has nothing to do with the treacherous terrain.

The first observation post sits on a natural plateau halfway up Thunder Ridge. The position offers clear sightlines to two of the fire sites while remaining sheltered by a granite outcropping. A perfect vantage point—invisible from below but commanding views of the valley.

"This is ideal," Martinez says, already unpacking surveillance equipment. "We can monitor both the north and west approaches from here."

"There's a small spring fifty yards south," I tell them, marking it on their field map. "The ridge above is unstable after last winter's freeze-thaw cycle. Don't climb higher without radio confirmation first."

Williams nods, laying out solar charging equipment. "How often do the winds shift here?"

"Afternoon thermals pick up around two. Expect sixty-degree directional changes until sunset." I scan the horizon, reading familiar weather patterns in the cloud formations. "Storm system moving in from the northwest. Probably hit by tomorrow evening."

"You can tell that just by looking?" Williams sounds impressed.

"The mountains talk if you know how to listen." My father's words spill out from me; his mantra lives with me.

I check my watch, calculating our next leg. "That cloud formation over the western peak only appears when a low-pressure system is building behind it."

Mac finishes the communications check, nodding his satisfaction. "You're set. Check in every two hours. Report any movement immediately, but do not engage. Clear?"

"Crystal, Cap," Martinez confirms, already settling into observation position.

As we descend toward the next drop point, Mac keeps pace beside me. "That was good. They respect your expertise."

I shrug, uncomfortable with the praise. "They'd better. Their lives might depend on it."

"You really can read the weather patterns that accurately?" There's genuine curiosity in his question.

"My father taught me." I duck under a low-hanging

branch. "He used to say the mountains never lie, but they don't always speak plainly. You have to learn their language."

"Your father sounds like a wise man."

"He was." The past tense slips out before I can catch it.

Mac notices—of course he does—but doesn't push. Instead, he asks, "Were you always going to follow in his footsteps?"

"I never planned to." I navigate around a fallen log. "I was studying environmental science at CSU when he died. Heart attack on Widow's Peak. By the time another hiker found him, it was too late."

"I'm sorry."

"It was seven years ago." I keep my voice neutral, as if discussing a stranger instead of the man who taught me everything I know about these mountains. "Sheriff Donovan asked if I'd take over as safety coordinator temporarily. Temporary turned permanent."

"You're good at it." His observation carries no flattery, just a simple acknowledgment.

"I was better before." The admission slips out before I can stop it.

Mac's expression softens with understanding. "Before Sarah."

I nod once, not trusting my voice.

"What happened to her? After the accident."

"Multiple surgeries to minimize the scarring." I focus on a distant peak, memories rising unbidden. "Last I heard, she recovered, but is wheelchair bound for life. The family moved to Arizona afterward."

"Away from the mountains."

"Away from me." The truth of it still stings. "Can't blame them."

Mac is quiet for several paces, then says something unexpected. "You blame yourself enough for everyone."

The observation hits too close to home. I pick up the pace, putting distance between us as we approach the next ridgeline.

By midday, we've positioned four of the six teams. Each location I've chosen offers strategic advantages—natural cover, clear sightlines, proximity to water, and multiple escape routes. With each successful placement, the knot of anxiety in my chest loosens incrementally.

Maybe I can do this. Maybe the weight of responsibility won't crush me this time.

The fifth position proves more challenging. The original location I marked on the map has changed since my last visit—a recent rockslide altered the approach, making it too exposed for safety.

"We need an alternative," I tell Mac, studying the terrain. "There's a hunter's blind about half a mile north, but it won't give the same coverage of the southern approach."

Mac consults his GPS, frowning at the readings. "What about that ridgeline?" He points to a rocky outcropping just visible through the trees.

"Too exposed." I shake my head. "First place lightning would strike in a storm."

"Underground options?"

"There's an old mine shaft entrance nearby, but—"

"No." His refusal comes sharp and immediate, startling me with its intensity. "No underground positions."

Burke and Nguyen exchange glances but say nothing.

"It's stable," I counter, confused by his vehemence. "I've mapped it myself."

"No underground." Mac's voice carries an edge I've never heard before—something raw and final that brooks no argument. "Find another option."

The sudden shift in his demeanor raises questions, but his expression warns against asking them now. Instead, I scan the terrain, recalculating.

"There's a natural depression beyond that copse of aspens." I point to a barely visible dip in the landscape. "Good cover, decent sightlines. We'd need to clear some brush for optimal visibility, but it could work."

Mac studies the location, then nods curtly. "Show us."

As Burke and Nguyen follow me toward the new position, I catch Mac taking a deep breath, one hand pressed briefly against his sternum before dropping away. The gesture seems unconscious, almost like he's steadying himself.

The new position proves workable with minimal adjustments. As Burke and Nguyen set up their equipment, Mac performs a perimeter check, his earlier tension still evident in the rigid set of his shoulders.

When we leave them to continue to our final drop point, Mac maintains an uncharacteristic silence. I match his quiet, sensing whatever triggered his reaction isn't something he wants to discuss in the field.

The radio crackles to life, Parker's voice breaking through static. "Alpha Leader, this is Base. Come in."

Scout's ears perk forward at the radio static, her body tensing with the same alertness she shows before storms. She's always been sensitive to changes in atmospheric pressure, and her reaction tells me something significant is happening before Parker's words confirm it.

MAC UNCLIPS HIS RADIO. "ALPHA LEADER. GO ahead, Base."

"New hotspot reported near Lookout Point. Tourist called it in. Appears to be fresh, within the last hour."

My stomach drops. Lookout Point is crawling with day-hikers this time of year.

"Size?" Mac's voice turns clipped, professional.

"Small, currently contained to a fallen log and surrounding brush. Fire team en route, but we're detecting unusual ignition patterns. May be connected to our arsonist."

Mac's eyes meet mine, the unspoken question clear. Lookout Point is at least four miles from the pattern established by the previous fires—a significant deviation.

"Civilian presence?" he asks, already calculating.

"Heavy. Weekend hikers, a tourist group from the lodge. Sheriff's coordinating evacuation."

"Acknowledged. Diverting to Lookout Point. Have Rodriguez and Williams maintain their position; all other teams proceed as planned. Alpha Leader out." Mac clips the radio back to his belt, decision made. "Change of plans."

Angel's Peak

CHAPTER 9

———

NEW FIRES

WE REACH LOOKOUT POINT IN FORTY-THREE minutes, lungs burning from the pace Mac sets over technical terrain. The scent hits us first—acrid smoke threading through pine and summer wildflowers. Then the sound: the hungry crackle of flames consuming dry timber.

Scout's hackles rise the moment we crest the approach trail. She stops dead, nose working the air, a low whine escaping her throat—the sound she makes when something is fundamentally wrong.

Her ears flatten against her skull as the acrid smoke hits us, and she looks back at me with worried eyes that seem to ask if we're really going toward that smell.

"I know, girl," I murmur, one hand finding her head for reassurance—mine or hers, I'm not sure. "But we have a job to do."

I crest the ridge and my stomach plummets.

What Parker described as a "small, contained" fire has spread to encompass nearly an acre of mixed woodland. Orange flames lick hungrily at the base of mature pines while smoke billows upward in a gray column visible for miles.

Worse, the fire burns in three distinct points—not the chaotic spread of natural wildfire, but deliberate ignition sites.

"Shit." Mac's assessment echoes my own as he studies the scene through binoculars. "That's not accidental."

Below us, Sheriff Donovan coordinates the civilian evacuation. Day-hikers stream down the main trail in loose groups, some moving too fast, others too slow. A family with young children struggles to keep pace, the father carrying a toddler while the mother herds two older kids ahead of the advancing smoke.

"There." I point to the family lagging behind. "They won't make it to the parking area before the fire reaches the trail junction."

Mac follows my gaze, jaw tightening as he calculates distances and wind patterns. "Alternate route?"

"The old service road loops around the north face. Longer but safer." I trace the route on my map, mind racing. "If they can reach it before the fire jumps that ridgeline."

"How long?"

"Twenty minutes if they move fast. Thirty if they don't."

Mac's radio crackles. Rodriguez's voice cuts through static: "Alpha Leader, we've got movement on the western perimeter. Two individuals heading toward the new fire site, not away from it."

"Civilians?" Mac asks.

"Negative. Moving with purpose, carrying equipment. Definitely not tourists."

My pulse spikes. Someone set this fire as a distraction, drawing attention while they operated elsewhere. Or worse— they're still here, watching their handiwork.

"Visual on suspects?" Mac demands.

"Lost them in the tree line. But they were heading straight for the active blaze."

Mac curses under his breath, torn between responding to

the immediate threat and protecting the civilians below. Command decisions in crisis—the weight I remember too well.

"I'll guide the family out." The words escape before I fully process them. "You coordinate with Rodriguez."

Scout moves to my side immediately, sensing the shift in my energy. She's already oriented toward the trail junction where the family struggles, her training kicking in.

She knows what "guide" means—it's what we do, what we've always done together in these mountains.

"Absolutely not." Mac's refusal comes swift and final. "You're not separating from the team."

"They need help now." I check my watch, calculating time against the fire spread. "Every minute they lose ground puts them deeper in the danger zone."

"Then we go together."

"And leave the arsonists free to operate? Rodriguez needs backup, and those civilians need guidance they're not getting from anyone else."

Mac's expression hardens, command authority warring with something more personal. The same protectiveness that kept him from letting me guide strangers into uncertain terrain.

"Josephine—"

"You know I'm right." My correction comes sharp, fueled by adrenaline and the familiar surge of purpose I haven't felt in three years. "This is what I do. What I'm good at."

Or, at least, it's what I used to think I was good at.

For a heartbeat, we stare at each other across the divide between safety and necessity. Then his radio crackles again—Parker requesting status updates, Rodriguez reporting the suspects have vanished completely, Sheriff Donovan calling for additional evacuation support.

Donovan's voice crackles over the comms. "Requesting additional support. Four hikers stranded near the upper switchbacks. Visibility dropping fast."

"Twenty minutes." Mac turns to me, voice all business. "Get them to the service road and hold position until the all-clear."

"Yes, sir." The words leave me automatically—efficient, clipped.

But something shifts. His eyes flick to mine with a sudden, sharp heat.

I'm already cinching my pack tighter, fingers moving fast through practiced motions. Knife. Gloves. Flare. Emergency beacon clipped front and center. Everything is exactly where it needs to be.

Then Mac steps closer, looming behind me like a storm wall. Heat radiates from him. His hand catches my wrist before I can go. Not restraining—just anchoring.

"Be careful out there."

"Always am."

His grip tightens just enough to make me gasp—and then I'm yanked flush against his chest. The impact steals my breath.

"I mean it, Josephine." His voice is low, rough gravel laced with steel. "No heroics. No unnecessary risks." Hard. Demanding. Possessive.

I open my mouth to argue—of course I do.

He doesn't let me.

His mouth crashes down on mine, a brutal collision of heat and command. It tastes like smoke and need, and the sharp tang of warning. His tongue claims, unapologetic. One hand knots in my hair, the other clamps over my hip like he owns it.

Owns me.

Like he's staking a claim before we walk into hell.

The storm howls around us, wind screaming through the treetops. I barely hear it. He kisses me like punishment.

Like promise.

Like this is the only moment we'll ever have, and he refuses to waste it.

When he pulls back, we're both breathless. His fingers still wrap tight around my wrist.

"Consider it an order," he growls. "Get in. Get out. No heroics. Just... just come back to me."

My breath hitches. I don't look away.

He doesn't let go.

"And if you disobey me out there..." His mouth brushes my ear, velvet and dark. "We'll have words. Real ones. The kind you'll feel."

A beat. My spine lights up with heat. My breath falters.

"You understand me?"

God, I do. I nod. The smallest motion.

"Say it."

"I understand." My voice cracks.

He stills. Something shifts in him—like a fault line snapping under pressure.

"There's something you need to know," he murmurs, voice a shade lower. Rougher.

"What?"

"I liked it." His pupils dilate. Hunger. Heat. A flash of something primal beneath the surface.

"Liked what? That I understand?"

"No." His gaze hooks mine. Dark. Blazing. Molten and locked in. Possession threaded through every syllable. "The way you said *Yes, sir.*"

My stomach plummets. I swallow hard. The air thickens until it sticks in my lungs.

"You have no idea what that does to me." He steps in

again, close enough to smother thought, close enough that I feel the shape of his restraint—and how little holds it back. His eyes drop to my mouth like he's imagining exactly how he'll take it.

I can't breathe.

"You say that again," he growls, low and lethal, "and I swear…" His hand slides up, fingertips grazing the side of my throat—just a hint of pressure, a phantom claim. "You'll find out exactly what kind of man you called sir."

My whole body coils, breath catching. My thighs clench, heat blooming low and wicked. I sway toward him, needing contact, needing friction.

He leans in, his breath hot at the shell of my ear.

"Now go." His voice is pure sin. "Before I fuck you up against this tree with your pack still on."

Scout waits a few feet away, her intelligent eyes tracking between Mac and me. She shifts her weight from paw to paw, the canine equivalent of checking her watch—urgent business to attend to, humans being ridiculous.

When I finally step back from Mac, she immediately moves to my side, ready to work.

My knees buckle a little. I back away, legs shaky, the fire in my blood a live thing. Pulse pounding in my throat—and between my thighs.

I don't look back.

Because if I do, I won't leave.

I'll let him take me apart right here in the middle of a goddamn emergency.

I stumble once, catching myself with a curse.

Behind me, he laughs. Low. Dark. The kind of laugh that coils around your spine and stays there.

"You feel it, don't you?" he says softly. Almost smug. "The fire burning between us…"

"Yes, sir," I tease, then spin around before he can react. Did he intimate what I think? He liked me calling him *Sir?*

What else does Mac enjoy? I'm eager to find out.

I descend through loose shale and scattered pine needles, each step carefully calculated to avoid triggering a rockslide that would create a different emergency.

The family is still visible on the main trail, moving too slowly, the children's energy flagging as smoke thickens the air.

Scout ranges ahead of me, following scent trails only she can detect, automatically choosing the most stable footing through the treacherous terrain. When we reach the family, she immediately approaches the children—no sudden movements, just a gentle canine presence that makes their eyes light up despite their fear.

"Is that your dog?" the little girl asks, reaching out tentatively.

"This is Scout," I tell her as Scout sits patiently for small hands to pet her head. "She's going to help us find the best way out."

The boy's tears stop as Scout nuzzles his palm. Nothing calms frightened children like a confident dog who knows what she's doing.

The father, mid-thirties, soft around the middle, clearly not an experienced hiker, keeps looking over his shoulder at the advancing fire. Fear radiates from his movements, the kind of barely controlled panic that leads to poor decisions. The mother carries the family pack, too heavy for her frame, while trying to encourage two kids who've reached their physical limits.

I intercept them at the trail junction, emerging from the tree line.

"I'm Jo Mackenzie, wilderness safety coordinator." I pitch my voice to carry reassurance. "I'm here to redirect you to a safer route."

"Thank God. We heard the fire wasn't contained." The father stops so abruptly that his wife nearly collides with him.

I kneel to get down at the children's eye level—a girl, maybe six, a boy who can't be more than four. Both are flushed and breathing hard, tiny faces streaked with ash. "Hey there. I bet you guys are tired."

"Mommy said we have to walk fast because of the fire," the girl says solemnly. "But Tommy can't keep up."

"That's okay. I know a special trail that's easier for tired legs." I stand, addressing the parents. "The main evacuation route is compromised. I can guide you to the service road. It's farther, but the grade is gentler and there's no smoke."

"Is it safe?" Relief floods the mother's face.

"Safer than staying here." I gesture toward the approaching fire, now close enough that we can feel its heat on the wind. "But we need to move now."

The family follows without question, desperation over-riding any concerns about trusting a stranger. I set a pace the children can maintain while keeping us ahead of the fire's advancing edge. The service road is abandoned, less main-tained than the main trail, but it loops around the fire's path.

"You live here?" The father breathes hard as we climb.

"All my life." I duck under a low branch, holding it back for them to pass. "These mountains are my backyard."

"How bad is it? The fire?"

I consider lying. Instead, I choose truth tempered with hope. "It's serious, but professionals are handling it. This route gets us clear of the immediate danger."

We continue in silence, broken only by the children's questions—why is the sky gray, where do the animals go when there's fire, will their car be okay in the parking lot?

I answer each with patience born of genuine concern, watching their faces relax incrementally as we put distance between ourselves and the flames.

Twenty-two minutes later, we emerge at the service road junction. The family is tired but unharmed, the children's energy returning as cleaner air fills their lungs. Below us, the parking area is visible—cars departing in an orderly evacuation, no panic, no chaos.

"From here, just follow the road down," I tell the parents. "Park service personnel are directing traffic at the bottom."

"What about you?" the mother asks. "Aren't you coming?"

"I need to check in with the fire response team." I hand her my card with emergency contact numbers. "If you have any problems on the way down, call that number."

The father extends his hand. "Thank you. I don't know what would have happened if—"

"You would have figured it out." I shake his hand briefly. "People are more capable than they think in crises."

After they disappear around the first bend, I radio Mac. "Family secured and en route to staging area. Requesting status update."

"Good timing. We've got a problem." His voice comes through immediately, tight with controlled tension.

"What kind of problem?"

"The kind that suggests our arsonist isn't finished for the day. Meet me at coordinates..." He rattles off numbers that put him near the old mining claims, deep in the backcountry where yesterday's fires burned. "And Josephine? Bring your geological survey maps. All of them."

"On my way."

I change direction, climbing back into the high country where Mac's coordinates place him. The urgency in his voice sets my nerves on edge, but underneath the anxiety runs something else—satisfaction at a job completed successfully.

The family is safe. I guided them out without incident, without hesitation, without the paralyzing fear that's haunted me since Sarah's accident.

Maybe I'm not as broken as I thought.

The meeting coordinates are a forty-minute hike through terrain I know intimately. I make good time despite the elevation gain, adrenaline sustaining me through technical sections that would normally require careful planning.

By the time I reach Mac's position, the sun hangs low in the western sky, painting the surrounding peaks in shades of copper and gold.

Mac stands at the edge of what was once the Silver Creek Mine's processing facility—rusted equipment scattered among foundations overgrown with wildflowers and young aspens. Rodriguez and Martinez flank him, all three studying something that has their full attention.

Scout's behavior changes the moment we approach the old mining facility. Her nose goes to the ground, following scent trails with intense focus. She circles the area twice before stopping at a specific spot, looking back at me with the alert expression that means she's found something significant.

"What is it, girl?" I follow her lead, and that's when I see the signs of recent habitation that the men missed—disturbed vegetation and the faint depression where someone recently slept.

"What've you got?" I ask, slightly breathless from the climb.

Mac turns, relief flickering across his features before professional focus reasserts itself. "Evidence our fire-setter has been busy."

He leads me to what appears to be a hastily abandoned campsite. Sleeping bag still warm to the touch. Coffee dregs in a metal cup. And scattered across a flat rock, detailed maps of the entire Angel's Peak region—marked with locations that match perfectly with yesterday's fire sites.

"Whoever was here left in a hurry," Rodriguez explains.

"We found this site maybe twenty minutes ago. Still smoldering embers in the fire ring."

"These are mine." I study the maps, recognition dawning cold in my stomach. "Older versions, but definitely mine."

"What?" Mac's voice sharpens.

"These maps. The style, the notations—I drew these." I pick up the topographical sheet showing Lookout Point, my precise pencil work visible in the margin notes. "But I've never seen these particular copies before."

"How is that possible?"

"I don't know." My hands shake slightly as I examine each map. All mine. All unauthorized copies. All marked with fire locations I never designated. "Someone's been reproducing my work."

Mac and Rodriguez exchange glances laden with implications I'd rather not consider.

"Who has access to your original maps?" Mac asks carefully.

"Official copies are on file at the visitor center, the sheriff's office, and park service headquarters." I set the maps down with deliberate care. "But I update my copies constantly. Anyone could have photographed my maps at the visitor center, or anywhere else I've displayed them publicly. The detail and accuracy suggest someone had extended access to study my work."

What chills me isn't the accessibility of my work, but the sophistication of the operation. This isn't some amateur with a grudge. This is someone who understands both fire behavior and my mapping techniques well enough to weaponize my expertise against the mountains I love.

My radio crackles. Parker's voice cuts through the charged silence: "All teams, be advised. Fourth fire reported at Crystal Falls. Estimated start time thirty minutes ago. This is now a coordinated arson investigation."

"We need to get back," Mac says quietly.

The return hike passes in focused silence. Mac leads, setting a punishing pace through terrain that blurs past in shadow and fading light. I follow, mind churning through possibilities—who had access to my maps, when they could have been copied, how long someone might have been planning this coordinated attack.

By the time we reach base camp, full dark has settled over Angel's Peak. Emergency vehicles fill the parking area—fire trucks, sheriff's deputies, state investigators. The coordinated response suggests this is no longer being treated as random vandalism.

Back at base, the chaos hums around us—radio static, clipped orders, the sharp scent of smoke riding the wind.

Mac stands near the command tent, legs braced wide, arms crossed over his chest as he listens to another report from dispatch. All control and steel and that unreadable calm that only makes me want to tear into him and demand he lose it—just once—with me.

Parker meets us at the staging area, expression grim. "Cap, we've got problems."

"Report."

"The Crystal Falls fire was set with an accelerant. Professional job—multiple ignition points, strategically placed for maximum spread."

Mac's jaw tightens. "Someone with serious expertise."

"Has to be," Parker says. "The fire placement shows an intimate understanding of both terrain and firefighting protocols."

"Find out who's behind it." Mac in command has never looked sexier.

"Trying, Cap." Parker glances over at me, then back at Mac. Something shines in her eyes, and a slight chuckle escapes her.

I step closer, Mac's presence solid and reassuring, while my mind replays our last conversation, about words I'll feel and titles I'll use. Instead of addressing *that*, I force myself to focus on the fires.

"Someone weaponized my work against these mountains. But they made one mistake."

"What's that?"

"They picked the wrong fight." My voice hardens with resolve. "These are my mountains. My maps. My responsibility to protect them."

"Then let's hunt this bastard down." Mac's voice is low and certain, but his eyes aren't on the fireline. They're on me. Pinning me with the kind of look that strips away my layers until I'm bare beneath it.

He steps closer. Not enough for anyone else to notice. But I feel it.

The shift. The pull.

"You were thinking something just now," he murmurs, voice pitched for my ears alone. "Back when you said those were your mountains. Your maps."

I straighten, trying to be professional. "I was just—"

"Don't lie." His head tilts, the edge of a smile tugging at his mouth. "You're too honest in your eyes. Try again."

Heat crawls up my throat. I glance past him, anywhere but those knowing eyes.

"I was thinking about what you said," I admit finally. "Back at the ridge."

His smile turns lethal. "Be more specific."

"I was thinking about..." I swallow. "What it would feel like..."

"Be *very* specific." His gaze turns molten hot, and his fingers graze the back of my neck—just a whisper of touch.

Still, I tremble.

Not from fear. From want.

I open my mouth, but the words don't come. They catch somewhere in my throat, heavy and hot, too tangled to speak aloud.

He notices. Of course he does.

"Can't answer?" A slow smirk curves his mouth, all heat and dark promise.

I shake my head, barely.

His voice drops to a growl. "Tell me, Josephine. Are you thinking about calling me *Sir...* or about being punished for the way your voice shakes when you do?"

My breath leaves me in a rush, knees suddenly weaker than I want to admit.

He leans in, brushing his lips along my jaw like he's tasting the answer. "Because either way, sweetheart... I will find out."

His palm splays low on my back, anchoring me there. And I can't move. Don't want to.

"When this fire's out, you're mine." He leans in, mouth brushing just beside my ear. "Don't worry, sweetheart. I plan to discover every one of your fantasies. And then I'll make damn sure you feel them. All of them." His fingers graze the back of my neck—just a whisper of contact, and yet I tremble.

"Soon." He pulls back before I can speak, his expression unreadable, voice sharp again as he turns to Parker. "Send a recon drone to the north flank. I want eyes on the old forest service road."

And just like that, Captain Mac is back.

But I'm still standing in the wreckage of his words, my body lit up like a lightning strike...

Aching to obey.

Around us, the controlled chaos of incident command continues—radios crackling, personnel moving with urgent purpose, the machinery of crisis response grinding into action. But between Mac and me, something solidifies.

Partnership. Purpose. Passion.

Somewhere in the darkness above us, another fire blooms against the mountainside—a fifth ignition point in what's an escalating campaign of destruction. As I watch the orange glow reflect off low-hanging clouds, one thought fills my mind. The arsonist isn't finished. They have a goal. Find that and we can anticipate rather than react.

Angel's Peak

CHAPTER 10

PATTERN RECOGNITION

MAPS SPREAD ACROSS MY KITCHEN TABLE LIKE A battlefield. Coffee rings stain wood around scattered maps, photographs, and incident reports. My grandfather's brass compass sits beside Mac's tactical GPS, two generations of navigation technology united by necessity. Outside, dawn threatens the horizon with pale fingers of light.

Scout lies beneath the kitchen table, her chin resting on my boots as I work. She's been there all night, a warm, steady presence while Mac and I pored over evidence and planned our next moves.

Every so often, she lifts her head when our voices get too intense, brown eyes tracking between us with the patient wisdom of a dog who's seen her humans through countless crises.

When I shift to reach for another map, she follows the movement, ensuring she's always touching some part of me. She knows tension when she feels it.

"Five fires in eighteen hours." Mac traces the locations with his finger, each red X a scar across my carefully drawn terrain.

"All in remote locations. All requiring extensive local knowledge to access."

I lean over his shoulder, close enough to smell coffee and smoke clinging to his uniform. The scent should comfort me. Instead, it reminds me that we're fighting an enemy who understands these mountains almost as well as I do.

"There's a pattern here." I tap the northwestern cluster. "These three fires form a triangle around the old Silver Creek mining claims. And these two—" I indicate Crystal Falls and Lookout Point, "—they're positioned to cut off the main evacuation routes from that area."

"Evacuation routes or access routes?" Mac's voice carries a dangerous edge.

The question hits like cold water. I grab my most detailed survey map, the one marked with every abandoned claim, every forgotten trail, every geological feature that might interest someone besides hikers and firefighters.

"The Silver Creek Mine closed in 1993." My finger traces the old mining road that winds through the fire triangle. "But the claims were never officially abandoned. Just... neglected."

"Who owns them now?"

"That's the problem." I pull out a folder of legal documents I researched years ago for a trail mapping project. "The ownership is tangled. Multiple shell companies, dissolved partnerships, and unresolved legal disputes. On paper, dozens of entities have potential claims to different sections."

Mac studies the documents, his expression growing darker with each page. "Someone's been patient. Very patient."

"What do you mean?"

"These fires aren't random destruction." He spreads the incident reports across the table. "They're strategic. Someone is using fire to clear legal obstacles."

The implications crawl up my spine like ice. "Clear them how?"

"Environmental surveys, safety inspections, historical preservation reviews—all the bureaucratic hurdles that prevent mining operations from resuming." His finger traces the fire perimeter. "But if the land is damaged by wildfire, classified as fire-prone, those protections might be waived for 'economic recovery' purposes."

My stomach drops. "You think someone's burning my mountains to restart mining operations?"

"I think someone's using your maps to identify the most efficient way to make that happen."

The coffee turns bitter in my mouth. Years of careful conservation work, decades of environmental protection, sacrificed for what? Profit margins and extraction permits?

Mac's radio crackles. Sheriff Donovan's voice cuts through the dawn quiet: "All units, be advised. Sixth fire reported at Eagle's Nest Trail. This one's bigger."

Scout's ears perk at the radio static, her body tensing with the same alertness she shows before storms. She rises from her position under the table, moving to the window where she can see the orange glow beginning to stain the horizon. A low whine escapes her throat—not fear, but recognition that we're about to head toward danger again.

WE DRIVE TOWARD EAGLE'S NEST IN PRE-DAWN darkness, Mac's SUV eating miles of winding mountain road. The fire's glow is visible long before we reach the staging area —a hungry orange smear against the gray sky that speaks of serious fuel consumption.

Scout sits alert in the back seat, her nose pressed to the partially opened window. Her nostrils work constantly, processing scents carried on the wind that tell her more about the fire's behavior than any of our instruments. Her ears swivel toward sounds I can't hear—the distant roar of flames, the crack of falling timber, the chaos of evacuation efforts miles ahead.

She knows we're driving toward something big. Something dangerous. But she doesn't hesitate, doesn't try to redirect us to safety. She trusts me to make the right choices, even when those choices lead us straight into hell.

"Jesus." Mac brakes at the first overlook, both of us staring at the inferno below.

This isn't the controlled burns we've been chasing. This is wildfire unleashed—acres of mixed woodland consumed in a roaring cathedral of flame. Smoke billows upward, darkening the sky.

"That's not possible." I grab my binoculars, scanning the burn pattern. "Eagle's Nest is surrounded by granite. Natural firebreaks on three sides. There's no way a surface fire could spread like that."

"Unless someone gave it help." Mac's voice is grim.

Through the binoculars, the fire's leading edge races through tree crowns with unnatural speed, jumping gaps that should stop its advance. This isn't arson. It's ecological warfare.

"We need to get closer." I lower the binoculars, my decision made. "I need to see the ignition pattern."

"Absolutely not." Mac's refusal is immediate. "That fire is beyond containment. The area's too dangerous for reconnaissance."

"Then, how do we identify the methodology? How do we anticipate the next strike?"

"We don't." His hands tighten on the steering wheel. "We respond and investigate after the fact."

"By then, it might be too late."

We stare at each other across the vehicle's interior, two

different approaches to crisis management grinding against each other.

His training emphasizes protecting personnel, gathering intelligence safely, and responding with overwhelming force. Mine says, 'Understand the enemy's pattern, get ahead of their strategy, and use intimate knowledge to outthink them.'

"There's an old fire lookout tower about two miles north." I point toward a barely visible structure on the distant ridge. "We could observe the fire behavior from there, identify how it's spreading so fast."

"How old?"

"Built in the 1940s. Decommissioned but structurally sound."

Mac considers this, weighing risk against intelligence value. "Access route?"

"Service road most of the way. Last half-mile on foot."

"Time to position?"

"Forty minutes if we leave now."

His radio crackles with updates. Fire teams are deploying. Evacuation routes are being established. Air support has been requested. The machinery of crisis response is grinding into action, but it's reactive, always behind the curve.

"Twenty minutes," he says finally. "Observation only. We see anything that puts us at risk, we abort immediately."

The service road is rough, overgrown with brush that scrapes against the SUV's sides. Mac drives with controlled aggression, balancing speed against vehicle damage. In the passenger seat, I study the fire's advance through binoculars, noting details that make my skin crawl.

"The fire's moving upslope against natural wind patterns." I adjust the focus, trying to make sense of what I'm seeing. "And it's burning too hot for available fuel loads."

"Accelerants?"

"Has to be. But distributed over how wide an area? This

isn't ignition points. Someone prepared this entire section of forest to burn."

"How long would that take?"

"Weeks. Maybe months." The scope of the operation hits hard. "Someone's been planning this for a very long time."

The fire tower emerges like a skeletal sentinel. Fifty feet of steel and wood, weathered gray by decades of mountain storms. A narrow ladder leads to the observation cabin at the top—glass on four sides, designed to provide panoramic views of the surrounding wilderness.

Scout balks at the base of the fire tower, her training warring with instinct. She's climbed plenty of technical terrain with me, but the narrow metal ladder and swaying structure trigger her caution. I clip her into her harness, checking the connections twice.

"We do this together," I tell her, and she settles, trusting my judgment even when her senses scream danger.

The climb is slow—Scout moving carefully from rung to rung while I spot her, both of us hyperaware of the growing heat and smoke that make the metal ladder slick with condensation.

We climb in silence, boots ringing against metal rungs. At the top, the cabin's interior is sparse—a chair, a table, and communication equipment that has long since been removed. But the views are exactly what I remember.

"There." I point through the southern windows. "See how the fire jumps that creek bed? Water should stop surface spread, but it's moving like there's a bridge."

Mac raises his binoculars, studying the pattern. "Fuel ladder. Someone created artificial connections between the ground and the canopy."

"More than that." I trace the fire's advance with my finger. "The spread pattern is too regular. Too predictable. This isn't natural fire behavior."

"What are you thinking?"

Someone didn't just prepare ignition points. They engineered the entire burn pattern." My voice hardens with growing certainty. "This fire is following a predetermined path."

"Toward what?"

I study my maps, comparing the spread of fires to topographical features. The answer emerges with chilling clarity.

"The old processing plant. The main facility for Silver Creek Mine." I tap the location on my map. "If this fire reaches the plant site, it'll destroy the last structural evidence of historical mining operations."

"Evidence of what?"

"Environmental damage. Safety violations. The reason the mine was shut down in the first place." My hands shake as the full scope becomes clear. "Someone's not just clearing legal obstacles. They're erasing evidence."

Mac's radio erupts with urgent chatter. Parker's voice cuts through static: "Alpha Leader, Priority One. We've got civilians trapped at Eagle's Nest campground. Evacuation route compromised by fire spread."

Scout's head snaps up at Parker's voice, her body going rigid with the focus she reserves for search and rescue operations. She knows that tone, understands what "civilians trapped" means in our shared vocabulary. She moves to the window, pressing her nose against the glass as if she can already scent the people who need our help.

When I move toward my pack, she's already there, sitting in the perfect position to be harnessed for a rescue operation. Ready. Willing. Trusting me to lead us toward people who need saving.

Eagle's Nest campground sits directly in the path of the engineered fire. And if my analysis is correct, the fire will reach the campground in less than two hours.

"How many?" Mac demands.

"Twelve confirmed. Family groups, including children. Fire cut off vehicle access. They're on foot with minimal supplies."

Mac looks at me, the same calculation running through both our minds. The campground sits three miles into the backcountry, accessible only by hiking trails. In normal circumstances, a three-mile hike with children might take two hours. But with smoke limiting visibility and panic affecting decision-making...

"Alternate extraction routes?" Mac asks.

"Negative. The fire's spread has eliminated all standard evacuation paths."

"What about air support?"

"Smoke's too thick for helicopter operations. And the wind patterns are too erratic for safe landing zones."

Mac stares at the fire, jaw working as he processes options. Command decisions in crisis—life and death choices made with incomplete information under time pressure. I've watched him carry this weight before, but never with stakes this high.

"There's another way out." My voice comes quietly, but certain.

Mac turns to me, tension bracketing his jaw. The fire rages downhill, a living, devouring thing. And still, he looks at me like I'm the fire he can't control.

"The old mining road," I continue, tracing the line on my map. "It connects to the campground through a tunnel system carved into the mountain. It'll bypass the worst of the flames. Shield them from the smoke."

"How do you know about these tunnels?"

"My father mapped them before the mine closed. I've walked sections of them myself." I meet his eyes. "It's risky, but it's their only chance."

Mac studies the map, clearly torn between multiple impossible choices. Save civilian lives by risking more lives? Trust my knowledge of tunnels I haven't fully explored? Send his team into unknown underground terrain?

"You're sure about this route?" His voice carries the weight of command responsibility.

"I'm sure the tunnels exist. Like I said, I mapped them with my dad before the mine shut down. Can't promise they're stable."

"That's not exactly confidence-inspiring."

"It's the truth." I hold his gaze steadily. "Sometimes, truth is all we have to work with. Besides, it's my fault this is happening."

The second I say it, something shifts. His posture. His breathing.

He doesn't respond. Just stares at me—too long, too hard.

My knowledge, my maps, my expertise—all of it weaponized against the mountains I love. The violation burns deeper than any physical wound.

Scout moves to my side, pressing her warm body against my legs as my voice breaks. She can read my emotional state better than any human and knows when the weight of responsibility threatens to crush me. Her steady presence grounds me, reminds me that I'm not carrying this burden alone.

She's been with me through every mountain crisis, every rescue, every moment of doubt. Her faith in me is absolute, unshakeable. If Scout believes I can handle this, maybe I can.

"Hey." Mac steps closer, reading the shame in my expression. "This isn't your fault."

"My maps—"

"Were used by someone else for purposes you never intended." His voice carries absolute conviction. "You didn't cause this."

"But my work made it possible."

"Your work is also going to stop it." His voice is low. Steady. Dangerous. He steps in, closer, until my back bumps the edge of the map table, and I have nowhere left to go. "Your knowledge. Your expertise. Everything they tried to steal and corrupt—you're taking it back."

His hands rise, framing my face, rough fingers surprisingly gentle as his thumbs brush my cheekbones. The reverence in his touch clashes with the fire in his gaze.

"You're fucking brilliant."

It's a growl. A confession. A claim.

"The way your mind works... the way you see through chaos." His voice roughens to a rasp, barely more than a breath against my skin. "Watching you piece this together— fuck, Josephine. I've never wanted anyone the way I want you right now."

His hands flex against my hips. "I shouldn't be doing this."

I still. Heat coils low in my belly.

"But I have to." His forehead drops to mine. "I have to ease this ache. I need to feel you. Then maybe I can think straight again."

"Mac..."

"I need to fuck you."

He grabs my hips and yanks me into him—hard—until my thighs hit the map table with a dull thump. Paper crumples beneath me. Topographic lines wrinkle under my ass. Elevation grids scatter at our feet like confetti at a warzone wedding.

Angel's Peak

CHAPTER 11

THE FIRE INSIDE US

"I've been hard for you all morning." His confession scrapes the air between us, low and raw. "Watching you work, seeing your intelligence in action. The way you command respect. The way you own every damn inch of your expertise."

Scout shifts restlessly near the fire tower entrance, her ears flattening against the sexual tension crackling between Mac and me. She's learned to give us space during these moments, but her brown eyes track our every movement with the patient resignation of a dog whose humans have terrible timing. A low whine escapes her throat—not distress, but the canine equivalent of *"seriously, now?"*

His hands slide from my face to my shoulders, then down—wrapping around my wrists. Not holding. Testing. Daring me to pull away.

I don't.

My breath hitches. My thighs part.

And he smiles—dark, possessive, absolutely feral.

"I was holding it together," he murmurs, hot against my neck. "I was doing just fine until you said *it*," he murmurs, voice low and sharp as a blade. "Back at the ridge."

"What?"

His gaze scorches. "When you called me, Sir." Dark heat floods his expression—dangerous, unfiltered want. "Instant fucking hardon. And now I need relief before I go back out there. I need you. Right here. Right now. On top of everything you've built."

Heat rushes to my core, a breath stolen by the memory.

Before I can respond, he lifts me onto the table, scattering maps and documents. My legs part instinctively as he steps between them, the position putting us at eye level.

"Tell me you need it too." His fingers trace the pulse hammering at my throat.

"Yes, sir." The words escape in a whisper. A surrender. A goddamn invocation.

"*Fuuuck*, you did that on purpose." His mouth crashes down on mine—consuming, claiming.

There's no pretense. No softness. Just raw possession. One hand knots in my hair, the other already working at my belt, my pants, my body.

Within moments, he has me bare from the waist down, the cool air of the fire tower raising goosebumps across my exposed skin.

I shudder, exposed and wanting.

"Look at you." His voice roughens with appreciation as his fingers trace the evidence of my arousal. "Dripping for me. Spread out on your maps like an offering."

He captures my wrists, pinning them above my head with one hand while the other wraps around my throat—not choking, but controlling, claiming. Just enough pressure to make the room tilt. Just enough to make me dizzy with want.

A flex of power, of intent. My breath hitches. My core pulses. He's not guessing what I want. He knows.

"Mine." The word rumbles from his chest as he thrusts inside me, hard and deep. "My brilliant, stubborn, impossible woman."

My mouth opens, but no sound comes out—not until he moves.

Every stroke is punishing. Worshipful. Fierce.

"You're not just mine," he growls, voice rough silk over granite. "You're perfect when you give it all over like this. Arms pinned. Throat under my hand. Needing me."

I moan—sharp, involuntary. The sound barely escapes before he captures it with his mouth. His kiss is rough and consuming, all heat and hunger and teeth. His hips slam forward again, pushing me back across the maps. My arms strain against his hold, but I don't want freedom. I want more.

His fingers shift from my throat to my breast, pinching my nipple hard enough to make me gasp.

"Louder," he demands, rolling the sensitive peak between callused fingers. "Let me hear you."

I arch under him, the sudden spark of pain blooming into raw pleasure. "Mac—please—"

"Sir." His voice is low. Commanding. "Say it. See what it does to me." His grip tightens. Not painful—yet the pressure slices clean through thought. My airway compresses. Breath thins.

My thighs quiver. The word's there, perched behind my lips. I whisper it, barely a breath.

Something deep inside me... yields.

"Sir..."

He growls. Low. Primal.

"There she is." He watches the surrender flash across my face, and his smile turns savage. "Goddamn right."

The map table rocks under us, wood groaning beneath the force of his need.

From her position by the door, Scout lets out a soft huff and deliberately turns her back to us, settling into a perfect down-stay with her nose pointed toward the window.

She's a professional working dog, and she knows when to ignore her humans' questionable life choices. Her tail twitches once—the only sign she's aware of the chaos happening behind her.

I ARCH INTO MAC'S DOMINANCE, MY BODY desperate for the possession he offers. He fucks me on the table where my life's work spreads beneath us, each thrust punctuated by the crinkle of paper and the distant roar of fire.

"You like being taken? Claimed?" he growls against my mouth.

"Yes, very much."

"You want to be used like this? Hard and rough."

"Yes, god yes!" I arch into him, back bowing, the slap of skin against skin joining the crinkle of paper and the low rumble of fire beyond the tower walls.

Then he pulls out fast and rough, leaving me empty and gasping.

"Hands flat," he orders, turning me with ruthless precision. I end up on my belly, hips dragged to the edge of the table. "You like it like this, don't you?"

My mouth is dry. I nod. Shakily. "Yes."

"Say it," he demands again, one hand gripping my hip, the other skating up my spine to press between my shoulder blades. Holding me down.

"Yes, sir," I gasp. "I like it when you take me like this. When it's rough. When I feel it after."

A growl tears from his chest, and he surges forward, burying himself inside me with one brutal thrust. I cry out—raw, undone.

"Look at you," he rasps, thrusting deep and hard. "Bent over your maps. Taking everything I give you. And begging for more."

I can't speak. I can only moan—his name, his title, words without meaning except that they're his. That I'm his.

"You belong to me when I'm inside you like this," he bites out. "You come because I give it to you."

His hand slides around my throat again, guiding my head back, forcing me to arch. I choke on a gasp as his hand tightens just enough to make my eyes flutter. To take my breath. To give me something else in return.

Fire.

He fucks me like he's burning from the inside out, like the wildfire chasing his team doesn't touch the urgency consuming him here, now, inside me.

My moan fractures in the air. He presses his body against mine, his mouth to my ear.

"You're going to save those people." His voice stays steady despite the rhythm of his hips. "Because you're the best guide these mountains have ever seen."

Pleasure and heat rise, fierce and immediate.

His hand presses harder. My oxygen dips.

I arch beneath him, thighs clenching, body writhing under the weight of him—under him.

He ruts like a man possessed.

"Say you know how fucking good you are." His grip tightens just a little more on my throat, the pressure perfect. Stars burst behind my eyes.

"I—I..." The pleasure is too much, too big. I can't hold it.

"Say it, Josephine."

"I'm good at this," I choke out, the words ripped from my soul. "I know these mountains. They're mine."

"Come for me."

I convulse around him, every muscle locking as the orgasm rips through me like a detonation. Hard, bright, shattering around him in pulses so strong they ripple through my legs, my arms, my soul.

"That's my girl." His approval sends me over the edge, my body clenching around him as waves of pleasure crash through me.

He doesn't stop. He drives into me with fierce, claiming strokes until his release hits like an avalanche, his groan rough and broken against my neck.

The weight of his body presses me deeper into the scattered maps. His hips jerk. He curses low and raw as he buries himself to the hilt.

Only then does he ease the pressure on my throat. Air floods in. My lungs expand. So does the ache in my chest— wanting more. Everything.

He holds me there, pressed against scattered maps and graphite smudges, his forehead resting against mine.

We collapse into stillness. Breathing. Shaking. My body sprawled beneath him, bare and bruised by pleasure, surrounded by crushed maps and proof of who I am. He pulls back just enough to meet my eyes—still dark, but now soft.

Reverent.

His arms wrap tight around me from behind, grounding me in the aftermath. His voice drops to a near whisper.

"You're mine, Josephine. All of you. And I'm never letting go." His voice holds a tenderness that steals my breath. "Now," he says, brushing his fingers down the side of my throat. "Let's go save some lives."

Scout rises immediately at the shift in our voices, recognizing the transition from personal to professional. She approaches as I straighten my clothes, her nose briefly checking me over with the clinical efficiency of a partner ensuring I'm ready for work.

When I clip her harness into place, she settles into mission mode—alert, focused, ready.

"Good girl," I murmur, and she wags once. Back to business.

Mac keys his radio. "Base, this is Alpha Leader. We have an alternate extraction plan. Prepare for tactical insertion at coordinates..." He rattles off numbers that mark the tunnel entrance I've indicated.

"Roger, Alpha Leader. Deploying teams now."

Mac clips the radio to his belt; the decision is made. "You're guiding us through those tunnels."

"Mac—"

"No arguments." His voice carries absolute authority. "You know the route. My team knows rescue operations. We do this together."

I nod once, acceptance and terror warring in my chest. Twelve civilians, including children, trapped by fire, depending on tunnels I've never fully explored and knowledge I pray is accurate.

"There's something else." I force the words out. "The tunnel system connects to the old mine shafts. If we get lost down there..."

Scout's ears perk at the word "tunnels," and her body tenses slightly. She's been in underground spaces with me before, but she doesn't like them—too many scents trapped in confined spaces, too many echoes that confuse her hearing. Still, when I meet her eyes, she holds my gaze steadily. Whatever her reservations, she'll follow me anywhere.

"Scout's been through the upper sections with me," I add, one hand finding her head. "She knows the scent markers, the air currents. She'll help us navigate if the maps aren't enough."

"We won't get lost." His conviction sounds absolute.

"How can you be sure?"

"Because you won't let us." He steps closer, close enough that I can see gold flecks in his blue eyes. "You know these mountains better than anyone. You've never led anyone astray."

"Sarah—"

"Was an accident." His voice is gentle but remains firm. "This is a choice. Your choice. Trust your knowledge, Josephine."

The way he says my name—certain, reverent, like a prayer—steadies something inside me that's been shaking since we found those copied maps.

"Okay." I square my shoulders, pushing fear aside for focus. "We'll need rope, headlamps, and emergency breathing apparatus. The tunnels may have unstable air quality."

"Done." He's already moving toward the ladder. "Anything else?"

"Yeah." I follow him down, boots ringing against metal. "Pray my father's maps were as accurate as I think they were."

As we descend toward ground level, the fire's roar grows louder, hungry flames consuming everything in their predetermined path. Somewhere ahead of that wall of destruction, twelve people wait for a rescue they don't know is coming.

Scout moves ahead of us as we approach ground level, her nose working constantly to process the chaotic scents of smoke, fear, and approaching danger. She pauses at the base of the tower, looking back at me with the focused intensity she reserves for the most serious operations. Her message is clear: she's ready. Ready to follow me into darkness, into danger, into whatever those tunnels hold.

I check her harness one more time, ensuring every buckle is secure. In the tunnels, we'll need each other more than ever.

Angel's Peak

CHAPTER 12

INTO THE DARKNESS

THE TUNNEL MOUTH GAPES BEFORE US LIKE A wound in the mountainside, dark and forbidding. Fallen timber partially obscures the entrance, nature's half-hearted attempt to reclaim what man carved decades ago.

"This is it?" Mac studies the narrow opening with professional skepticism, already assessing structural integrity and escape routes.

"Silver Creek's secondary access tunnel." I run my fingers along the weathered support beam, feeling the rough grain beneath my skin. Wood groans under the pressure of my touch —a subtle warning that makes my stomach tighten. "Not on any official mining records, but my father mapped it extensively before the operation shut down."

Rodriguez whistles low, shining his tactical flashlight into the darkness. The beam disappears into black nothing, swallowed by stone. "Tight quarters."

"It widens about fifty feet in." I pull my headlamp from my pack, securing it over my hair. The elastic catches on a tangle, and I wince as I work it free. "The initial passage was kept narrow to prevent unauthorized access."

Martinez checks his oxygen meter, frowning at the readings. "Air quality's decent for now, but we should still use emergency breathing apparatus if smoke starts filtering through."

The scent hits me as I step closer to the entrance—earth and rust, the metallic tang of old iron mixed with something deeper.

Decay.

Time.

The weight of the millennium.

The mountain's slow, patient breath exhales decades of stored air. My father's voice echoes in memory: *The mountain always tells you what it's thinking if you know how to listen.*

Scout approaches the tunnel mouth with visible reluctance, her nose working overtime to process the complex scents emanating from the darkness.

Her hackles rise slightly—not from fear, but from the overwhelming sensory input of a place that holds decades of human activity, mineral deposits, and stagnant air.

She looks back at me once, brown eyes questioning, before settling into her working stance. If I'm going in, she's going in. That's never been a question.

Mac's radio crackles with Sheriff Donovan's voice. "Fire's jumped the ridge line. The main evacuation route is completely compromised. How's that alternative looking?"

"WE'RE PROCEEDING VIA TUNNEL EXTRACTION." Mac's response is crisp and authoritative. "Estimate thirty to forty minutes to reach the civilians. Will advise when contact is made."

"Copy that. Be advised, air support is grounded due to

smoke density and wind conditions. You're on your own down there."

Mac's eyes meet mine over the radio. "We've got this, Sheriff."

The confidence in his voice should sound hollow given the circumstances. Instead, it lands like a promise—not just to Donovan, but to me.

"Team check." Mac turns to our small rescue unit—Rodriguez, Martinez, Burke, and Williams, each loaded with emergency equipment and rescue gear.

The rest of his crew remains on the fireline with Parker, fighting the leading edge of the blaze while we attempt this underground extraction. The division of his forces weighs on him—I can see it in the tension around his eyes, the way his jaw works as he calculates risks on multiple fronts.

"Comms?" he asks.

"Check."

"Check."

"Check."

"Check."

Four voices respond in unison.

"Oxygen?"

"Four primary tanks, eight emergency backups."

"Medical?"

Williams pats her extensive kit. "Everything from bandages to burn treatment."

Mac nods, satisfied, then turns to me. "Navigation?"

I unroll my father's map across a flat rock, anchoring the corners with small stones. The paper crackles under my fingers, edges soft with age and handling. The faded lines detail a web of interconnecting passages, notations in his familiar handwriting marking air shafts, water sources, and potential danger zones.

Scout sits at attention beside me as I spread the map, her

eyes tracking my finger as I trace the route. She's been through enough briefings to understand this ritual—the careful study of terrain, the marking of waypoints, the measured discussion of hazards.

Her ears swivel constantly, processing sounds from the tunnel that my human hearing can't detect. When I fold the map and secure it in my jacket, she rises smoothly, ready to lead us into whatever darkness awaits.

"MAIN TUNNEL RUNS NORTHWEST FOR approximately half a mile before branching." I trace the route with my finger; the pencil marks are still sharp, despite the years. "We take the eastern fork, follow it until we hit the old vertical shaft. There is a maintenance tunnel located there that cuts directly toward the campground area. Total distance is just under a mile."

"Underground hazards?" Mac studies the map with intense focus.

"Two sections with known structural weakness." I indicate the areas marked with my father's careful hatch marks. "And one low area that floods during heavy rain. Given the current conditions, that shouldn't be an issue."

Mac commits the route to memory, his eyes tracking each turn, each junction. Then he rolls the map carefully and hands it back to me.

"You lead, I'll follow." He says it simply, like it's the most natural arrangement in the world. "Your mountain, your tunnels."

The trust in those words hits harder than any praise he's ever given me.

"Let's move." I adjust my headlamp and step into the darkness.

Scout takes point immediately, her training overriding her discomfort with confined spaces. Her paws find purchase on loose stone with the sure-footed confidence of a dog bred for mountain work.

Every few steps, she pauses to scent the air, cataloging information I can't process—air currents, mineral deposits, the faint traces of wildlife that occasionally use these passages. Her white-tipped tail moves in careful semaphore, signaling "all clear" as we descend into the mountain's heart.

Cold air rushes past my face, carrying the scent of mineral water and old timber. My boots crunch on loose gravel—a sound that echoes ahead and behind, creating a symphony of footsteps that seems to come from everywhere at once. The darkness beyond our headlamps feels alive, pressing against the thin cones of light like something with weight and intention.

"Temperature drop." Mac's voice comes from directly behind me, close enough that I feel his breath on my neck.

"Twenty degrees cooler than outside." I duck beneath a low-hanging beam, the wood so close it brushes my hair. "The mountain holds the winter down here. Stores it in stone."

Our lights reveal rough-hewn walls, chiseled by hand and time into something that feels more like a throat than a passage. Support beams arch overhead every ten feet—massive timbers that have turned silver-gray with age. Some sag slightly under the mountain's weight. Others stand straight as the day they were installed, defying decades of pressure.

Water drips somewhere ahead. The sound echoes off stone walls, creating a percussion that's both rhythmic and random.

Drip. Drip-drip. Drip.

My father used to say you could tell the mountain's mood by the sound of its water. Tonight, it sounds restless.

"Airflow's good." Rodriguez's voice carries an edge of relief. "Must connect to multiple surface points."

I feel it too—a subtle current that moves past us, carrying

the scent of pine and smoke from the world above. Underneath that familiar smell lurks something else. Something older. The mountain's perfume of iron and quartz, limestone and time.

We continue deeper, the tunnel gradually widening as promised. The floor slopes gently downward, taking us into the mountain's heart. I check landmarks against memory—a distinctive quartz vein running through the left wall, like frozen lightning, an alcove where miners once stored their tools, and the remains of an old ore cart track embedded in stone.

My boots find different sounds as we progress. Gravel gives way to packed earth, then to stone worn smooth by decades of foot traffic. Each surface change registers through the soles of my feet, telling stories of the men who worked these tunnels when they were new.

The walls change, too. Here, a natural rock face where miners followed a vein. There, carefully mortared stone was used where reinforcement was needed. The textures shift under my fingertips as I trail one hand along the wall—rough granite, smooth limestone, the occasional patch of quartz that catches our light and throws it back in scattered sparkles.

"How much farther to the first junction?" Mac's voice sounds different down here, rounded by stone and distance.

"Another hundred yards." I pause to consult my father's map, the paper rustling loudly in the enclosed space. "There's a chamber ahead where three passages meet. We take the center route."

A sound drifts from somewhere far ahead—a low moan that might be wind through stone crevices, or might be something else entirely. The mountain's voice, speaking in frequencies that make my teeth ache.

Williams shifts nervously behind me. "What was that?"

"Air pressure equalizing." I maintain a steady and professional tone. "The mountain breathes. You'll hear all kinds of sounds down here."

But my father's warnings echo in memory. *The mountain talks, Jo. Sometimes it whispers. Sometimes it shouts. You learn to tell the difference between conversation and warning.*

We reach the junction—a circular chamber carved from living rock, with passages branching off like spokes of a wheel. Our lights reveal tool marks in the stone, evidence of the hands that shaped this space. The air moves differently here, as currents mix and separate as they flow through multiple openings.

Scout circles the chamber twice, nose to the ground, reading scent trails that tell stories I'll never understand. She pauses at each tunnel entrance, testing air currents with the methodical precision of a professional. At the center passage—our chosen route—she sits and looks back at me, tail wagging once. Her message is clear: this way feels right to her superior senses.

"This is incredible." Burke's voice carries genuine awe as he studies the craftsmanship. "How long did this take to carve?"

"Three years, according to the mining records." I lead them toward the center passage, our footsteps echoing in the larger space. "They worked through two winters."

The air grows warmer as we continue, and I catch the first hint of smoke threading through the mineral scents. Not heavy yet, but enough to remind us why we're here. Above us, the mountain is burning.

"Masks." Mac's order comes immediately. "Air quality's about to change."

We don the emergency breathing apparatus, the filtered air

cool and metallic against my tongue. The change in how sounds reach us is immediate. Everything is muffled, and the equipment amplifies our breathing. But we can still hear the mountain around us. Still feel its presence pressing in.

The tunnel narrows again, forcing us into a single file. Here, the walls press close enough that I can touch both sides with outstretched arms. The stone feels different—warmer, somehow alive with the heat of the fire above. Condensation beads on the rock face, trickling down in streams that catch our light.

A deep rumble vibrates through the stone beneath our feet. Dust sifts down from overhead, visible in our headlamp beams like golden snow. I freeze, one hand pressed flat against the wall, feeling the mountain's distress transmitted through solid rock.

"Seismic activity from the fire above." Mac's voice carries through the mask filters. "Keep moving."

We continue deeper, the passage gradually opening into another chamber. This one feels different—larger, with air that moves more freely. Our lights reveal a vertical shaft rising into darkness above, iron rungs embedded in the stone creating a ladder to nowhere. The upper access was sealed decades ago, but the shaft still breathes, pulling air through hidden fissures.

From somewhere ahead comes a new sound. Voices. Human voices, muffled by distance and stone, but unmistakably real.

"Contact." Mac's voice sharpens with purpose. "Two hundred yards, maybe less."

My pulse quickens as we approach the final stretch. The tunnel here shows signs of more recent use—less dust, occasional boot prints in patches of damp earth, evidence of modern reinforcement on some of the support beams.

"Park service uses this section occasionally," I explain, stepping carefully around a puddle that reflects our lights like a black mirror. "Winter access to the campground when the main road's impassable."

The voices grow clearer as we advance. Children crying. Adult voices trying to maintain calm. The unmistakable sound of fear barely contained by willpower.

We're close. So close to the people we came to save. But in these mountains, close doesn't always mean safe."

Angel's Peak

CHAPTER 13

WHEN MOUNTAINS FALL

"SMOKE'S GETTING THICKER." MARTINEZ CHECKS HIS readings, frowning at the display. "They've been breathing this for hours."

We round the final bend and find them. Twelve civilians huddle in a small natural cavern where the mining tunnel intersects with what appears to be an ancient water channel. Two families with young children, a middle-aged couple, and three college-aged hikers. Their faces, illuminated by failing flashlights and chemical light sticks, transform from fear to cautious hope as we appear.

Scout reaches the cavern first, her excited whine announcing the discovery of the people we've come to save. She approaches the frightened group with the confidence of a trained search-and-rescue dog, allowing the children to see her before the intimidating sight of armed rescuers in breathing apparatus. Her presence immediately calms the youngest victims.

Nothing says "safety" like a confident dog who knows what she's doing.

The cavern itself tells a story of water and time. Smooth

walls carved by underground streams, a ceiling that disappears into darkness above our lights. The air here feels different, moving with purpose, suggesting multiple connections to the outside world.

Above us, the fire rages like a living thing with teeth and hunger. Through the thin layer of stone and earth, I can hear it—a low rumble that's part freight train, part beast breathing. It's not the gentle crackle of a campfire or even the controlled burn of a prescribed fire. This is something primal and furious, chewing through timber with ravenous hunger, racing toward anything combustible with unstoppable momentum.

The campers fled here, thinking stone would save them. The cavern seemed safe, cool, damp, and far from the flames that cut off their escape routes. They didn't count on smoke being a liquid thing, flowing downhill like water, seeping through cracks in the ceiling, and pooling in the lowest places. Now gray wisps curl around our lights, and the bitter tang of burning pine coats my tongue even through my mask.

The mountain that was supposed to shelter them is slowly filling with the same poison that drove them here.

"Angel's Peak Fire and Rescue." Mac steps forward, authority radiating from every line of his body. "We're here to evacuate you to safety."

Relief crashes over the group. Questions tumble over each other. How long until we're out? Is it safe? Will the tunnel hold? Mac handles them efficiently while Williams moves among them to check for injuries.

I scan the group, taking a quick inventory of what we're dealing with.

Near the back wall, a young couple clutches a small boy between them—the father's arm protective around his son's shoulders, the mother's hand smoothing the child's hair with nervous, repetitive strokes.

The boy can't be more than seven, his wide eyes

taking in everything with the mixture of fear and curiosity that only children possess. His parents whisper reassurances to him, but I can see the barely controlled panic in their faces as they try to stay strong for their son.

The boy keeps looking toward our rescue team with fascination, especially at Scout, who sits calmly near the cavern's entrance. Despite his parents' protective grip, there's something in his posture that suggests resilience, a quiet bravery that reminds me why I love working with kids in the mountains.

A little boy's face lights up at the sight of Scout. "Is that your dog?" he asks, momentarily forgetting his fear.

"This is Scout," I tell him, removing my mask briefly. "She's the one who found you. Do you want to pet her?"

Danny looks up at his parents, who turn to each other, nod, then smile at me as if I've lifted a great weight off their shoulders. It's incredible what the power dogs hold to ease human fears.

The young boy approaches me with wide, solemn eyes. His face is streaked with dust and tear tracks, but he's not crying now. He kneels to pet Scout. Meanwhile, Mac organizes the campers.

"Are you really going to get us out?" the boy asks.

I crouch to his level, removing my mask momentarily to meet his gaze directly. "Yes. I promise."

The word slips out before I can stop it. *Promise.* The same word I said to Sarah before everything went wrong.

But this time feels different. This time, I know the way.

"What's your name?" I ask.

"Danny." He wipes his nose with his sleeve. "My mom says the mountain might fall down."

"Your mom's scared, and that's okay. But this mountain has been here for millions of years. It's not going anywhere." I tap my map case. "My name is Jo, and I've got the secret way out."

His eyes brighten slightly. "Secret?"

"Really secret. Want to help me navigate?"

He nods eagerly, and something tight in my chest loosens. This is what I've been afraid of—this trust, this responsibility, but it doesn't feel crushing anymore. It feels like coming home.

"Is everyone able to walk?" Mac asks quietly as I stand.

"One sprained ankle, but manageable with assistance. No serious injuries." Williams reports. "They're dehydrated and scared, but they can move."

"Then let's get these people home."

Mac's voice is calm yet authoritative as he assigns positions. "Stronger adults will assist anyone who needs help. Parents, keep your children close. We move as one unit—no one gets ahead, no one falls behind."

Danny's parents exchange a worried glance as they prepare to move. His mother adjusts her small backpack while his father checks their water supply. Danny's attention is fixed on me, his young face serious with the weight of what we're about to attempt.

He tugs on his mother's sleeve. "Mom, can I walk with Miss Jo? She knows the secret way out."

His mother looks uncertain, protective instincts warring with the recognition that their son has found something to focus on besides his fear. "Danny, you need to stay with us—"

"It's okay," I interrupt gently, meeting the parents' eyes. "He can help me navigate. Sometimes having a job makes the scary parts easier."

Danny's father nods slowly. "If Miss Jo doesn't mind..."

"I'd be honored to have such a brave navigator," I tell Danny, extending my hand.

Danny looks up at his parents one more time for permission. When they nod, he slips his small hand into mine with a trust that both humbles and terrifies me.

The return journey begins with Mac taking point, his broad shoulders cutting through the darkness ahead. I watch him organize the civilians—stronger adults supporting the injured woman, teenagers helping with the smaller children. His voice carries back to us, calm and authoritative, as he sets the pace.

"Single file. Stay close to the person in front of you. If you need to stop, call out immediately."

I bring up the rear, Danny's small hand gripping mine with surprising strength. The role reversal feels strange—following instead of leading, watching Mac's headlamp bob ahead while I scan behind us for threats that shouldn't exist but somehow feel possible.

"Why aren't you in front?" Danny whispers, his voice barely audible over the crunch of so many feet on loose stone.

"Someone needs to make sure nobody gets left behind." I squeeze his hand gently. "That's my job now."

The tunnel feels different on the return trip. Longer somehow. The walls seem to press closer, and shadows dance at the edges of our lights in ways that make my skin crawl. Every sound echoes strangely. Footsteps multiply. Voices bouncing off stone until I can't tell if what I'm hearing is real or just the mountain playing tricks.

Behind us, the passage stretches into absolute darkness. Nothing but black air and the weight of stone pressing down. My father's voice whispers in memory: *Never trust your back to the mountain, Jo. It's got a sense of humor, and not always a kind one.*

Danny stumbles, his weight pulling on my arm. I steady him, feeling how his legs shake with exhaustion. The boy's been breathing smoke for hours and dealing with his fear in equal measure, but he doesn't complain, just looks up at me with eyes that trust me completely.

That trust sits in my chest like a physical weight.

The smoke grows thicker as we progress, seeping through cracks in the ceiling where the fire burns above. My mask filters most of it, but I can still taste ash on my tongue. Can still smell the familiar scent of burning pine mixed with something else—something chemical and wrong.

Accelerants. Someone engineered this hell.

"Mac." I call softly, not wanting to alarm the civilians. "Smoke's getting worse."

His acknowledgment comes back immediately. "Picking up the pace."

But the children are struggling. I see it in the way they lean against their parents, in the increasing frequency of stumbles and whispered complaints. The woman with the sprained ankle moves with visible pain despite Williams' support.

We're moving too slowly.

The mountain groans around us—a sound like settling timbers but deeper, more fundamental. Stone is adjusting to heat and pressure, expanding, finding new configurations as the fire above changes everything. Dust sifts down from overhead, visible in our headlamp beams like falling stars.

I know that sound. It's the same one I heard the day before Sarah's accident, when unseasonable rain saturated the trail above Crystal Falls. The mountain is warning me that something is wrong.

I ignored it then.

Now my skin prickles with awareness, every nerve ending attuned to the subtle vibrations traveling through stone. The mountain is trying to tell me something.

"Mac," I call again, more urgently. "We need to—"

The rumble starts deep in the mountain's bones.

Not the gentle groaning, but something massive and final. The passage shudders around us like a living thing screaming in pain. Loose stone rains down, pinging off our helmets and shoulders.

"Cave-in!" Mac's shout echoes ahead of us. "Everyone down!"

Scout's warning bark comes a split second before Mac's shout—her superior hearing detecting the subtle shift in stone that precedes catastrophic failure. She pushes Danny and me, shoving us back as rock crashes around us.

The boy's small body trembles against mine, and I cover his head with my arms, feeling the mountain's fury crash down around us. Rock dust fills the air, choking our lights and turning everything into a gray, suffocating fog.

When the dust settles, Scout's already on her feet, nose working to assess our situation while keeping herself between us and any remaining danger.

I lift my head cautiously. My headlamp cuts through the dust, revealing devastation. The passage ahead is blocked—not completely, but enough. A wall of fallen stone separates Danny and me from Mac and the rest of the group.

"Danny." I check him frantically, hands running over his small arms and legs. "Are you hurt?"

"I don't think so." His voice shakes, but he's alert. Responsive. "Ms. Jo, where did everyone go?"

The wall of debris stretches from floor to ceiling, massive chunks of granite and limestone wedged together like puzzle pieces. Through the gaps, the dim glow of headlamps is visible on the other side, and muffled voices call out.

"Mac!" I press my face to the largest gap, tasting rock dust and fear. "Mac, can you hear me?"

"Josephine!" His voice comes through clearly, blessed relief flooding through me. "Status report."

"Danny and I are okay. The passage is completely blocked

from this side." I examine the collapse with growing dread. These aren't loose rocks that shifted. This is structural failure—tons of stone that won't be moved without heavy equipment.

"Can you clear it?"

I run my hands along the debris, testing stability. A smaller rock shifts under pressure, triggering a small avalanche that makes Danny yelp and press closer to my side. Any attempt to clear this blockage could cause the ceiling to collapse further.

"Negative. Too unstable."

Silence stretches between us, filled with the terrible mathematics of our situation. Mac has civilians to evacuate and a clear route back to the entrance. I have one small boy and a blocked passage, deep in a mountain that's actively trying to kill us.

"Alternative route?" Mac's voice stays steady, but I hear the strain underneath.

I close my eyes, visualizing my father's map. The maintenance tunnel I mentioned earlier connects to this section somewhere ahead. However, I've never walked it, nor have I verified its stability or condition. It was marked as an emergency route, one my father mapped but cautioned against using except in desperate circumstances.

This qualifies as desperate.

"There's an emergency route that bypasses this section." I keep my voice calm for Danny's sake, though my heart hammers against my ribs. "I can't guarantee its condition, but it should connect to the surface near the old equipment shed."

"How far?"

I calculate distance and elevation, factoring in Danny's small legs and our limited supplies. "Maybe forty minutes if we're lucky. Longer if we run into problems."

"Take it." Mac's decision comes without hesitation. "We'll

continue back the way we came, retrace our route to the entrance."

Relief and terror war in my chest. Relief that Mac has an escape route. Terror that I'm about to lead a seven-year-old boy through unknown passages based on a map drawn years before he was born.

"Understood." I pull out my father's map, the paper crackling in the sudden quiet. "We'll rendezvous at the equipment shed."

"Josephine." Mac's voice softens, carrying all the weight of what he can't say through a wall of stone. "You know these mountains better than anyone. Trust your instincts."

The sound of my full name stops my breath. Not Jo, not Mackenzie—*Josephine*. The name he whispers against my skin when he's buried deep inside me, when control fractures and tenderness bleeds through his dominance. He's the only one who says it like that, like it means something sacred.

To hear it now, separated by tons of stone with death pressing close, feels like the most intimate thing he's ever given me. A promise wrapped in syllables. A claim that reaches through rock and fear to anchor me.

"Yes, sir." The words slip out before I can stop them, automatic and reverent. "Take care of them."

Even separated by stone and crisis, the dynamic between us pulses like a living thing. His sharp intake of breath echoes through the gap, and I know he feels it too—that electric current that runs beneath everything else, the way I yield to his authority even when he can't touch me.

"Take care of yourself." His voice roughens, dropping to that register that makes my spine liquid. Even through stone and static, I feel the promise threaded beneath his words—the unspoken *because you're mine, and I'm not done with you yet.* "That's an order, Josephine."

I fold the map carefully, tucking it into my jacket pocket.

When I turn around, Danny is watching me with eyes too serious for his age.

"Are we lost?" he asks quietly.

The question hits harder than the falling stone. Three years ago, I would have lied, offered false comfort to avoid frightening him, but Sarah's accident taught me that mountains don't forgive pretty lies.

"We're separated from the others," I tell him honestly. "But I know another way out. It's going to be an adventure."

Scout approaches the debris wall, sniffing carefully at the gaps where voices filter through. She whines softly, not in distress, but communicating with me. She smells Mac and the others on the far side, hears their movements, but understands instinctively that this barrier is beyond her ability to overcome.

When I call her away from the wall, she comes immediately, pressing against my legs in a gesture of solidarity. Whatever happens next, we face it together.

"WHAT KIND OF ADVENTURE?" DANNY ASKS.

I adjust my headlamp, checking the battery indicator. Still good for at least two hours. "The kind where we get to be explorers. Like the miners who first carved these tunnels."

Danny considers this, then nods solemnly. "Okay. But if we find treasure, we split it fifty-fifty."

"Deal." Despite everything, I laugh.

I take his hand and lead him away from the blocked passage, toward a branching tunnel marked on my father's map with careful notations. As we walk deeper into the mountain's embrace, the weight of responsibility settles across my shoulders.

Behind us, the sound of Mac's team retreating grows fainter, then fades to silence. The tunnel ahead stretches into darkness I've never explored, guided only by pencil marks on aging paper and the trust of one small hand in mine.

But I'm my father's daughter, and this mountain has been my home for twenty-eight years.

We're going to make it out.

I have to believe that.

For Danny's sake, and my own.

Angel's Peak

CHAPTER 14

SURFACE

THE EMERGENCY TUNNEL STRETCHES AHEAD LIKE A throat carved from living stone. Danny's hand grips mine with surprising strength, his breathing steady despite the fear that radiates from his compact frame.

Scout moves ahead of us in the narrow emergency tunnel, her compact frame perfectly suited for the tight passage. Her nose works constantly, testing air currents for the sweet scent of surface access while her paws find the most stable footing on loose stone.

Every few steps, she pauses to look back at Danny and me, her brown eyes reassuring in the headlamp's glow. She's our early warning system, our pathfinder, our anchor to the world above.

"How much farther?" His whisper echoes off damp walls.

"Not much."

I hope I'm telling the truth.

The map shows this tunnel connecting to an old equipment shed, but distances underground can be deceptive. What looks like a quarter-mile on paper might be twice that when you're navigating by headlamp through stone that was never meant for human passage.

The air grows cooler as we climb, a subtle shift that makes my pulse quicken with hope. Fresh air means surface access. Means we're close.

Scout's pace quickens as she catches the first hint of surface scents—pine needles, smoke, the complex mix of the world above. Her tail begins a tentative wag, and she looks back at me with what I swear is relief. She can smell freedom ahead, can detect the end of this underground journey that's tested even her considerable courage.

Danny stumbles on loose scree, his small boots sliding on stones worn smooth by decades of groundwater. I catch him before he falls, steadying him against my hip.

"I'm okay." He looks up at me with eyes too brave for his age. "I won't slow us down."

"You're not slowing anything down." I adjust my headlamp, checking our progress against the map. "You're the best hiking partner I've ever had."

"Better than the fire captain?"

Despite everything, I smile.

"Different kind of partner."

We continue upward, the tunnel gradually widening until I can see daylight—actual daylight—filtering through what appears to be a grated opening ahead. The equipment shed. My father's route was accurate down to the last detail.

"Danny, look." I point toward the light. "We made it."

"We're really out?" His face transforms, fear melting into pure relief.

"We're really out."

Scout reaches the equipment shed first, her nose pressed to the grate as she confirms what her senses have been telling her. We found our way to safety. The moment I lift the grate, she bounds out into daylight, shaking rock dust from her coat before turning back to ensure Danny and I follow.

Her joy is infectious, tail wagging as she breathes deeply of clean mountain air.

The shed's interior is dim after hours underground, but the air tastes sweet with pine and freedom. Through grimy windows, the emergency staging area my father marked is visible—a cleared space where vehicles can access the backcountry. Mac's SUV sits in the clearing, and I spot two figures pacing anxiously beside it.

Danny's parents.

The moment we step into daylight, Danny releases my hand and sprints toward them.

"Mom! Dad!"

They crash together in a tangle of arms and tears, his mother dropping to her knees to clutch him against her chest while his father's shoulders shake with relief.

Scout bounds alongside Danny toward his parents, her presence adding to the chaos of the joyful reunion. Danny's mother looks up through her tears to see the German Shepherd who helped bring her son to safety, and she reaches out to pat Scout's head with trembling fingers.

"Thank you, too, girl," she whispers, and Scout accepts the praise before returning to my side.

"Danny! Oh, baby, we were so scared—" His mother's voice breaks as she runs her hands over him, checking for injuries.

"I'm okay. It was amazing!" Danny's voice bubbles with excitement despite his parents' tears. "Miss Jo knows all the secret tunnels, and we saw where the old miners worked, and she taught me how to read the mountain's breathing."

"When the tunnel collapsed, we thought—" His father ruffles Danny's hair, voice thick with emotion.

"Miss Jo took care of me. She's the bravest person in the

whole world." Danny's exuberance can't be contained. "She promised she'd get me out, and she did."

Mac stands apart from the reunion, radio in one hand, but his eyes are locked on me. The professional mask he wears for everyone else dissolves the moment our gazes meet, replaced by something raw and intense.

He crosses the distance between us in three long strides.

Scout immediately moves to Mac's side as he approaches, her tail wagging in recognition of the man who's become important to both of us. She seems to sense the emotional intensity between us, positioning herself nearby but giving us space for whatever reunion is about to unfold. Even she understands the gravity of what we've just survived.

"You're okay." His hands frame my face, thumbs brushing over my cheekbones as if confirming I'm real. "You got him out."

"We got each other out." I lean into his touch, allowing myself this moment of weakness. "The route was stable. My father knew what he was doing."

"So do you." His arms circle me, pulling me against his chest. "I knew you'd find a way." His voice carries an edge I recognize, relief mixed with something darker, hungrier.

I feel it then, the hard length of him pressing against my hip as he holds me close. Heat floods my core despite everything around us.

"I was too worried, too focused on getting everyone else out. But now—" His grip tightens, pressing me more firmly against him. "Now that you're safe, now that you're in my arms again, I can't think about anything except getting inside you."

My breath catches at his raw admission.

"I need you, Josephine. Need to remind myself you're mine." His mouth finds the sensitive spot below my ear. "The second we're alone, I'm going to take you apart piece by piece until the only thing you remember is how it feels to belong to me."

Danny's mother walks over to us, tears still tracking down her soot-streaked face, and extends her hand. "I don't know how to thank you."

"Take care of him." I glance down at Danny, who beams up at me. "He's got the makings of a real mountaineer."

After Danny and his parents are loaded into Mac's SUV, his expression shifts back to command mode. His radio crackles with updates that grow more dire by the minute.

"Fire's jumped the creek line," Parker's voice cuts through static. "We've got maybe four hours before it hits the outer residential areas."

Mac keys his response. "Understood. Status on the fire-break construction?"

"Slow going. We need more personnel."

Mac meets my eyes over the radio, a question passing between us without words.

"How are you at drumming up volunteers?" he asks.

"Pretty good, Angel's Peak will come together. We're a family like that."

"Good, because I need you to whip up an army to fight this thing."

The forward staging area buzzes with controlled chaos. Fire trucks, equipment trailers, and personnel carriers form a semicircle around a command tent, where Parker directs operations. Her blonde hair is pulled back in a severe bun, her yellow uniform is dirty after hours of coordinating firefighting efforts.

"Captain." She approaches as we arrive, relief evident in her weathered features. "Successful extraction?"

"All civilians evacuated safely." Mac's response is crisp, professional, but his hand finds the small of my back—a possessive touch that doesn't go unnoticed. "What's our current situation?"

Parker unrolls a tactical map across the hood of a truck, red markers indicating fire positions that have advanced significantly since our tunnel rescue. "The main blaze is here, moving southeast at fifteen miles per hour. Wind's pushing it directly toward town."

I study the fire's path, recognition dawning cold in my chest. "It's jumping the old logging roads. The fire's ignoring natural barriers that should stop it."

Parker's expression darkens.

Mac's radio squawks with another update. Rodriguez's voice cuts through the static: "Alpha Leader, we need you on the line. Fire's threatening the fuel depot."

Mac's jaw tightens as he processes multiple crisis points requiring his attention. The weight of command settles across his shoulders, transforming him from the man who kissed me desperately into Captain Sullivan, responsible for containing an ecological catastrophe.

"I have to go." He turns to me, something vulnerable flickering behind his professional mask. "The fuel depot—"

"I know." I understand the implications. If the fire reaches the depot, it won't just be Angel's Peak at risk. "Do what you have to do."

He steps closer, close enough that I can smell smoke and sweat and the familiar scent that's purely him. His hand slides to the back of my neck, fingers tangling in my hair.

"Stay safe." It's an order and a plea wrapped in two words.

"Yes, sir." The response comes automatically, and his eyes darken at the acknowledgment.

Then his mouth is on mine again, harder this time, more desperate. A claim that speaks of unfinished business and promises neither of us dares voice. When he pulls away, my lips feel bruised and my pulse hammers with more than adrenaline.

"I'll find you when this is over," he growls against my ear.

"You'd better."

"Well, that's one way to boost morale before a mission." Parker's dry voice cuts through our moment. She approaches with a knowing smirk, tactical gear slung over her shoulder. "Captain, if you're done marking your territory, we've got a fuel depot that's about to become a very expensive firework."

Mac's jaw tightens, but he doesn't step away from me immediately. If anything, his arm around my waist becomes more possessive.

"Just ensuring our guide knows her value to the operation," he says smoothly.

"Right." Parker's grin widens. "Is that what they're calling it these days? Because from where I'm standing, it looks more like—"

"Parker." Mac's voice carries a warning that would silence most subordinates.

"Yes, Cap." But her eyes dance with mischief as she turns to me. "Ms. Mackenzie, try to keep him focused out there. Man's been impossible to work with since you disappeared into that tunnel."

Heat creeps up my neck at her implication, but Parker's already moving toward the vehicles, calling over her shoulder, "Clock's ticking, Cap. Romance later, save the town now."

Mac mutters something under his breath that sounds distinctly uncomplimentary about smart-mouthed sergeants.

He strides toward his team, authority radiating from every line of his body as he shifts into crisis mode. His shoulders stretch the fabric of his uniform with each purposeful step, muscles coiled with controlled power that makes my mouth water.

Parker follows, barking orders into her radio as they coordinate the defense of the fuel depot, but I barely register her presence. All I can think about is the controlled violence in Mac's movements, the coiled strength that promises he'll take me apart with the same focused intensity he brings to everything else.

The way Mac moves, all predatory grace wrapped in discipline, sends heat spiraling through my core.

God, the things that man can do.

The way those broad shoulders cage me beneath him, how his hands span my ribs while he drives into me with animalistic ruthlessness. My thighs clench involuntarily at the memory of his weight pinning me down, the delicious ache of being thoroughly fucked.

Tonight. The promise burns in my chest, spreading downward until I'm liquid with want. Those hands will map every inch of my skin. That mouth will issue crisp orders I can't wait to obey.

When he's done with me, when I'm marked and sated and trembling beneath him, I'll beg him for more.

I can't wait to burn beneath him.

Scout sits beside me as Mac's vehicle disappears. Her ears track the sound of engines long after they've vanished from sight. She leans against my leg—a warm, steady presence that grounds me while my mind races with worry for the man who's just driven toward the most dangerous part of this crisis.

Scout's calm acceptance reminds me that we have our own responsibilities to attend to.

Sheriff Donovan approaches as Mac's vehicle disappears down the mountain road, his weathered face grim with the weight of what's coming.

"Nice work out there, Jo." He tips his hat, a gesture of respect that acknowledges our shared history. "You just pulled off a hell of a rescue."

"Thanks. Just doing my part."

"Your part is about to get a lot bigger." He spreads his map across the truck hood, this one marked with evacuation routes and civilian staging areas. "Fire's moving faster than we anticipated. We're calling in every volunteer we can muster. I could use your help organizing them."

I study his annotations, seeing immediately how the path of the engineered fire will render standard evacuation procedures ineffective.

"You need different routes. The main roads will be cut off within two hours."

"That's what I was hoping you'd say." Donovan's smile is grim but determined. "I need someone who knows every back road, every trail, every way in and out of these mountains."

"What about Mac's team?"

"They're fighting the fire itself. We're fighting to save the people." He meets my eyes directly. "I'm coordinating on-site fire suppression. I need you to coordinate volunteer evacuation efforts from town."

The request hits hard. He's asking me to take responsibility for the civilian population of Angel's Peak—hundreds of people whose lives will depend on my knowledge of escape routes and my ability to coordinate complex logistics under pressure.

But I can do more.

"You need more hands fighting this blaze. I'll get everyone out who needs to go, and I'll get you able-bodied people to fight that fire."

Three years ago, I would have refused. The weight of that responsibility would have crushed me.

Now, with Danny's trust still warm in my memory and Mac's faith burning in my chest, I nod.

"Where do you need me?"

"The Haven's ballroom. Lucas Reid offered it as an emergency command center." Donovan rolls up his map, the gesture decisive. "Every volunteer firefighter, every search and rescue team, every person willing to help—they're meeting there in thirty minutes."

"Understood." I check my watch, my mind already racing through logistics. "What resources do I have?"

"Whatever you need. Angel's Peak is fighting for its life." His radio crackles with another urgent update, and he keys the response before looking back at me. "The town's counting on you, Jo."

As his vehicle disappears toward the fire line, I stand alone in the staging area, watching smoke columns rise like pillars against the afternoon sky. Somewhere in that inferno, Mac and his team are fighting to contain an ecological disaster.

Scout moves to my side, pressing against my legs as if sensing the weight of what comes next. Her brown eyes follow my gaze to the smoke columns, and her nostrils flare as she processes the scents carried on the wind—smoke, fear, the complex chemistry of a town under siege.

Angel's Peak

CHAPTER 15

CALL TO ARMS

THE HAVEN'S GRAND BALLROOM HAS NEVER SERVED a purpose more distant from its design. Where crystal chandeliers usually illuminate elegant gatherings, they now cast harsh light over maps spread across banquet tables pushed together in a makeshift command center. The air tastes of smoke that clings to everyone's clothing, mixing with fear and determination in equal measure. My throat burns with each breath, a constant reminder of the disaster pressing against our town's borders.

Scout lies beneath the main table, her chin resting across my boots as I address the assembled crowd. She's been my shadow since we emerged from the tunnels, refusing to leave my side even in this crowded, chaotic space.

Her brown eyes track every movement in the room, ears swiveling toward radio chatter and urgent conversations. The stress radiating from every person here affects her too—I can feel the tension in her body where she presses against my legs, offering comfort while drawing it in return.

Every chair is filled. Every face is grim.

Somewhere out there, Mac fights alongside his team on

the front lines, facing the engineered inferno head-on. The knowledge sits in my chest like a weight, worry threading through every decision I make here in relative safety.

I stand at the head of the main table, trying to channel the authority Mac displayed before he left for the front lines. Maps ready, pulse still racing from our tunnel rescue and the passionate goodbye that followed. The memory of his hands on my skin, his promise to find me when this is over, grounds me even as my nerves sing with tension about where he is now, what he's facing out there with Parker and his team.

"The situation is critical." I don't waste time with preambles; I echo Mac's direct approach. My voice carries through the room, steadier than I expect despite everything we've faced. "We're facing a fire unlike anything these mountains have seen in recorded history. Captain Sullivan and his hotshot crew are fighting the main blaze on the front lines, while we coordinate civilian evacuation and volunteer firefighting efforts."

Lucas Reid, The Haven's owner, leans forward. The polished businessman looks haggard, expensive shirt wrinkled, usually perfect hair disheveled.

"What resources do we have for civilian operations?" he asks.

"Local fire services. Volunteer firefighters. Search and rescue teams." I gesture toward the assembled crowd, drawing strength from their determined faces. "And everyone in this room who knows these mountains."

Murmurs ripple through the assembled crowd—a cross-section of Angel's Peak's residents summoned for this emergency council. I spot familiar faces etched with worry throughout the ballroom.

Eleanor Morgan, her silver braids coiled regally atop her head, sits with her spine straight despite her age, her sharp eyes already calculating logistics. Beside her, Hunter Morgan leans forward intently, flour still dusting his forearms from whatever he abandoned in his restaurant kitchen to be here.

Drs. Cole Blake and Tess Carrington cluster near the medical supply station, their trained eyes scanning the crowd for potential volunteers with relevant skills. Jackson Hart, mountain rescue specialist and wilderness guide, studies the fire projection maps with the intensity of someone who's pulled bodies from burning mountains.

Caleb Donovan stands by the window with arms crossed, his forest ranger uniform wrinkled from hours on the fireline, watching smoke columns rise in the distance.

Lucas Reid paces near the windows, his usual corporate polish replaced by genuine concern as he calculates what resources The Haven can contribute. Near the back, I spot Riley Bennett, the journalist who returned to cover Angel's Peak's revival, her notepad forgotten as she absorbs the gravity of our situation.

Ruth Fletcher, owner of The PickAxe bar, stands with her weathered hands clasped, having closed her establishment to be here. Beside her, Marianne Cox from Mountain Metalworks nods grimly—both women representing the artisan community that's helped transform our town.

Even Dominic Mercer from Silverleaf Vineyards has come down from his mountain vineyard, soil still under his fingernails from whatever harvest work he abandoned. His dog Merlot sits alert beside him, both of them radiating the same coiled tension.

The diversity of faces—business owners, artists, medical professionals, emergency responders, and longtime residents—reflects everything Angel's Peak has become. All of them now united by a single purpose: saving their home.

The chandelier light catches the dust motes floating through the air, tiny particles of ash that infiltrated even this sealed space. My skin feels gritty with it, the taste bitter on my tongue.

"What are you asking of us?" Eleanor's voice cuts through the whispers, direct as ever. Her hands rest steady on her walking stick, but I catch the slight tremor in her fingers—the only sign of the fear she won't let show.

I meet her gaze steadily, drawing on every ounce of authority Mac trusted me with. "Everything. Your knowledge. Your skills. Your hands." I gesture toward the map, the paper crinkling under the weight of our collective attention.

"This fire was deliberately engineered to cause maximum destruction. Captain Sullivan believes the ultimate target is the old Silver Creek mining complex, but the path there runs straight through Angel's Peak."

My stomach clenches at my own words. Someone wants my mountains to burn, wants my town reduced to ash for reasons I can't yet fathom.

Noah Morgan stands, the movement drawing all eyes. His chair scrapes against the polished floor—a sound too loud in the sudden quiet. As fire chief, his authority here is crucial in Mac's absence.

"For those who don't know, Captain Sullivan's team are elite firefighters specifically trained for wilderness blazes." Noah's respect for Mac is evident in his tone, but his voice carries the weight of someone who's seen what untrained volunteers can do in crisis situations.

"Jo coordinated a successful civilian rescue earlier today. If she says we need everyone, we need everyone."

"What's the strategy?" Jackson Hart's question comes sharp and precise, the voice of someone accustomed to life-or-death decisions in unforgiving terrain.

I step forward, feeling the weight of thirty pairs of eyes. The maps beneath my fingers feel familiar, comforting—years of work distilled into lines and symbols that could save or damn us all.

"The fire is using natural features to accelerate." I indicate the map's topography, my finger tracing the paths I've walked countless times. "Canyons acting as chimneys, ridgelines creating wind tunnels. We can't match its power, so we need to break its momentum."

Scout rises from her position under the table, moving to stand beside me as I trace routes on the map. Her presence draws a few glances from the assembled volunteers—several of whom know her reputation as a search and rescue dog.

When Jackson Hart nods approvingly at her, I realize they're not just seeing my expertise, but our partnership. The team that's already proven itself in today's rescue operations.

I trace a curved line across the map, the pencil marks showing elevation changes that most people couldn't read. But these people can. These are my neighbors, people who've spent their lives learning the mountain's moods.

"We create a containment line here, along this natural fire-break. The ridge drops nearly vertical on the north side— approximately two hundred feet of bare rock the fire can't easily jump."

"What about the access points?" Noah asks, already seeing the weakness. His pen hovers over his notepad, ready to capture every detail.

"Three valleys interrupt the ridge." I tap each location, feeling the weight of what I'm asking. These gaps are natural funnels, places where wind and flame will converge with devastating force. "These are our critical defense points. If we can hold these three gaps, we force the fire to climb the rock face, which will slow its advance significantly."

"Captain Sullivan's team is handling the northern position— the most dangerous." I continue, my voice catching slightly as I think of Mac facing that hell. "Caleb and Jackson, I figure you're the best to lead volunteer crews. Noah will get your crews set and lead the volunteers. I'll coordinate the civilian evacuation."

Noah studies the map intently, his weathered finger tracing distances. Jackson and Caleb join him. I can almost see them calculating personnel, equipment, the terrible mathematics of men against wildfire.

"That's nearly seven miles of containment line," Noah pulls at his chin. "We don't have enough personnel to cover it effectively."

"That's why we're here." I let my gaze sweep the room, meeting each face individually. The chandelier light catches the determination in their eyes —the absolute conviction that makes people believe in the impossible. "We need every able-bodied person who knows these mountains. Guides, hunters, rangers—anyone who can safely navigate the terrain and follow directions under pressure."

Jackson Hart, all lean muscle and contained energy, speaks up. "Mountain Rescue can contribute ten experienced guides, all with wildfire training."

"The lodge staff are at your disposal." Lucas Reid's offer comes as a surprise, given his usual corporate detachment. "We know the trails."

"I'll coordinate supply lines and base camp operations." Eleanor Morgan rises, commanding attention despite her diminutive stature. Her walking stick taps once against the floor—a sound like a gavel calling court to order. "The community center can serve as a staging area."

"Eleanor..." I hate to say it, but it needs to be said. "You should evacuate with the—"

"And leave my town when it needs me most? Not going to happen. You've got enough on your plate with the evacuations. I can ferry up water and snacks to the frontline."

One by one, Angel's Peak's residents step up, offering

skills, equipment, and knowledge accumulated over generations of mountain living. I watch in silent amazement as the community coalesces around a single purpose: protecting their home. The air in the room shifts, fear transforming into something harder, more determined.

Caleb Donovan, normally reserved to the point of reclusiveness, approaches me directly. His uniform is wrinkled, boots dusty from whatever fire line he's just left. "The Forest Service has detailed fuel maps for the entire region. Recent updates show deadfall concentrations and beetle-kill zones. Might help predict where the fire will burn hottest. We'll get them distributed."

"Thank you."

As the meeting transitions to specific assignments, Sheriff Donovan draws me aside, his weathered hand warm against my elbow. His voice drops low beneath the room's organized chaos.

Noah approaches. "We need more detailed maps of those three gaps. Everything you've got—water sources, terrain features, potential safety zones."

I'm already nodding, mind racing through the files in my office. "I have them at my office. Comprehensive surveys from last spring."

"Let's grab them. I'll drive. Jackson and Caleb look like they've got the volunteers handled."

The room is organized into functional groups, each with assigned leaders and clear objectives.

Outside, the afternoon sun glows unnaturally orange through smoke that thickens by the minute, casting Angel's Peak in apocalyptic light. The wind carries ash and the distant roar of approaching devastation—a sound like thunder that never ends, growing closer with each gust.

The sheriff and I slip out and head to the visitor center.

It stands empty, evacuated hours earlier as part of the town's emergency protocols.

Scout trots between Sheriff Donovan and me as we cross the parking lot, her nose working constantly to process the smoky air. She pauses once, looking back toward the mountains where the fire rages, a low whine escaping her throat.

She can smell what's coming. The acrid scent of destruction carries on winds that shift unpredictably. When I call her name softly, she falls back into step, trusting my judgment even when her instincts scream warnings.

My footsteps echo in the unnatural silence as I unlock my office, the keys jingling in my shaking hands. The familiar space feels alien in the eerie light filtering through smoke-stained windows.

"Here." I pull open a flat file drawer, extracting rolled maps labeled with ·dates and locations in my careful handwriting. The paper feels substantial under my fingers, years of field-work distilled into precise lines and measurements. "Complete terrain surveys of all three gaps, updated within the last six months."

Sheriff Donovan spreads them across my desk, his focus intense as he absorbs every detail. The desk lamp casts a pool of yellow light, throwing sharp shadows across his weathered features. His finger traces elevation lines, water features, and vegetation patterns.

"These are incredible." The admiration in his voice is genuine, sending warmth through my chest despite the circumstances. "The detail is... Mac was right to trust your expertise."

"I walked every inch." I move beside him, close enough to feel the weight of shared responsibility, to catch the scent of smoke and determination that clings to his uniform.

My shoulder brushes his as I indicate features too subtle for standard mapping. "This small ravine provides a natural

fire break if we can clear the brush at the entrance. And here
—" I tap a blue line barely visible on the paper, "—spring-fed
pool that doesn't appear on any forest service maps. Reliable
water source even in drought conditions."

He studies each feature, asking precise questions that
reveal a tactical mind working through scenarios, contingen-
cies, and worst-case possibilities. For twenty minutes, we bend
over the maps, planning a defense for mountains we both love,
sharing the burden of command that Mac carried alone just
hours earlier.

"This is our best chance." Donovan straightens finally,
rolling the maps carefully for transport. His hands are steady,
sure, but I catch the tension in his shoulders, the weight of
responsibility that settles on anyone who must make life-or-
death decisions. "If we hold those three gaps, we can force the
fire to burn itself out against the ridge."

"If." The weight of that small word hangs between us like
smoke.

His eyes meet mine, brown and steady despite the magni-
tude of what we're facing. "You've done everything possible to
prepare us. Mac chose well when he put you in charge of
civilian coordination."

"And weather." I glance toward the window where smoke
now obscures the mountains entirely, turning day to prema-
ture dusk. The wind rattles the glass, a sound like restless spirits. "If the wind shifts..."

"We adapt." His certainty echoes Mac's earlier words,
grounding me to something solid in a world that feels like it's
burning around us. "That's what your maps give us—options
for adaptation."

My radio crackles to life, cutting through the charged
silence. Mac's voice comes through static, professional but
strained.

"Base Command, this is Alpha Leader. Requesting imme-

diate supply drop at northern position. We're holding, but barely."

Scout's ears perk immediately at the sound of Mac's voice crackling through the radio. She moves closer, pressing against my leg as if she can sense the tension in his transmission.

Her eyes fix on the radio with the same intensity she shows when tracking scents—as if she's trying to reach through the static to the man who's become important to both of us. When the transmission ends, she looks up at me with worried brown eyes that mirror my fears.

I key the radio with steady hands despite my racing pulse.

"Alpha Leader, this is Base Command. Supply drop coordinates acknowledged. Status on crew welfare?"

"All personnel accounted for. Fighting extreme conditions. Fire behavior unlike anything we've seen." The controlled tension in his voice tells me more than his words.

They're facing hell out there.

"Copy that, Alpha Leader. Sheriff Donovan coordinating supply drop now. Additional volunteer teams deploying to support positions."

A pause, filled with static and what sounds like the roar of a freight train. "Roger, Base Command. Tell the volunteers... tell them this is brutal. Alpha Leader out."

The radio goes quiet, leaving me staring at its display as if it might provide more connection to the man fighting for his life somewhere in that orange hell visible through my window.

"He's the best there is. He'll bring his team home." Sheriff Donovan's hand settles on my shoulder, steadying.

I nod, swallowing past the tightness in my throat. "Then let's make sure he has a home to come back to."

We return to The Haven, where the ballroom has transformed into a fully operational command center. Teams cluster around assigned leaders, equipment is distributed, and communication networks buzz with constant updates.

I oversee it all, trying to channel the calm authority I watched Mac display, directing resources and personnel like pieces on a complex chessboard.

"Complete terrain analysis for our volunteer teams." I spread the detailed surveys across the main table, the paper crackling under the bright chandelier light.

Noah Morgan studies the map, absorbing details. His finger traces the contour lines, reading the terrain like text. "What about natural shelter positions? Safety zones if our volunteers need to pull back?"

"Two locations." I indicate the rock formations marked in red. My father's careful notations are still visible in faded ink. "This outcropping provides coverage from three sides. And this cave system extends approximately thirty feet into solid rock. Both are last resorts, but they'll withstand direct flame passage."

"That cave system might be our best emergency option." Jackson Hart joins us, his experienced eye evaluating escape routes with the methodical assessment of someone who's pulled bodies from burning mountains. "I've used it during winter rescues. Stable air flow, multiple chambers."

The briefing continues, each team leader absorbing critical information about their assigned sector. I move among them, answering questions, adjusting deployments based on individual skills and experience.

It feels strange to be in command, to have Mac's authority transferred to me in his absence, but the responsibility settles across my shoulders with surprising comfort.

Eleanor Morgan approaches, her silver head barely reaching my shoulder, but her presence commanding absolute attention. "The supply lines are established. Hot meals and clean water every four hours to all positions."

"Thank you." I squeeze her weathered hand gently. "Mac's

team especially needs consistent supplies. They're facing the worst of it."

"You care for him." Her eyes, sharp despite her age, study my face with knowing assessment.

"More than I should." It's not a question, but I answer anyway.

"Love isn't about *should*, child." Her smile carries decades of wisdom. "It's about *is*. And what's between you two is worth fighting for."

Before I can respond, my radio crackles again. This time it's Parker, Mac's second-in-command. *"Base Command, this is Alpha Two. We need immediate evacuation for injured personnel. Request medical team at northern staging area."*

Scout senses the shift in my emotional state before I fully process Parker's words. Scout presses closer, her warm body a steadying presence as my hands shake while keying the radio. Her training has taught her to recognize medical emergencies, and the urgency in Parker's voice triggers her alert posture. She remains perfectly still during the radio exchange, understanding instinctively that this is a critical moment requiring absolute focus.

My blood turns to ice. "Alpha Two, this is Base Command. Nature and severity of injuries?"

"Two personnel down. Burns and smoke inhalation. Conscious but need immediate medical attention."

Not Mac. Please not Mac. "Copy that, Alpha Two. Medical team dispatching now. Status on Alpha Leader?"

"Alpha Leader is... Alpha Leader is operational. Continuing fire suppression operations."

The relief nearly buckles my knees. He's alive. He's fighting. He's coming home.

"Roger, Alpha Two. Medical support en route. Base Command out."

I turn to find Drs. Blake and Carrington grabbing their medical go bags. They race for the door.

The room buzzes with urgency as teams mobilize to support the frontline fighters, who risk everything to save our town.

Sheriff Donovan catches me coordinating supply distribution, his expression approving.

The radio crackles again—routine updates, supply confirmations, position reports. But no more word from Mac himself. I stand in the elegant ballroom turned war room, staring at maps that show his position as a simple red dot, wondering if those careful lines and measurements can possibly capture the reality of what he's facing out there.

Scout moves to my side, pressing her head against my hand in a gesture of comfort that grounds me. Her steady breathing and warm presence remind me that I'm not facing this alone.

She's weathered every crisis with me today, from underground rescues to command decisions, proving once again that the bonds forged in these mountains run deeper than fear.

Angel's Peak

CHAPTER 16

CHIMNEY ROCK

THE RADIO CRACKLES TO LIFE AT 1847 HOURS, JUST as the sun disappears behind a wall of smoke thick enough to choke out daylight. I'm bent over supply manifests in The Haven's ballroom, tracking water deliveries to the fire line, when Mac's voice cuts through the static—tight, controlled, but carrying an edge I've never heard before.

Scout's head snaps up from her position beneath the command table, ears pricked forward with sharp attention. She's been restless all evening, pacing between the radio station and the windows, her nose constantly working the smoky air.

Now she moves to my side, pressing against my leg as if sensing the gravity of what's about to come through that radio. Her brown eyes fix on the device with the same intensity she shows when tracking a scent trail, as if she can hear something in Mac's voice that my human ears might miss.

"Base Command, this is Alpha Leader." His usual steady composure has steel beneath it now, sharp and dangerous. *"We have a problem."*

My hand freezes over the manifest. Around me, the

command center's controlled chaos dims as heads turn toward the radio.

"Alpha Leader, this is Base Command. Go ahead."

"Fire jumped the containment line. My entire team is cut off." A pause, filled with the distant roar of destruction. *"Repeat—we're cut off from our primary and secondary evacuation routes."*

Ice slides down my spine. I grab the radio, my voice steady despite the fear clawing at my throat.

"Alpha Leader, what's your current position?"

"Grid reference 847-291. North of Widow's Peak." Static crackles, then his voice returns, strained but controlled.

I trace my finger across the map spread before me, finding their position.

My stomach drops.

They're trapped.

"Alpha Leader, how many personnel total?"

"Twelve. Full crew complement." A pause filled with the distant roar I recognize as wildfire consuming everything in its path. *"We've got maybe thirty minutes before this position becomes untenable."*

Thirty minutes. I stare at the topographical lines surrounding their location, my mind racing through escape routes. The main trail they used to reach that position is now blocked by fire. The eastern slope is too steep for safe descent. The western approach leads directly into the fire's path.

That leaves north.

Straight up the mountain face.

"Alpha Leader, stand by." I key off the radio and grab my most detailed survey map of Widow's Peak—hand-drawn, every cliff face and hidden ledge marked from personal reconnaissance.

Sheriff Donovan appears at my shoulder. "What are we looking at?"

"Mac's team is trapped on the north face of Widow's Peak." My finger traces their position to the surrounding terrain. "Fire cut off their retreat. They need an alternate extraction route."

"Air support?"

I check the weather station readings posted on the wall. "Wind gusts to forty-five mph. Visibility is near zero. No pilot's going to risk it in these conditions."

Noah Morgan joins us, his face grim. "What about the old mining trail? The one that connects to Thunder Ridge?"

"Washed out last spring." I point to my notations on the map. "Flash flood took out the bridge. There's a twenty-foot gap now."

The radio goes quiet except for static. Around me, the command center has gone absolutely silent. Every face turns toward me, waiting for the miracle that will save twelve of the best firefighters in the country.

I stare at the map, but the lines blur as my mind processes what Mac just told me.

"Jo." Sheriff Donovan's voice cuts through my paralysis. "What do you need?"

I blink, focusing on the map with laser intensity. The terrain features sharpen back into clarity—elevation lines, water sources, and rock formations. My father's notations in faded ink along the margins.

There.

A thin line marking shadows where they would naturally collect. Too small for the official surveys, but I walked it two summers ago during drought conditions. It cuts north through a narrow canyon, connecting to Hidden Lake above the fire line.

But it's a box canyon. One way in. One way out.

"There's a route." My finger traces a line on the map where shadows would naturally collect. "Blind canyon. Runs north through Devil's Canyon—looks like a dead end from the outside, but there's a chimney formation at the back wall."

Noah frowns, studying the terrain. "Devil's Canyon? That's suicide. It's a box canyon."

"Exactly why the fire can't follow them." The fire won't, but the heat and smoke will. I grab my radio, my pulse hammering. "The walls funnel wind away from the interior. But Noah's right—it's a one-way trip. If they can't climb the chimney..."

Jackson Hart, who's been silent until now, shakes his head. "I know that formation. Sixty-foot vertical climb through a rock chimney barely wide enough for a man's shoulders. In perfect conditions, it's challenging. In smoke?"

"It's their only chance."

I key the radio, my decision made.

"Alpha Leader, this is Base Command. I have an extraction route, but it's extreme risk."

"Go ahead, Base Command."

"North-northwest from your position, approximately four hundred yards through burned timber. Look for a narrow canyon entrance—it appears as a shadow cut into the rock face."

Static crackles as Mac processes the information. When his voice returns, it's strained.

"Found it. Looks like a dead end."

"The canyon extends two hundred yards into the mountain, then terminates at a vertical wall. But there's a chimney formation—a natural shaft carved by water erosion. Sixty feet straight up through solid rock."

A pause. When Mac speaks again, his voice carries the weight of command decision balanced on a knife's edge.

"How narrow is this chimney?"

I close my eyes, remembering the formation from my exploration three years ago. The terror of being trapped in that vertical shaft, shoulders scraping rock on both sides, sixty feet of darkness above.

"Shoulder width. Maybe less in places. It's a one-person climb. If someone gets stuck halfway up..."

"Game over for everyone behind them." Mac finishes grimly. *"How sure are you about the exit?"*

The question that could doom or save twelve lives.

"I've climbed it. It opens onto a ledge system above Hidden Lake—a small alpine lake about forty feet below the chimney exit. You'll need to rappel down to the water, then swim across to the north shore where the fire hasn't spread. Evacuation can pick you up from there." I pause, needing him to understand. "Once you enter that canyon, there's no other way out. If the chimney proves impassable..."

"We cook." His voice is flat, matter-of-fact. *"Understood. Moving to canyon entrance now."*

I watch the clock on the wall, tracking their progress in my mind. Four hundred yards through burning forest to reach the canyon mouth. Then two hundred yards into the blind canyon. Then, a sixty-foot vertical climb while superheated air rises beneath them.

The radio crackles with updates as they move through the hellscape. Mac's voice, professional despite the chaos: *"Alpha Leader moving to canyon entrance. Visibility near zero. Ground temperature extreme."*

Long minutes pass. I track their progress on the map, imagining them stumbling through superheated air and falling ash toward what might be salvation or a death trap.

"Base Command, Alpha Leader at canyon entrance. Confirm—this terminates at a rock wall?"

"Affirmative. The chimney entrance is at the back wall, northeast corner. Look for a vertical crack in the granite."

"Moving into the canyon now."

The radio goes quiet except for static. I stare at the map,

knowing they're now committed to a route with no alternatives. If the chimney is blocked, if someone gets trapped in the narrow shaft, if the exit is compromised...

"Alpha Leader, status?"

Static.

"Alpha Leader, respond."

More static, then a burst of noise that might be voices or might be wind through stone.

Minutes crawl by. Even if they survive the climb, they might emerge to find the world above them consumed by flame.

Scout begins pacing, her agitation mirroring my own as the radio remains silent. She moves between the windows and the command table, occasionally returning to press against me before resuming her restless circuit.

Her ears swivel constantly, as if she's trying to pick up sounds beyond human hearing—the distant roar of fire, the crackle of burning timber, any sign that the men we're trying to save are still alive. When she finally settles beside my chair, her brown eyes reflect the same worry that gnaws at my chest.

Then Mac's voice cuts through the silence, tight with strain: *"Base Command, we've got a problem."*

My blood turns to ice. "Go ahead, Alpha Leader."

"The chimney's blocked. Rockfall, maybe twenty feet up. We've got Williams trying to clear it, but..." A pause filled with the sound of falling stone. *"It's unstable. Every rock she moves threatens to bring down more."*

"Can you clear it?"

"Unknown. And we're running out of time. Fire's reached the canyon mouth."

I close my eyes, visualizing the chimney formation. There had been loose rock when I climbed it—old fractures, water damage, the slow work of freeze-thaw cycles weakening the granite.

"Alpha Leader, how big is the blockage?"

"Maybe four feet of loose rock. But it's wedged tight. Williams is..." Static drowns out his words, then, *"Shit. She's stuck. Her pack's caught on something."*

My heart pounds as I imagine Williams trapped in the narrow shaft, rock walls pressing from both sides, loose stones threatening to bury her alive, while superheated air rises from below to cook her and the rest of Mac's team.

"Can she back down?"

"Negative. Pack's jammed. Rodriguez is going up to help, but there's no room for two people."

This is the nightmare scenario—multiple people trapped in a vertical chimney while fire fills the canyon below them like a furnace.

"Alpha Leader, you need to cut her pack free."

"Working on it. But if we destabilize the blockage..."

He doesn't finish the sentence. Doesn't need to. If the rockfall shifts, it could crush Williams and trap everyone below her.

The radio crackles with urgent voices—Rodriguez calling up to Williams, Burke reporting that the canyon floor is heating rapidly, Martinez coordinating the evacuation of personnel who haven't yet entered the chimney.

"Still stuck. Rodriguez got her pack cut free, but the loose rock is shifting. If it comes down..."

I imagine Rodriguez positioned just below Williams, trying to help stabilize the rockfall while she works to clear the passage, ten people waiting below as fire fills their refuge.

"Base Command, this is Alpha Leader." Mac's voice cuts through the chaos. *"Fire's entered the canyon. Ground level becoming untenable."*

I grab the radio, my mind racing through alternatives that don't exist. "Alpha Leader, status on Williams?"

Then Williams' voice cuts through, exhausted but

triumphant: *"Got it! I cleared the blockage!"* A pause, then her voice drops with grim realization. *"But Captain... the opening I made is only about eighteen inches wide. I can barely squeeze through myself."*

"Shit." Mac's voice carries the weight of understanding. *"How many of us can fit through that gap?"*

"Maybe Parker, Flint, Burke if he sucks it in real good. But you, Rodriguez, Martinez, Nguyen—no way in hell. You're all too broad in the shoulders."

Static fills the radio as Mac processes this. Then his voice, calm and tactical. *"Alright, here's what we're going to do. Rodriguez, climb back down. Williams, you continue up. Parker, Flint, Burke—you four get through that gap and climb to the top. The chimney opens up past the blockage, right?"*

"Affirmative," I say. "Wide enough for normal climbing once you're past the squeeze."

"Good. Reach the summit and secure anchors. Drop belay lines down the exterior face of this formation. Rodriguez, Martinez, Nguyen, and I will climb the outside."

"Captain, that's suicide," Parker's voice cuts through. *"The exterior's fully exposed to the heat—"*

"It's our only option. We've got maybe five minutes before this canyon floor becomes uninhabitable." Mac's voice hardens with command authority. *"Parker, you're in charge of the top team. Get those anchors set."*

Relief and terror war in my chest as the radio erupts with coordinated activity. Williams squeezing through the narrow gap. Parker following, her gear scraping against rock. Flint barely making it through. Burke cursing as he forces his larger frame past the blockage.

"Top team at the summit." Parker's voice reports. *"Setting anchors for exterior belay."*

Long minutes pass while I track their progress. Parker's team rigging solid anchors while Mac, Rodriguez, Martinez, and Nguyen prepare for the most dangerous climb of their lives—up the exterior face with fire licking at the rock below them.

"Two belay lines secured and deployed down the exterior face." Parker reports. *"Beginning dual evacuation."*

Two by two, the larger firefighters are hauled up the outside of the chimney formation—Rodriguez and Martinez on the first pull, their bodies silhouetted against the flames below. Then Nguyen paired with gear, leaving Mac alone on the superheated canyon floor.

"Alpha Leader, you're last up?"

"Affirmative. Exterior face fully engaged now. Heat extreme."

I track his ascent in my mind—sixty feet of vertical climbing up the exterior rock face, hauled by belay lines while superheated air and flames surround him like the breath of a dragon.

"Alpha Leader, halfway point."

Static.

"Alpha Leader, status?"

More static, then his voice, labored: *"Exterior surface too hot. Can't maintain grip much longer."*

My heart stops. The granite is absorbing heat from the fire below, turning the chimney into a vertical oven.

"Can you continue?"

"Have to." His breathing is labored, desperate. *"No choice."*

Long seconds pass. I imagine him pressed against burning stone, fingertips seeking purchase on rock hot enough to sear flesh, sixty feet of vertical hell between him and safety.

Finally: *"Alpha Leader clear. All personnel accounted for and clear of immediate danger. We're at the lake—forty feet below us, crystal clear water. Beginning rappel operations now."*

The relief nearly buckles my knees. I grip the edge of the table, breathing for what feels like the first time in an hour.

Scout seems to sense the shift in my emotional state before I fully process Mac's words. Her tail gives a tentative wag—the first sign of optimism she's shown all evening. She moves to my side as my knees threaten to give out, her solid body providing support as relief crashes through me.

When I reach down to pat her head with trembling fingers, she leans into the touch, sharing both my fear and my relief. Her brown eyes hold the same exhausted gratitude I feel—*our pack leader is coming home.*

"Roger that, Alpha Leader. Once you're across the lake, you'll be clear of the thermal column and in the green zone for evacuation. Status on injuries?"

"Minor burns and smoke inhalation. Nothing that won't heal." A pause, then his voice drops lower, intimate despite the open channel. *"Outstanding work, Base Command. You just saved twelve lives with that route."*

"Just bringing you home, Sir."

"On our way to you now."

As the radio goes quiet, I become aware of the silence around me. Every person in the command center is staring at me with expressions ranging from amazement to respect.

Sheriff Donovan breaks the silence first. "That was extraordinary."

I sink into a chair, the adrenaline finally catching up with me. My hands tremble as I roll up the map that just saved the man I love and eleven of his teammates.

But even as relief floods through me, this isn't over. Mac's team may be past this threat, but the main blaze still burns. Angel's Peak still faces destruction.

And somewhere in those flames, an arsonist watches his engineered disaster unfold, probably congratulating himself on a plan that's working exactly as intended.

The radio crackles one more time. Mac's voice, quiet but carrying clearly: *"Josephine."*

I grab the radio instantly. "Yes?"

"When I get back..." His voice drops to that dangerous whisper that makes my skin tighten with anticipation. *"We're going to have a very thorough conversation about exactly what happens when you save my life."*

Heat pools low in my belly despite everything. "Is that a threat or a promise?"

"Both." The single word carries weight that has nothing to do with fire suppression and everything to do with the way he's going to take me apart when this is over. *"Now get back to saving our town. I have work to finish."*

The radio goes quiet, leaving me staring at it while my pulse hammers against my throat. Around me, the command center returns to its controlled chaos, but I remain frozen by the promise in his voice.

Scout tilts her head at the sudden change in my scent—the shift from fear to something warmer, more anticipatory. She's learned to read the subtle changes that indicate when Mac and I are focused on each other rather than the crisis at hand.

Her tail thumps once against the floor, and I swear there's amusement in her brown eyes. Even she knows what's coming when this fire is finally out.

When this fire is out, when Angel's Peak is safe, when the adrenaline fades and we're alone, he's going to remind me exactly who I belong to.

But first, we have a town to save.

Angel's Peak

CHAPTER 17

FIRE TORNADO

THIRTY-SEVEN MINUTES LATER, MAC'S SUV PULLS into The Haven's circular drive, followed by a Forest Service transport carrying his team. Through the ballroom's tall windows, twelve soot-covered firefighters emerge from the vehicles.

Alive.

Moving.

Whole.

My knees nearly buckle with relief.

Mac strides through the entrance, his uniform torn and blackened, face streaked with ash and sweat. But his eyes are clear, focused, scanning the room until they find mine. The intensity in his gaze stops my breath—gratitude, possession, and something darker that promises our earlier conversation is far from over.

Scout beats me to him by several seconds, launching herself from beneath the command table the moment Mac crosses the threshold. Her tail whips back and forth as she reaches him first, pressing against his legs and inhaling deeply —cataloging the scents of smoke, granite, and survival that cling to his uniform.

Mac's stern expression softens as he crouches briefly to accept her enthusiastic greeting, one soot-stained hand scratching behind her ears.

"Hey, girl," he murmurs, and I catch the relief in his voice—not just at being alive, but at being home.

Scout's entire body wiggles with joy, and for a moment, the dangerous tension between Mac and me takes a backseat to the simple reunion of a dog with her pack.

"Base Command." His voice carries across the room, professional despite the heat that flares between us. "Requesting status update."

I force myself to remain seated, to keep my voice steady. "Fire's continued to spread. Three new ignition points reported in the last hour. We deployed volunteer teams to the containment positions you designated."

He approaches the main table, where our maps are spread out. His team files in behind him. Parker looks exhausted but alert, Rodriguez favors his left arm, Williams moves stiffly but under her own power. They're battered but functional. Exactly what I'd expect from elite firefighters.

"Casualties?" Mac asks, studying the updated fire positions marked in red across my carefully drawn terrain.

"Minor injuries only. Burns, smoke inhalation, exhaustion." I point to the medical station Eleanor has set up near the kitchen. "Dr. Blake and Dr. Carrington are treating everyone. Your team should be checked over."

"Negative. We don't have time." Mac's finger traces the fire's advance on the map, his jaw tightening as he processes how much ground the blaze has gained during their extraction. "How long until it reaches the first residential areas?"

"At the current rate of spread? Maybe four hours."

Four hours to save Angel's Peak.

Mac's hand finds the small of my back as he leans over the

map. The brief touch sends electricity racing through me despite everything. His thumb brushes against my spine, a subtle claim that makes my breath catch.

"You did well, Josephine." The words are quiet, meant only for me. "Damn well."

Before I can respond, Parker clears her throat. "Cap, we need to get back out there. Fire's not going to contain itself."

"Five-minute equipment check. Water, medical supplies, communications." Mac straightens, command mode reasserting itself. "Then we redeploy."

As he coordinates with his team, he watches me with that dangerous intensity. Our reunion will be explosive when this crisis ends.

Sheriff Donovan approaches, radio in hand. "Fire's jumped another ridge line. Moving faster than predicted. We need to deploy now if we're going to establish positions before it hits."

"All teams move out. Follow your assigned leaders to staging areas." Mac's voice carries without shouting, his command presence filling the room. "Radio check-ins every fifteen minutes. If conditions change, fall back to designated safety zones. No heroics."

The room empties as teams move toward vehicles and equipment caches. Within minutes, only the core command staff remains—Mac, Parker, Sheriff Donovan, Noah Morgan, and me.

"I'll coordinate from here." Sheriff Donovan indicates the communications setup. "Direct link to state emergency services and evacuation centers."

"I'm with Alpha Team at the northern gap." Mac turns to me. "You're staying at command. We need your terrain knowledge centralized where all teams can access it."

The logical assignment still strikes like a blow. "I should be in the field."

"You're more valuable here." His tone leaves no room for argument. "Every team needs your expertise. That only works if you're at the communication hub."

I want to protest and demand a place on the front line, but the strategic logic is unassailable. My knowledge serves more people from the command center than it would at any single location.

"Fine." I concede with poor grace. "But I'm monitoring all positions. Any terrain questions, any route adjustments, I need immediate notification."

Mac nods, already moving toward the door. "Parker, you've got Beta Team at the central position. Work with Chief Morgan's crew on containment lines."

"Copy that, Cap." Parker grabs her gear.

"Communications test at position, then every fifteen minutes thereafter." Mac pauses at the door, eyes finding mine one last time. Something passes between us—unspoken but undeniable. Then he's gone, striding into smoke-tinged daylight with the confidence of a man who's faced fire before and expects to do so again.

Scout follows Mac to the door, her brown eyes tracking his movement with the focused attention she reserves for important departures. She knows the difference between him leaving for routine business and leaving for danger—her posture tense, ears forward, tail still.

When the door closes behind him, she returns to my side, settling beneath the command table with a soft whine. Her eyes remain fixed on the entrance, as if willing him to return safely through sheer canine determination.

The next hours pass in controlled chaos. I remain at the command table, surrounded by maps and communication equipment, fielding questions from team leaders and tracking the fire's advance through periodic reports. The blaze moves like a living thing, accelerating through canyons, climbing slopes, creating its own weather systems as it consumes everything in its path.

Eleanor Morgan joins me, her calm presence a counterpoint to the tension thrumming through the command center. She organizes supply chains for those on the ground, ensuring water, food, and equipment flow steadily to the defensive positions.

"You care deeply for him." She says it without preamble as we study updated fire projections.

I don't pretend to misunderstand. "Is this really the time for that conversation?"

Her smile holds the wisdom of decades. "Crisis has a way of clarifying what matters, child."

Before I can respond, Mac's voice cuts through the radio chatter: *"Command, this is Alpha Leader. Fire front advancing on northern position. Estimated contact in fifteen minutes. Containment lines established."*

"Copy, Alpha Leader." Sheriff Donovan responds. "Status of personnel?"

"All in position. Weather conditions deteriorating rapidly. Wind speed increasing, shifting easterly."

I grab the radio. "Mac, easterly wind will funnel directly through the canyon to your west. Expect accelerated spread and possible spot fires behind your position."

"Copy that." His voice remains steady despite the implications. *"Adjusting defensive line to accommodate."*

The radio falls silent as teams prepare for imminent contact with the fire front. I stare at the tactical display, watching icon markers that represent real people—Mac, Parker, dozens of Angel's Peak residents standing against an inferno engineered for maximum destruction.

"They're well-prepared." Eleanor's voice cuts through my spiraling thoughts. "Every person on that line knows these mountains and respects fire's power."

"It may not be enough." I trace the fire's projected path. "If the wind continues to shift east..."

"Then they'll adapt." She places a weathered hand over mine. "That's what we do here. We don't defeat the mountain. We learn to move with it."

Minutes stretch into hours as reports flow in from all three defensive positions. The northern gap—Mac's position—takes the brunt of the fire's initial assault. Radio reports paint a grim picture: flame heights exceeding sixty feet, wind-driven embers igniting spot fires, temperatures so extreme that equipment fails.

Yet they hold.

Through skill, determination, and the natural barrier of the ridge, Mac's team forces the fire to climb rather than advance. The central gap, under Parker and Noah's direction, establishes a secondary containment line reinforced by the only available bulldozer. The southern position, manned primarily by volunteers under Sheriff Donovan's coordination, prepares for the fire front, still hours away from their location, cutting vast swaths of firebreak as quickly as possible.

Night falls, but darkness doesn't come. The fire illuminates the sky in hellish orange, visible for miles as it consumes acre after acre of wilderness. From The Haven's elevated position, we can see the distant battle lines marked by the headlights of emergency vehicles and the rhythmic flash of warning beacons.

Scout moves restlessly between the windows and the command table, her behavior reflecting the anxiety that permeates the room. She pauses at each window to stare out at the orange glow painting the mountains, nose working as she processes the complex scents of smoke and destruction carried on the night wind.

When she returns to my side, she presses against my legs with unusual intensity—not seeking comfort, but offering it.

Her steady presence grounds me as we monitor the distant battle for Angel's Peak's survival.

"Command, this is Alpha Leader." Mac's voice comes through just after midnight, strained but determined. *"Fire has crested the ridge. Containment holding at northern position."*

Relief washes through me, short-lived but powerful. "Casualties?"

"Negative. Two minor burns treated on site. All personnel accounted for."

I close my eyes briefly, offering silent gratitude to whatever forces govern such things. "Central and southern positions?"

"Central holding steady. Southern position reports fire front approaching, estimated contact within the hour."

"Copy that." I check the latest weather data. Wind is continuing to shift eastward. Central position should prepare for increased pressure on their eastern flank."

As if summoned by my warning, Parker's voice breaks through: *"Command, this is Beta Leader. Wind shift confirmed. Eastern flank taking heavy ember fall. Spot fires developing behind our position."*

Noah Morgan's voice follows immediately: *"Requesting additional personnel to address spot fires. Main line fully committed."*

Sheriff Donovan scans our resource board. "All available units already deployed. Reserve teams committed to evacuation security."

The implications settle heavily. The central position is developing into a crisis with no additional resources to address it.

"I can redirect two units from the southern position." Donovan offers. "But it leaves them critically undermanned if the fire intensifies there."

Before I can respond, Mac's voice cuts through: *"Alpha*

Leader to Command. We're stable at northern position. I can send Rodriguez with four team members to support central."

"Negative." The refusal comes automatically. "Northern position could destabilize if the wind shifts again. You need your full complement."

"Assessment indicates northern ridge is containing primary spread as predicted." Mac's voice carries absolute certainty. *"Greater risk now at central position. Making the call. Rodriguez team departing for central support."*

The strategic logic is sound, but fear still clutches at my chest. Weakening one position to strengthen another carries inherent risk—risk that falls squarely on Mac's shoulders.

Scout lifts her head from her position beneath the table, ears swiveling toward the radio as if she can sense the tension in Mac's voice despite the static. She moves to my side, pressing her warm body against my leg in a gesture that's become familiar during this crisis.

Her brown eyes meet mine with the same worried expression I feel—our pack leader is making dangerous decisions, and we can only wait and trust.

"Command copies." I maintain a professional tone despite the concern churning beneath. "Beta Leader, be advised: reinforcements en route from northern position."

The next hour passes in tense monitoring as the fire continues its relentless advance. The central position stabilizes with the additional personnel, managing to contain the spot fires before they develop into a secondary front. The southern position engages the fire with less intensity than predicted, the ridge's natural barrier functioning as designed to slow the blaze's momentum.

Scout's hackles rise suddenly, her body going rigid with the same alertness she shows before severe weather hits. She moves to the window, a low whine escaping her throat as she stares out at the fire-lit mountains. Her superior senses are detecting something my human awareness hasn't yet processed; a change in air pressure, a shift in the wind, or some subtle alteration that speaks of approaching catastrophe.

Maybe all three.

When she looks back at me, her brown eyes hold a warning I've learned never to ignore.

Angel's Peak

CHAPTER 18

LEAD US THROUGH THE DARK

"COMMAND, THIS IS BETA LEADER." PARKER'S VOICE carries an edge I haven't heard before. *"Fire behavior changing. Multiple vortices forming along the eastern flank."*

Fire vortices—tornado-like columns of flame and superheated air that can transform a controlled burn into an unstoppable force.

"Intensity?" I grab the radio, dread pooling in my stomach.

"Extreme. Flame heights now exceeding ninety feet. Rotating columns visible at three points along the containment line."

I check the topographical map, confirming my worst fears. "The canyon system east of your position creates perfect conditions for vortex development. If they merge..."

"Fire tornado." Sheriff Donovan finishes my thought, face grim.

Before we can process this new threat, Mac's voice cuts through: *"Alpha Leader to all units. Major wind event developing. Central position at critical risk. All personnel prepare for rapid change in fire behavior."*

As if his words were prophecy, Parker's next transmission

comes through garbled and desperate: *"Beta Leader to Command. Fire tornado forming. Eastern flank compromised. Multiple spot fires behind our position. Route to safety zone cut off."*

The command center falls silent as the implications register. Parker's team—including half of Mac's hotshot crew and Noah Morgan's local firefighters—are now trapped between an advancing fire tornado and a rapidly developing secondary fire that blocks their retreat.

"Beta Leader, report positions." Mac's voice remains controlled despite the crisis. *"Exact coordinates of all personnel."*

Parker responds with precise grid references that I immediately mark on the tactical map. Two groups, separated by the developing fire tornado, both cut off from established escape routes.

"Command, this is Alpha Leader." Mac's transmission comes through crisp and determined. *"I'm moving with Jackson Hart and four team members to Beta position. We'll establish a corridor through the secondary fire for evacuation."*

"Negative, Alpha Leader." Sheriff Donovan responds immediately. "Fire intensity exceeds safety parameters for rescue attempt. Maintain position."

"Not a request, Command." Mac's tone brooks no argument. *"Alpha position stable under Williams' direction. Hart has identified a potential route using natural features for protection. We're moving now."*

The radio falls silent as Mac disconnects, already committed to his course of action. Sheriff Donovan curses under his breath, frustration warring with grudging respect.

"He'll get himself killed." Donovan mutters, turning to me. "That route—is it viable?"

I study the map where I've marked Parker's coordinates, tracing potential approaches through terrain I know intimately. Every path seems blocked by advancing flame or impassable in current conditions.

Then I see it—a possibility so slim it barely qualifies as an option.

"The ridge system west of their position." I trace the feature with my finger. "If they follow this spine, they might—*might*—be able to approach from behind the secondary fire."

"But?"

"But it's incredibly exposed. No natural cover. Directly in the path of ember fall from the main fire." I swallow hard. "And even if they reach Parker's position, getting everyone out along that same route would be nearly impossible with the fire's current rate of spread."

Donovan studies the map, the grim reality settling between us. Mac is attempting what might be a suicide mission, with minimal chance of successfully extracting the trapped firefighters.

"There has to be another way." I pull out my most detailed maps, searching for alternatives missed in our initial planning. "Something we've overlooked."

Eleanor joins us, her keen eyes scanning the topography. "What about the old mining tunnels? The ones you used for the camper rescue?"

I shake my head. "Too far south. They don't extend to Parker's position."

"Not those." Eleanor taps a section of the map marked with faded notation. "The high country system. The one Jacob Mackenzie mapped in '87."

My father's name jolts me. "That system was never fully documented. Dad only explored the southern entrance before the company restricted access."

"But you have his notes." It's not a question. Eleanor knows my father kept meticulous records of every exploration, whether official or not.

I hesitate, mind racing through possibilities. "The tunnels might—*might*—extend beneath that ridge system. If they do..."

"They'd provide shelter from the fire." Donovan finishes my thought. "A way to ride out the worst of it until conditions improve."

Hope flickers, fragile but persistent. I pull out my father's old journal, filled with handwritten notes and hand-drawn maps from decades of mountain exploration. The pages on the high country tunnel system are sparse—rough sketches, partial measurements, observations cut short by corporate interference.

"Here." I locate a relevant entry. "Dad noted a vertical shaft that vented near Whiterock Ridge. If it's still accessible..."

"It would be within half a mile of Parker's current position." Donovan traces the potential route. "But how do we know if it's still open? If it's stable enough to shelter that many people?"

"We don't." The admission costs me. "But it's their best chance."

Donovan makes the call instantly. "All units, this is Command. Alternative shelter option identified near Beta position. Possible underground system with access via vertical shaft near Whiterock Ridge."

Static answers, followed by broken transmission fragments as the fire's electromagnetic interference disrupts communications. Then Mac's voice cuts through, remarkably clear: *"Alpha Leader copies. Location of shaft entrance?"*

I grab the radio, heart pounding. "My father's notes show a vertical shaft approximately four hundred yards northwest of Parker's position. Look for a rock formation shaped like a wolf's head. Entrance should be at the base, partially obscured by brush."

"Copy that." The connection wavers. *"Stability assessment?"*

"Unknown." I force myself to deliver the complete truth. "Dad's exploration was limited. Notes indicate the main chamber extends at least fifty feet into solid rock, with possible additional passages. Air quality noted as good due to natural ventilation."

A pause stretches, filled with static and the distant roar of fire. *"Understood. Moving to investigate."*

"Mac—" I hesitate, aware of the command center staff listening. "The shaft may be collapsed. These notes are thirty years old."

"Then we'll dig." His determination carries through despite the deteriorating connection. *"Beta Leader reports fire tornado now fully formed. Their position will be overrun within twenty minutes. This is their only chance."*

The transmission ends, leaving us in tense silence broken only by the constant updates from other sectors and the evacuation coordination. I stare at the tactical display, watching Mac's icon move with agonizing slowness toward Parker's trapped teams, acutely aware that technology cannot capture the hell through which he moves.

"He'll find it." Eleanor's quiet confidence anchors me. "And your father's maps will save them, just as they saved those campers."

I nod, unable to speak past the knot in my throat. All we can do now is wait, and hope, and pray to mountains that have never shown particular interest in human survival.

Minutes stretch like hours. Radio communication becomes increasingly fragmentary as the fire intensity grows. The southern defensive position reports directly to command, their situation stable but tense as they watch the distant fire tornado tear through the central gap.

Then, like a miracle, Mac's voice breaks through: *"Alpha Leader to Command. Shaft located. Entrance partially collapsed but accessible. Proceeding to Beta position to guide personnel back."*

Relief crashes through me, so powerful my knees nearly buckle. "Copy, Alpha Leader. Status of shaft interior?"

"Initial assessment confirms your father's notes." The pride in Mac's voice is unmistakable despite the poor connection. *"Main chamber adequate for shelter. Natural ventilation functioning. Secondary passages extend further than documented."*

"Copy that." My voice steadies; the professional mask slides back into place. "Beta Leader status?"

"Moving to rendezvous now. Fire tornado tracking east of their position. Window narrowing rapidly."

The next forty minutes pass in excruciating slowness. Sporadic transmissions track the evacuation attempt—Mac reaching Parker's position, the firefighters regrouping for the push toward the shaft, the fire tornado changing direction to threaten their escape route.

"Command, this is Alpha Leader." Mac's transmission comes through broken but understandable. *"First group entering shaft now. Parker leading. Five personnel secured."*

Hope rises, cautious but persistent. "Copy, Alpha Leader. Remaining personnel?"

"Moving final group now. Fire conditions deteriorating rapidly. Air becoming unsuitable for—" His transmission cuts off abruptly.

"Alpha Leader, report." Sheriff Donovan leans toward the radio, tension evident in every line of his body. "Alpha Leader, do you copy?"

Silence answers, broken only by static and the distant sounds of emergency operations. Minutes pass with no further contact from Mac or Parker. The tactical display shows their last known positions, icons frozen in time at the edge of the advancing inferno.

"Command to any units near Whiterock Ridge." Donovan

broadcasts on all channels. "Status report requested for Alpha and Beta teams."

More silence. The command center staff exchange grim looks, the possibility of massive casualties settling like lead in the air.

"They made it." I speak with more certainty than I feel. "The shaft would shield radio transmissions. Once they're inside, communication would be impossible until they reach a point where the signal can penetrate."

Donovan nods, willing to embrace any hope. "All units continue operations. Southern position maintain containment line. Focus on preventing further spread."

The night deepens, the fire's glow casting an apocalyptic light across Angel's Peak. Evacuation continues from outlying areas, though the town itself remains intact, protected by the defensive positions established hours earlier. The fire tornado eventually dissipates, its brief but devastating path marked by a swath of destruction.

By dawn, exhaustion settles over the command center. Personnel work in shifts, maintaining the constant flow of information and resources needed to manage the ongoing crisis. I remain at the tactical table, unwilling to rest while Mac and Parker's teams remain unaccounted for.

"You need sleep." Eleanor appears at my side, offering coffee that smells strong enough to strip paint. "You're no good to anyone if you collapse."

"I'm fine." The lie comes automatically.

"Of course you are." Her dry tone carries no judgment. "Just like Noah was 'fine' after the Carson Ridge incident. Just like your father was 'fine' after the '97 rescue went bad."

I accept the coffee, the hot mug warming hands I hadn't realized were cold.

"They should have reported in by now."

"Perhaps." Eleanor studies the fire map, eyes sharp despite

her age. "Or perhaps they're exactly where they need to be, doing exactly what they need to do."

Before I can respond, the radio crackles to life: *"Command, this is Beta Leader. Do you copy?"*

Parker's voice—exhausted but unmistakable—sends a wave of relief through the command center. Donovan grabs the radio: "Beta Leader, this is Command. We copy. Status report."

"All personnel accounted for and secure. Sheltering in tunnel system as planned." The connection wavers but holds. *"Fire passed over our position approximately three hours ago. Conditions at surface still unsuitable for evacuation."*

"Copy that. Casualties?"

"Nothing critical." Parker's professional tone slips slightly. *"The shaft saved us. Exactly where Mackenzie said it would be."*

My eyes burn with sudden moisture. "Alpha Leader status?"

A pause, then: *"Stand by for Alpha Leader."*

Mac's voice comes through next, rough with smoke exposure but strong: *"Alpha Leader to Command. Confirm Beta Leader's report. All personnel secure in tunnel system. Conditions stable, but monitoring air quality closely."*

The command center erupts in subdued cheers, relief breaking through the professional veneer maintained through hours of crisis. Sheriff Donovan allows it briefly before restoring order.

"Surface temperatures still extreme. Significant burnover continuing. Estimate minimum six hours before safe evacuation possible." Mac's assessment is clinical, detached. *"Tunnel system more extensive than documented. Multiple chambers, good air circulation. Adequate for extended shelter if necessary."*

"Copy that." Donovan checks the latest fire projection. "Fire front continuing eastward movement. Your position is now behind the main advance. Will coordinate extraction when conditions permit."

"Understood." Mac pauses, then adds: *"Josephine's father saved our lives today. His maps were perfect."*

The use of my first name—so deliberate, so public—sends heat rising to my face. Eleanor's knowing smile doesn't help.

"Conserve radio batteries." Donovan advises. "Check in hourly unless conditions change."

"Copy that. Alpha Leader out."

As the radio falls silent, I allow myself to relax for the first time in hours. They're alive. Trapped, but alive, sheltered in tunnels my father mapped decades ago. The connection across time—his knowledge saving lives long after his own ended—fills me with a bittersweet pride I hadn't expected.

"You should rest now." Eleanor's suggestion carries more weight now that the immediate crisis is resolved. "The evacuation center has cots set up."

I shake my head. "I'll stay until they're out."

She doesn't argue; she simply pats my shoulder as she moves to coordinate the next phase of operations. The command center settles into a different rhythm—less frantic crisis management, more sustained response coordination as the fire continues its advance into less populated areas.

The hours pass in a blur of updates, resource allocations, and contingency planning. Fire conditions near Mac and Parker's position improve gradually as the central front moves eastward, leaving behind smoldering destruction and isolated hotspots.

By mid-afternoon, extraction becomes viable. A small team deploys with fresh oxygen supplies and medical equipment, guided by the GPS coordinates Mac provides from the tunnel entrance.

Three hours later, they emerge—smoke-stained, exhausted, but intact. The footage captured by Sheriff Donovan's body camera shows a procession of ghost-like figures emerging from the scorched earth, faces blackened with soot, uniforms singed and filthy.

Mac is among the last to exit, ensuring every member of both teams is accounted for. Even through the grainy video feed, his commanding presence is unmistakable. His shoulders are squared despite his exhaustion. His steady gaze constantly scans for threats, steadying those who stumble on weakened legs.

"Command, this is Extraction Team." The radio brings welcome news. *"All personnel recovered. En route to medical staging area."*

Relief crashes through me so powerfully that my knees buckle, forcing me to grip the table for support. Eleanor appears at my side, her weathered hand steady on my arm.

"Go to him." She says it like it's the most obvious truth in the world.

I hesitate, professional obligations warring with personal need. "The command center—"

"Can function without you for a few hours." She makes a shooing motion. "Noah's team has the southern sector well in hand. The main fire front is moving away from populated areas. Go."

Sheriff Donovan nods in agreement. "Take my truck. They're bringing them to the medical checkpoint at the community center."

Decision made, I move with renewed energy, despite having been awake for more than thirty hours. The drive to the community center takes less than ten minutes, but it feels like crossing an ocean.

Angel's Peak has transformed in the past day—streets empty from evacuation, ash falling like gray snow, the smell of smoke permeating everything. The mountains that frame the town stand partially blackened, the fire's path visible against slopes that remain defiantly green.

The community center parking lot teems with emergency vehicles—ambulances, fire trucks, police cruisers arranged in organized chaos. Medical personnel move between them, triaging firefighters as they arrive from various sectors. I scan the crowd, searching for Mac's distinctive height and bearing.

I spot him seated on the tailgate of a medical transport, oxygen mask covering his face. A paramedic checks his vitals while he issues instructions to Rodriguez, apparently unwilling to pause command responsibilities even for medical attention.

His uniform is nearly unrecognizable—blackened with soot, singed in multiple places, torn at one shoulder. His face bears the distinct raccoon-eyes of someone who wore goggles in heavy smoke. Despite this, his posture remains commanding, his focus absolute as he ensures his team receives care.

I approach slowly, suddenly uncertain of my place in this scenario. Before I can decide whether to interrupt, Mac looks up—some sixth sense alerting him to my presence. Our eyes lock across the distance, and something profound passes between us, more intimate than any touch.

He dismisses Rodriguez with a brief nod, standing despite the paramedic's obvious objection. Each step toward me seems to cost him, but he refuses to show weakness, maintaining the captain's bearing that defines him.

We meet in the neutral territory between vehicles, surrounded by the organized chaos of emergency response, yet somehow isolated within it.

"Your father's tunnels." His voice is rough from smoke, but his eyes hold something like reverence. "Exactly where you said they'd be. Exactly as you described."

"Dad was thorough." The understatement feels necessary, a shield against emotions too raw to expose.

Seventeen people are alive because of him. Because of you." Mac's intensity cuts through my defenses. "If you hadn't remembered that shaft..."

"But I did." I step closer, close enough to smell smoke and sweat and the undercurrent that is uniquely him. "And you found it. That's what matters."

His hand rises, hesitates, then settles against my cheek. The contact is gentle, despite his skin being roughened by heat and exertion. "When I thought we wouldn't make it out... when the fire tornado changed direction..."

"Don't." I cover his hand with mine, keeping it pressed to my face. "You're here now."

Something in his expression shifts, professional distance giving way to something more personal, more urgent. He glances around at the busy scene, then back at me.

"I need to finish here. Debriefing, team assessment, coordination with Noah and Parker." His thumb brushes my cheekbone. "But after..."

"After." I agree, understanding all he doesn't say.

"Find me when this is contained." It's not quite a request, nor is it quite an order. "When I can think beyond the next crisis point."

I nod, reluctantly stepping back as a medical officer approaches, clearly intent on dragging Mac to proper treatment. His hand falls away from my face, but his eyes hold mine for one moment longer—a promise more binding than words.

"Captain Sullivan." The medical officer's tone brooks no argument. "You're required in triage for respiratory assessment."

Mac's expression shifts seamlessly back to professional mode. "On my way." He turns to me one last time. "Josephine. Thank you." He walks away, back straight despite exhaustion that would cripple most people.

"He's something else, isn't he?" Parker appears beside me, her uniform in similar condition to Mac's, though she at least seems to have completed her medical assessment.

"He is." I don't bother denying the obvious.

"Never seen him like this." She accepts a bottle of water from a passing volunteer. "During a fire, sure, he's always the captain. But this—" she gestures vaguely toward where Mac now sits submitting to medical examination, "—this is different."

"Different how?"

Parker studies me with knowing eyes. "Five years, dozen major fires, I've never seen him look at maps the way he looks at yours. Never seen him trust someone's word over his tech." She takes a long drink. "Never seen him look at anyone the way he looks at you."

Before I can respond, Sheriff Donovan's voice cuts through on all emergency channels: "Command to all units. Fire containment is at seventy percent. Wind is shifting favorably. State resources are arriving within the hour. Maintain positions but prepare for relief rotation."

Parker straightens, professional responsibility reasserting itself.

"Duty calls. My team needs assessment and rest rotation." She hesitates, then adds, "He won't say it, so I will. What you did—remembering those tunnels, knowing exactly where to send us—it was extraordinary."

She walks away before I can respond, rejoining the organized chaos of emergency operations. I stand alone for a moment, watching Mac as he receives oxygen treatment while simultaneously reviewing tactical maps with Noah Morgan. Even exhausted and injured, he remains fully present and fully committed to the responsibility he carries.

And I realize, with startling clarity, that I've fallen for far more than his commanding presence or the way his hands feel on my skin. I've fallen for the man who carries the weight of lives with unflinching determination, who trusts my expertise when technology fails, who looks at my mountains and sees what I see—not obstacles to overcome, but forces to respect and work alongside.

The fire still burns across parts of Angel's Peak, but something else has ignited as well—something that will remain long after the last embers cool.

Angel's Peak

Chapter 19

Containment

Three days after the fire tornado, Angel's Peak exists in two states simultaneously—parts untouched and functioning almost normally, while others have been transformed into blackened moonscapes, where trees stand like skeletal sentinels against an ash-gray ground.

The fire continues to burn in the eastern wilderness, but coordinated efforts have contained its advance away from populated areas.

The Haven's ballroom has permanently transitioned from a command center to a recovery headquarters. Maps still cover the tables, but they track different data now—damaged structures, compromised watersheds, unstable slopes at risk for mudslides when rain eventually comes.

Scout lies beneath the main table, her chin resting on my boots as I work. The past three days have taken their toll on her, too, but she's adapted to this new normal, positioning herself where she can monitor both the entrance and my movements while staying out of the way of the constant foot traffic.

I bend over the latest assessment, marking areas where

emergency trail restoration will be needed before winter. The work grounds me, giving purpose to hours that might otherwise be spent processing everything that has happened.

Mac and his hotshot crew have been deployed continuously since the tunnel rescue, working in shifts to secure the fire's edge and prevent any resurgence toward town.

We've barely spoken—a few brief radio exchanges, a moment's eye contact during shift change, his hand brushing mine as we passed maps between us during tactical briefings.

Professional. Proper. Maddening.

"Jo." Sheriff Donovan approaches, looking marginally less exhausted than he did yesterday. "Got a situation that needs your expertise."

I straighten, rolling tight shoulders.

"What kind of situation?"

"Fire's contained along the northeastern sector, but we've got a new problem." He spreads a satellite image across my maps. "Heavy equipment team reports the old mining road has collapsed in three places. They can't get fire crews to the hotspots in Sector Seven."

I study the image and identify the problem immediately. "They're trying to use the main access road. It's built on unconsolidated fill that would be unstable after intense heat."

"Exactly. We need an alternate route for heavy equipment. Something that can support brush trucks at a minimum."

My mind shifts to the mental map I carry of that region— a combination of official surveys and personal exploration over years of hiking.

"There's an old logging road that parallels the mining access. It's not on official maps because it was abandoned in the 80s, but the roadbed is solid rock in most sections."

"Viable for vehicles?"

"It would need clearing—fallen trees, probably some erosion damage—but the underlying structure is sound." I trace the approximate route on the satellite image. "It would give access to most of Sector Seven, bypassing the worst collapse areas."

Donovan nods, already calculating logistics. "Can you guide the assessment team? They need someone who knows exactly where this road is. Satellite imagery shows nothing but tree cover."

"Of course." The opportunity to do something active instead of mapping from headquarters is welcome. "When do they need me?"

"Now. Team's assembling at the east checkpoint in twenty minutes." He hands me a field radio. "Check in every thirty minutes. Cell service is still down in that sector."

I gather my gear—detailed maps, GPS unit, emergency supplies that have become second nature after days of crisis response. The rhythm of preparation feels good, purposeful, pushing aside the constant awareness of Mac's absence.

Scout rises immediately when she sees me preparing field gear, her tail wagging with the first genuine enthusiasm I've seen from her in days. She knows the difference between my staying at command and heading into the field—and she clearly prefers action to waiting.

When I clip her working harness into place, she practically vibrates with readiness, eager to return to the mountains where we both feel most capable.

"You're coming with me, girl," I tell her, and her entire body language transforms from patient endurance to focused anticipation.

The drive to the east checkpoint takes me through progressively more damaged terrain. The town center remains largely intact thanks to the defensive lines that held, but moving eastward reveals the fire's true destructive power. Familiar landscapes have been transformed, recognizable only by topography, where all surface features have been consumed.

At the checkpoint, a small team awaits—two Forest Service engineers, a heavy equipment operator, and Jackson Hart, whose mountain rescue expertise has been invaluable throughout the crisis.

"Hey, Jo," Jackson nods in greeting, his weathered face showing the strain of days without proper rest. "Heard you're going to show us this magic road."

"Not magic. Just forgotten." I spread my map across the hood of the Forest Service truck. "It follows this ridgeline, staying on bedrock for most of the route. The mining company abandoned it when they built the newer access road, but the foundation should still be intact."

The senior engineer—Stevens, according to his vest—studies the route with skepticism. "No signs of this on any of our surveys."

"It wouldn't be. The forest reclaimed the surface decades ago." I trace the path with my finger. "But underneath the growth, you'll find engineered roadbed. My father documented it when he was surveying the watershed in the early 90s."

"Your father again." Jackson's expression holds respect rather than doubt. "His knowledge keeps saving our asses."

"He knew these mountains better than anyone." The simple truth comes without the pain that usually accompanies memories of my father. "I just try to maintain his maps."

"And add your own." Jackson gestures toward the detailed annotations I've made to the original survey. "Let's see if this road of yours is still there."

We load into a Forest Service truck modified for off-road conditions, Jackson taking the wheel with me in the passenger seat, navigating. The heavy equipment operator follows in a smaller bulldozer, transported to the edge of the access road.

Scout settles in the truck's back seat, her nose pressed to the partially opened window as we begin our ascent into the fire-damaged terrain. Her ears swivel constantly, processing sounds and scents that tell her more about the changed landscape than my eyes can detect.

When we pass through areas of complete devastation, she whines softly—not distress, but recognition that something fundamental has been altered in her familiar territory.

The going is rough immediately. The fire has transformed familiar landmarks, leaving behind a monochromatic landscape of ash and blackened trees. I navigate primarily by topography and memory, identifying subtle features that fire couldn't erase—a distinctive rock outcropping, a sharp bend in a stream bed, the gradual rise of a ridge that my father first showed me when I was twelve.

"Should be just ahead." I check the GPS coordinates against my memory. "The entrance was hidden by brush even before the fire. Look for a gap between those two boulder formations."

Jackson slows the truck, scanning the slope with experienced eyes. "There. That look right to you?"

I follow his gaze to a barely perceptible break in the terrain—more suggestion than obvious path. "That's it."

The small dozer moves forward, clearing carbonized brush and fallen timber to reveal what lies beneath. As the debris is pushed aside, a distinctly engineered surface emerges—not pavement, but deliberately placed stone forming a durable roadbed.

"I'll be damned." Stevens steps from the truck, crouching to examine the exposed surface. "This is professional road construction. Probably better than the official access we've been using."

"Told you." I can't help the satisfaction in my voice. "The mining company built things to last back then."

"Can it support the weight of fire apparatus?" Jackson asks the practical question.

Stevens nods, already calculating load capacities. "If it's consistent with what we're seeing here? Absolutely. This could handle engines, water tenders, everything we need."

"Then let's find out how far it goes." I return to the truck and pull out the detailed map showing the road's projected path. "According to my father's survey, it continues for approximately three miles, connecting to the main fire road just beyond the worst collapse point."

The bulldozer takes point, clearing just enough width for vehicles to pass while we follow slowly in the truck. The road reveals itself gradually—in some places completely obscured by decades of forest growth, while in others, it remains surprisingly intact despite years of neglect.

We maintain regular radio contact with command, reporting our progress as the forgotten road proves its value, yard by yard. The work is slow but satisfying, each section cleared bringing us closer to providing the access desperately needed by firefighting teams.

Two hours in, we reach a viewpoint that reveals the valley below—parts still actively burning, others reduced to smoldering ash. From this elevation, the fire's strategic pattern becomes unmistakable—engineered to cause maximum destruction to specific areas while creating a barrier of devastation around the old Silver Creek processing facility.

"It's the mine." I murmur, more to myself than the others.

Jackson overhears. "What is?"

"The fire pattern." I gesture toward the valley. "It's not *just* arson. It's surgical. Whoever did this knew exactly what they were targeting and how to ensure that the land around the mine was destroyed."

Before Jackson can respond, our radio crackles with unexpected static, then Mac's voice cuts through: *"Alpha Leader to Road Assessment Team. Do you copy?"*

"Road Assessment copies, Alpha Leader." Jackson answers.

"Status update on alternate access route?"

"Progressing well. Approximately one mile cleared so far. Road foundation is solid, capable of supporting all apparatus types." I hesitate, then add, "Your team should have access to Sector Seven hotspots within approximately two hours."

"Understood. Alpha Team standing by at rendezvous point. Will monitor your progress."

"Copy, Alpha Leader. Road Assessment out."

We continue our methodical progress, the bulldozer operator expertly clearing minimal width to preserve as much of the original roadbed as possible. The work develops its own rhythm. Identify the next section, clear debris, assess stability, and move forward. Despite the destruction surrounding us, there's satisfaction in revealing this hidden path, in making visible what time and nature had concealed.

Four hours after starting, we reach the junction where the forgotten road connects to the main fire access beyond the collapsed sections. Stevens immediately begins marking the route for the heavy equipment teams that will follow.

"Road Assessment to Command." Jackson radios our success. "Alternate route established and marked. Ready for apparatus access to Sector Seven."

"Copy that." Sheriff Donovan's voice carries rare satisfaction. *"First engine company deploying now. Alpha Team has been notified and is moving to hotspot locations."*

I check my watch, calculating the time against the remaining daylight. "We should head back. Light's failing, and this terrain is dangerous after dark."

"Agreed." Jackson starts the truck, waiting for Stevens and Martinez to secure their equipment. "Command wants us back at base for debriefing anyway. State fire teams are taking over most operations now that the immediate threat to the town is contained."

As we begin the journey back, I watch the devastated landscape with mixed emotions. So much destruction, yet Angel's Peak itself survived largely intact thanks to the defensive lines that held. The knowledge that my maps —my father's legacy —played a crucial role in protecting both the town and the firefighters fills me with quiet pride beneath the exhaustion.

The drive back takes us past the Sector Seven rendezvous point—a cleared area where fire apparatus now gathers in preparation for accessing the hotspots via our newly established route. Jackson slows as we approach, checking in with the incident commander coordinating the response.

That's when I see him.

Mac stands at the center of operations, a map spread across the hood of a command vehicle, directing teams with the focused authority that seems as natural to him as breathing. Even at a distance, his presence commands attention—his shoulders squared despite obvious exhaustion, his gestures precise as he indicates target areas.

Scout's head snaps up the moment she spots Mac through the windshield, her tail beginning a tentative wag—the first sign of pure joy I've seen from her since the crisis began. She presses against the window, clearly recognizing the man who's become as important to her as he has to me.

When I open the truck door, she bounds out before I can stop her, making a beeline for Mac with the single-minded determination of a dog greeting her favorite human.

He looks up as our truck approaches, his conversation pausing mid-sentence. Even through the windshield, the intensity of his gaze hits me like physical contact.

Jackson glances between us, then makes a decision. "I need to update the IC on road conditions." He puts the truck in park. "Coming?"

I follow Jackson toward the command area, maintaining my professional composure despite the awareness prickling across my skin. Mac watches our approach, his expression revealing nothing to casual observers, though I can read the tension in his jaw, the slight shift in his stance.

"Hart." Mac acknowledges Jackson first. "Road assessment successful?"

"Better than expected." Jackson gestures toward me. "Thanks to Jo. Road's solid enough for anything you need to deploy."

Mac's eyes shift to me, his professional mask firmly in place. "Good work. That access will make a significant difference to containment operations."

Before I can respond, Parker approaches with update requests, pulling Mac's attention back to immediate operational needs. The moment breaks, reality reasserting itself in the form of fire maps, deployment schedules, and resource allocations.

Jackson touches my arm lightly. "We should get back. Donovan's waiting for our report."

I nod, turning to leave, when Mac's voice stops me.

"Josephine. A word before you go."

He steps away from the command vehicle, creating a small pocket of privacy amid the organized chaos of the staging area. I follow, heart inexplicably accelerating despite the professional context.

"The road you found." His voice drops slightly, not intimate but less formal than before. "It saved us hours of critical time. The hotspots in Sector Seven were at risk of reactivating into a significant threat."

"I'm glad it helped." I match his tone, conscious of the operational activity surrounding us.

Something shifts in his expression, professional appreciation giving way to something more personal.

"You keep saving us."

The simple acknowledgment hits harder than any elaborate praise.

Mac glances toward the command center, clearly torn between duty and something else. "I need to finish here, but after we should talk."

"Talk?" I repeat the word, knowing it encompasses far more than mere conversation.

"Yes." His gaze intensifies. "About maps. Mountains. Where *we* go from here."

"I'd like that." My response is simple but honest.

Something like relief flickers across his features. "I'll find you when we're done here."

Jackson waits by the truck, tactfully pretending not to observe our exchange. As we drive back toward command headquarters, he maintains a diplomatic silence for all of thirty seconds.

"So." He finally ventures, eyes on the ash-dusted road. "You and Sullivan."

"It's complicated." I stare out the window, watching the gradual transition from burned landscape to partially preserved forest. It's not really complicated. Mac's tenure at Angel's Peak will come to an end when fire season officially ends. He'll return to California with the rest of his team, while I stay behind.

"Always is." He offers the wisdom of someone who's seen enough of life to know its patterns. "Especially when it matters."

We complete the drive in companionable silence, each lost in our private thoughts as twilight settles over Angel's Peak. At command headquarters, we deliver our report to Sheriff Donovan, providing detailed information on the alternate route and its capacity for supporting firefighting operations.

"Good work." Donovan studies the marked-up maps.

"The road's in remarkably good condition considering it's been abandoned for decades." Stevens adds his professional assessment. "Some sections will need reinforcement for continued heavy use, but it's immediately viable for emergency operations."

Donovan makes notes, coordinating with state resources now arriving to supplement local efforts. He turns to me. "Get some rest. You've been going nonstop for days." He glances specifically at me. "That's an order, Jo. Twelve hours minimum."

I start to protest, but exhaustion chooses that moment to make itself known—a wave of bone-deep weariness that makes even standing an effort.

"Fine. Twelve hours."

Eleanor appears as if summoned, her timing suspicious enough to suggest coordination with Donovan. "I'll drive you home. You're in no condition to operate a vehicle."

Too tired to argue, I follow her to her ancient Jeep, sliding into the passenger seat with limbs that suddenly feel made of lead. Scout jumps into the back seat.

The drive to my cabin passes in comfortable silence, Eleanor respecting my need for quiet after days of constant crisis communication.

As we pull up to my cabin—miraculously untouched by the fire that came within two miles of its location—she finally speaks. "You did your father proud, child."

The simple statement brings unexpected moisture to my eyes. "I hope so."

"I know so." She pats my hand, weathered fingers surprisingly strong. "Now rest. The mountains will still be here tomorrow, and so will all the handsome fire captains."

Despite my exhaustion, I laugh. "You're impossible."

"I'm observant." Her eyes twinkle with knowing amusement. "Been watching people fall in love in these mountains for seventy years. Recognize the signs."

I open my mouth to protest, then close it again. Denying the obvious to Eleanor Morgan is an exercise in futility.

"Rest." She repeats, suddenly serious. "What comes next requires strength."

With that cryptic statement, she waits until Scout and I are safely inside before driving away, her Jeep disappearing down the pine-lined drive leading back to town. I stand in my silent cabin, the familiar space feeling simultaneously welcoming and somehow empty.

I manage to shower before exhaustion claims me completely, falling into bed with hair still damp and thoughts of Mac lingering at the edges of consciousness. Sleep comes instantly, deep and dreamless.

Angel's Peak

CHAPTER 20

HOME

WHEN I WAKE, SUNLIGHT STREAMS THROUGH THE uncurtained windows, suggesting it's at least late morning. Scout stretches luxuriously beside my bed, her internal clock apparently as disrupted as mine by the past week's irregular schedule.

She's been my constant companion through every crisis, and even she seems to recognize that the immediate danger has passed, allowing both of us to finally rest deeply.

A glance at my phone confirms it—11:37 AM, nearly fourteen hours since Eleanor dropped me off. Dozens of notifications fill the screen—updates on fire operations, coordination messages, resource requests—but one text message stands out from the others.

Mac: *Fire contained. 94% controlled. Team standing down for 24-hour rest rotation. Need to see you.*

The timestamp shows 5:47 AM, sent while I was still deeply asleep. I check for further messages, finding none. My fingers hover over the keyboard, considering a response, when a knock at my door interrupts the deliberation.

I pull on a robe over my sleep clothes, running fingers

through tangled hair as I move toward the door. Through the side window, I catch sight of a Forest Service vehicle parked beside my Jeep.

Scout reaches the door before I do, her tail wagging with genuine excitement as she recognizes Mac's scent through the wood. When I open the door, she greets Mac with joy, pressing against his legs briefly before stepping back to allow us humans our reunion. Her brown eyes track between us with the satisfied expression of a dog whose pack is finally complete.

Mac stands on my porch, his uniform exchanged for worn jeans and a simple button-down that makes him look more imposing rather than less. His face shows signs of recent rest, though exhaustion still lingers in the shadows beneath his eyes.

"Josephine." He says my name like it's both a greeting and a prayer.

"Mac." I step back, inviting him in without words. "I just woke up. Donovan ordered twelve hours of rest."

"Smart man." Mac enters, his presence immediately filling the small cabin. "I got the same order from state command after containment was confirmed."

"Is the fire contained?" I close the door, suddenly conscious of my disheveled appearance.

"Controlled on all fronts relevant to Angel's Peak." He runs a hand through his hair, still damp from what I assume was his recent shower. "State teams are handling the eastern sectors now. My crew is on a mandatory rest rotation."

"That's... good." I struggle to find words that bridge the gap between professional relief and personal awareness. "Coffee? I was just about to make some."

"Please."

The familiar routine of measuring grounds and filling the reservoir gives my hands something to do while my mind races. Mac moves to the window, looking out at the mountains that have shaped both our lives in different ways.

"Your maps saved Parker's team." He speaks without turning. "Without that tunnel system... without your knowledge of where to find it..."

"You're the one who went into that inferno to guide them out." I keep my voice steady despite the emotion his words evoke.

He turns, eyes finding mine across the cabin's open space. "Because you showed me where to go."

The coffee maker gurgles to life, filling the silence that stretches between us. Mac moves from the window to the kitchen counter.

"I've been thinking about what happens next." His voice drops lower, the professional captain giving way to something more personal.

"Next?" I echo, hands braced against the counter.

"The fire's contained," he says quietly, voice low like he's trying not to spook the fragile peace that's finally settled. "Immediate crisis is over."

Relief rushes through me, but it doesn't quite reach the tight spot in my chest. Not yet. He steps closer, boots scuffing against ash and gravel. His presence stills the air the way it always does—steady, grounding. Safe.

"I've been offered a position here. Full-time." A pause. "Assigned permanently to Angel's Peak."

My breath catches. "You have?"

He nods. One hand lifts, hesitating a beat before brushing my cheek with his fingertips. Calloused. Warm. Surprising gentleness from someone forged in fire. His touch is careful, like he's not sure if he's allowed to hope.

"Yes," he says, then draws in a breath like the next part costs him something. "But there's a condition."

My stomach dips. "A condition," I repeat, trying for lightness but already bracing. "Should I be worried?"

His eyes stay locked on mine. Unflinching. Raw.

"We barely know each other," he says. "A week here. Another fighting this fire. That's it. But that doesn't change what I feel when I look at you. Doesn't change what I want."

My heart stumbles.

"I need to know if you want me to stay." His voice lowers, rich with quiet urgency. "Not just in Angel's Peak. In your life. Permanently."

The air between us tightens, thick with heat and hope and the sharp edges of fear. I can't breathe past it. Can't think beyond the ache he's awakened in me since the moment we met.

He takes a step closer, his hand rising to trace my jaw with the rough pads of his fingers. "The past week has been crisis conditions," he says, thumb brushing just beneath my lip. "Adrenaline. Life-or-death decisions. It changes how people connect and how they respond to each other. I think we've been building something real. Something more than amazing sex, but I need to know you feel the same. That what's between us isn't just trauma response."

I could dodge. Hedge. Take a breath and ask for more time. But that's not what this man deserves. Mac doesn't bluff or posture—he lays it all out, steady and real, and expects the same in return.

So I give it to him.

"I want you to stay."

The words fall between us like a flare tossed into dry timber.

He stills. Something sharp and possessive flickers behind his eyes, the quiet firestorm that always simmers beneath his surface breaking free.

"I need to be very clear about what that means." His voice drops to that commanding growl that makes my stomach twist with want. "I'm not talking casual. I'm not talking temporary. If you say yes, you get all of me, just as I will claim all of you."

His hand moves from my jaw to my throat, fingers wrapping around the column of it—not tight, just enough to feel the strength there. My pulse hammers against his thumb, frantic beneath his control.

The dominance in his tone, in his touch, should scare me.

Instead, it grounds me.

"Do you?" His grip tightens slightly. "Do you want that? I want to wake up beside you. I want to learn every trail on your mountains. I want to come home to you after fighting fire all day. And I want to take you apart in ways that will ruin you for anyone else."

"I do." My breath trembles as I answer. "In Angel's Peak. In my life. In my bed."

"Is that a yes?" He leans in closer, breath hot against my lips.

"Yes, *Sir*." The words come without hesitation, and something shatters in him.

His eyes darken—like storm clouds rolling in fast—and then his mouth is on mine, demanding and consuming, no pretense left between us. His hand slides from my throat into my hair, gripping tight, tilting my head back as he kisses me like he's starving.

I respond with equal hunger, fingers yanking at the buttons of his shirt, needing skin, heat, him.

"Too many fucking clothes," he mutters against my mouth, already pulling my robe down my shoulders.

"Bedroom," I gasp, tugging at his belt with shaking hands.

He doesn't hesitate. Lifts me like I weigh nothing, my legs locking around his waist as he carries me through the cabin. His mouth stays fused to mine, the kiss deepening with every step. It's not gentle—it's claiming. Every inch of me branded by the heat of him.

He kicks the bedroom door open and lays me out across the bed with a reverence that's rough and raw all at once. His shirt is half open, jeans barely hanging on. I'm spread beneath him in nothing but skin and need.

Mac braces over me, breathing hard, his body tight with control he's about to lose.

"When I was sitting in that damn hole," he says, voice thick with memory, "with fire closing in from every direction... all I could think about was you."

I reach for him, but he captures my wrists and pins them to the bed.

"I couldn't see a future without you in it. I didn't want one. I *don't* want one." His grip tightens just enough to make me gasp. "I want my life. I want you. I want every goddamn inch of you in my bed and in my world. And I love—"

He breaks off, jaw tight.

"I love the way you surrender to me."

My breath catches. That word—love—lands like a thunderclap in my chest. I arch beneath him, mouth open, but no sound comes.

"I love the fire in you. The way you fight me and melt for me in the same breath. The way you need control until you don't. I love the way you let go and give me your surrender."

I tremble beneath him, everything inside me unraveling.

"You're mine," he says, lowering his mouth to my neck, teeth grazing the sensitive skin there. "Say it."

"I'm yours."

He lets go of my wrists only to grab my thighs, dragging me down the bed and spreading me open for him. He doesn't undress slowly. Doesn't tease. He claims—stripping away every barrier between us until we're nothing but skin and sweat and the taste of forever.

The world narrows to his hands, his mouth, the low growl of his name on my lips. Every thrust, every touch, every whispered order drives me higher. Takes me apart. And when he wraps his hand around my throat again, his body moves over mine with lethal control. I break apart beneath him, crying out as heat crashes through me.

He follows with a groan that sounds like worship, collapsing against me, breath hot against my ear.

When the world stills, when my body stops shaking, I feel his arms wrap around me, tight, certain.

"I love you. I need you in my life. I want you as my wife."

What follows is unlike anything we've shared before—not the desperate coupling against my desk or the adrenaline-fueled claiming after the tunnel rescue. This is exploration, discovery, the careful mapping of bodies with the same attention we've given to mountains and fire lines.

Mac takes his time, learning what makes me gasp, what draws out the moans he seems to crave. His hands are both gentle and commanding, guiding without forcing, suggesting without demanding. When he finally enters me, the connection feels like coming home.

Afterward, we lie tangled in sheets damp with exertion, my head on his chest where I can hear the steady rhythm of his heartbeat. His fingers trace lazy patterns on my bare shoulder, touch gentle now that the urgency has been satisfied.

"When did you know?" I ask, the question emerging from comfortable silence.

"Know what?" His voice rumbles beneath my ear.

"That this was more than just..." I search for the right word, "physical attraction."

His hand stills momentarily, then resumes its gentle exploration. "The tunnel rescue. Watching you lead those people out, seeing your absolute confidence in your knowledge despite the risks." His arms tighten around me. "I've worked with the best firefighters in the country, people who run toward danger without hesitation, but you faced your deepest fear and still didn't falter."

The admission warms something deep inside me. "And after? In the fire tower, when you pinned me against that map table? That was about admiration?"

His laugh vibrates through his chest. "That was about wanting to claim every inch of you. Mind, body, soul." His voice drops lower. "Still do."

I rise on one elbow to look at him properly, finding his eyes dark with renewed hunger. "Your team's on rest rotation for how long?"

"Twenty-four hours." His hand slides into my hair, guiding me down for a kiss that promises much more to come. "And I intend to make the most of every minute."

A slow shiver rolls through me. That voice. That tone.

The promise of it.

I drag my fingers down his chest, nails grazing along the ridges of muscle, and feel him harden beneath my touch. Again. Still.

His control frays in real time as I shift, straddling his hips, naked and aching and utterly his.

"I could say no," I whisper, teasing, breath hot against his lips.

His grip tightens in my hair, just enough to sting. Just enough to make my breath hitch.

"But you won't." His voice is iron wrapped in velvet. "Because you need this. Crave it. And I'm not asking you to be my wife. I'm telling you."

I don't deny his words. I can't.

I meet his gaze and let him see it all—my need, my surrender, my choice.

"Well, then, if it's settled, you have my complete and undivided attention...*Sir*."

The effect is immediate.

His pupils blow wide, hunger replacing the warmth in his eyes like a fuse catching flame. In a single breath, the gentle Mac who cradled me moments ago is gone, replaced by the force of nature I've come to love. The man who commands fires and mountains—and me.

He flips me onto my back with a growl, pinning me to the mattress with his full weight, wrists trapped above my head.

"Say it again," he demands.

"Sir."

His mouth crashes down on mine, teeth, tongue, claiming. The kiss steals air, thought, and time. His hands are everywhere, mapping me with ruthless precision, dragging need from my body like it's his right.

And it is.

Because I give it to him. Because I want him to take it.

What follows is no longer gentle. It's possession—raw, unrelenting, earned. Every thrust, every whispered order, every rough stroke of his hands against my skin carves his name into me.

And I welcome it.

I arch beneath my future husband, body trembling, breath breaking on each desperate cry.

When release takes me, it's not soft. It's an explosion. A surrender. A promise.

Hours later, as golden afternoon light streams through the windows and Scout settles contentedly at the foot of our bed, Mac traces random designs on my shoulder.

"Your father would be proud," he murmurs against my skin. "You didn't just preserve his legacy—you built something beautiful on top of it."

I think of the maps spread across my desk, marked now with routes that saved lives, tunnels that brought people home, paths that led a lost fire captain to love. Think of the mountains that tested us, nearly broke us, then blessed us with everything we never knew we needed.

"We built it together," I whisper, turning in his arms to find his eyes—those impossible blue eyes that saw through every wall I built and claimed the woman hiding behind them. "The mountains brought you to me."

"No, Josephine." His thumb brushes away the tear I didn't realize had fallen, his voice soft with absolute certainty. "You brought me home."

And as the sun sets over Angel's Peak, painting our mountains in shades of gold and promise, I know he's right. This is home—not just the cabin, not just the town, but this: his arms around me and the whisper of wind through pine trees that have witnessed a hundred love stories but none quite like ours.

In these mountains that demand everything and give back even more, we've found what neither of us was looking for but both of us desperately needed.

Each other.

Forever.

Angel's Peak

CHAPTER 21

EPILOGUE

EPILOGUE: ONE YEAR LATER

Eighteen months after the fire that nearly destroyed Angel's Peak, I stand at the edge of Lookout Point, watching Mac coordinate a controlled burn with the precision of a master conductor leading an orchestra. The irony isn't lost on me—using fire to prevent fire, healing the mountain with the same force that nearly consumed it.

Scout sits at attention beside me, her brown eyes tracking Mac's movements through the smoke with the focused intensity she reserves for *important* work. She's learned to distinguish between crisis fires and beneficial ones, though her protective instincts remain unchanged when it comes to her humans venturing near flames.

The wedding ring on my left hand catches the afternoon sunlight, the simple band of white gold that Mac slipped onto my finger six months ago during a ceremony overlooking Mirror Lake. We kept it small—family, close friends, and half the population of Angel's Peak, which amounts to the same thing in a town this size.

"Mrs. Sullivan." Mac's voice cuts through my reverie, carried on radio static from his position half a mile downslope. *"How's it looking from the observation point?"*

I raise my binoculars, scanning the controlled burn's progress against the forest that's slowly recovering from last year's devastation. New growth pushes through ash-enriched soil—vibrant green shoots that speak of resilience and renewal.

"Burn pattern looks good from here, Captain Sullivan." I key the radio, maintaining the professional protocol we've established for field operations, even though his team knows exactly what happens when we get home. "Wind conditions stable. No spot fires detected on the eastern perimeter."

"Copy that. Proceeding to phase two."

The controlled burn is part of a larger restoration project —one that Mac has championed since accepting his permanent position as Angel's Peak's Fire Management Officer. Where the arsonist's engineered blaze sought destruction, we're using scientific precision to heal and protect.

The arsonist himself sits in federal prison, convicted of seventeen counts of arson and environmental terrorism. His plan to clear the old mining claims for renewed extraction failed spectacularly when the FBI traced the accelerants back to his shell company. Justice served, though it can't undo the ecological damage or restore what was lost.

"Looking good out there." Eleanor Morgan's voice makes me turn. She approaches with her signature walking stick, silver braids gleaming in the sunlight, carrying a thermos that probably contains coffee strong enough to strip paint.

"He knows what he's doing." I accept the coffee gratefully, inhaling the rich aroma that's become synonymous with Eleanor's presence at every major town event.

"I'm not talking about the fire." Her eyes twinkle with knowing amusement as she settles beside me on the flat rock that serves as our informal observation post. "Though that's going well too."

I follow her gaze to where Mac moves among his crew, issuing calm directions as they manage the controlled burn. Even at this distance, his commanding presence is unmistakable—shoulders squared, movements economical, the absolute confidence that makes trained firefighters follow his lead without question.

"He's a good captain," I agree, deflecting Eleanor's obvious direction.

"He's a good husband." She doesn't let me dodge. "Amazing what a year of steady love will do for a man. And a woman." Her keen eyes study my face with the thoroughness of someone who's been watching people fall in love on these mountains for seven decades. "You're both different. Settled. Complete."

The observation is accurate. Mac has found his place in Angel's Peak with the same determination he brought to fighting fires—learning every trail, befriending every local, becoming not just a resident but an integral part of the community's fabric. Sheriff Donovan calls him for everything from search-and-rescue to traffic control during tourist season.

And me? I've expanded my work beyond simple cartography to comprehensive fire management planning, collaborating with state and federal agencies to develop protection strategies for mountain communities throughout Colorado. My maps now carry weight in policy decisions that affect thousands of acres and dozens of towns.

"Any regrets?" Eleanor asks, voice soft with genuine curiosity rather than nostalgia.

I consider the question while watching smoke rise in careful columns from the controlled burn. A year ago, I was a woman haunted by a single, tragic decision, afraid to take responsibility for anyone's safety. Now I guide fire management teams, coordinate emergency responses, and sleep soundly beside a man who faces danger as naturally as breathing.

"None." The answer comes without hesitation. "Not one."

My radio crackles with an update from the burn crew, and I respond with current wind readings from my position. The easy collaboration between Mac and me has become second nature—a professional partnership that complements our personal relationship without overshadowing it.

"Phase two complete." Mac's voice carries satisfaction through the static. *"All parameters within acceptable range. Proceeding to final containment."*

"Copy that. Observation post maintaining overwatch."

As the controlled burn enters its final phase, my hand drifts unconsciously to my still-flat stomach, where the early signs of pregnancy create a secret flutter of anticipation. I haven't told Mac—the test confirmed what I suspected only three days ago—but the knowledge sits warm and precious beneath my ribs.

Scout's head snaps toward me, nose twitching as she processes scents my human awareness can't detect. Her tail gives a tentative wag, and I swear there's knowing approval in her brown eyes. Dogs always know first.

"When will you tell him?" Eleanor asks quietly.

I blink in surprise. "Tell him what?"

Her smile holds the wisdom of decades spent reading people and situations with uncanny accuracy. "Child, I've delivered enough babies in this town to recognize the signs. Plus, Scout's been treating you like precious cargo for the past week."

I glance down at Scout, who's positioned herself slightly in front of me—a subtle but unmistakable protective stance she's adopted without conscious direction.

"Tonight." The admission feels right as soon as I speak it. "When he gets home."

"He'll be over the moon." Eleanor's confidence carries absolute certainty. "That man's been father material since the day he set foot in Angel's Peak. The way he handles emergencies with kids, coordinates with the school district on fire safety education—he's been practicing without realizing it."

The observation warms me. I've watched Mac with Danny's family during their return visits to Angel's Peak, seen him coordinate youth fire prevention programs, and noticed how naturally children gravitate toward his calm authority. He'll be an extraordinary father.

"All units, controlled burn complete." Mac's voice announces success. *"Beginning final suppression and monitoring protocols. Site will be monitored for forty-eight hours per standard procedure."*

"Copy that. Observation post returning to base."

Eleanor and I pack up our equipment while Scout conducts a final perimeter check, her nose working to confirm no threats remain in the area. The controlled burn site below shows perfect execution—targeted vegetation removal without any escape or uncontrolled spread.

The drive back to town takes us through the recovering landscape where last year's devastation is gradually giving way to new growth. Mac's fire management strategies have accelerated healing, and green shoots now push through ash-enriched soil in carefully planned patterns.

At the fire station, Mac's crew completes their post-operation debriefing with the efficiency of professionals who've worked together long enough to anticipate each other's needs. I watch through the bay doors as Mac reviews reports, signs documentation, and coordinates with his team for tomorrow's planned educational program at the elementary school.

When he finally emerges, uniform dusty but spirits high, his eyes find mine immediately across the parking lot. Even after eighteen months, that first moment of contact still sends electricity racing through my veins.

Scout bounds toward him with unleashed enthusiasm, her greeting ritual unchanged despite the passage of time. Mac crouches to accept her attention, one hand scratching behind her ears while his eyes remain locked on mine over her head.

"Successful burn?" I ask as he approaches.

"Textbook execution." He stops close enough that I can smell smoke and sweat and the familiar scent that's uniquely his. "Your wind readings were perfect. Made all the difference in containment timing."

The professional acknowledgment gives way to something more personal as his hand finds my waist, thumb brushing against my ribs in a touch that speaks of possession and familiarity.

"Hungry?" I ask, though food isn't really what I'm thinking about.

"Starving." The double meaning in his voice sends heat pooling low in my belly. "For several things."

The drive to our cabin—no longer just mine, but ours, expanded with a workshop where Mac builds furniture and a larger office where we both work on fire management planning—passes in comfortable conversation about the day's successes. Scout settles in the back seat with the contentment of a dog whose pack is complete and safe.

At home, Mac heads for the shower while I prepare dinner, my mind rehearsing how to share the news that will change everything. Scout positions herself where she can monitor both of us, her protective instincts heightened by whatever scents she's detecting.

When Mac emerges, hair damp and wearing the jeans and

flannel shirt that make him look more mountain man than fire captain, I'm standing at the kitchen counter with my back to him, summoning courage.

"Josephine." His voice carries a note of concern. "Everything alright?"

I turn, meeting his eyes across the space that's become our sanctuary. "Remember when you said you wanted all of me? Permanently?"

Something shifts in his expression—wariness mixed with hope. "I remember. Why?"

Instead of words, I pull the pregnancy test from behind my back, holding it where he can see the unmistakable positive result. "Because you're about to get more than you bargained for."

The silence stretches for three heartbeats while he processes what he's seeing. Then his face transforms—wonder, joy, and something deeper blazing in his eyes as he crosses the kitchen in two long strides.

His hands frame my face, thumbs brushing over my cheekbones as he stares down at me with an intensity that steals my breath. "Are you...? We're...?"

"Pregnant." The word comes out soft but certain. "About six weeks, I think."

His response is immediate and overwhelming—arms wrapping around me, lifting me off my feet as he spins us both in a circle, his laughter rich with pure joy. When he sets me down, his hands immediately move to my stomach, palms spread wide over the place where our child grows.

"A baby." His voice holds wonder, as if he's afraid speaking too loudly might make it disappear. "Our baby."

"Are you happy?" The question arises from old insecurities —the part of me that still sometimes fears being too much trouble, too much responsibility.

"Happy?" He looks at me like I've lost my mind. "Josephine, I'm..." He shakes his head, searching for words adequate to the moment. "I never dared hope for this much. You, this life, this town, and now..." His hand moves protectively over my stomach. "A family."

The kiss that follows is gentle, reverent, filled with promises for the future we're building together. When we break apart, his forehead rests against mine, breath mingling in the space between us.

"The baby will grow up on these mountains," I whisper, the realization filling me with fierce joy. "Learn the trails, understand the risks, respect the power."

"Like their mother." His voice roughens with emotion. "Strong, capable, absolutely fearless when it matters."

"And like their father." I trace the line of his jaw, feeling the slight tremor that runs through him at my touch. "Protective, determined, willing to run toward danger to keep people safe."

Scout approaches, pressing her nose gently against my stomach in a gesture so deliberate it can't be a coincidence. Her tail wags slowly, approval evident in every line of her body. She's already accepted her new role as guardian of the family's newest member.

"Think she knows?" Mac asks, one hand finding Scout's head while the other remains protectively over our growing child.

"She's known for days." I scratch behind Scout's ears, earning a contented sigh. "Dogs always know first."

We spend the evening on the porch, watching sunset paint the recovering mountains in shades of gold and rose. Mac's hand never leaves my stomach, as if maintaining physical contact with the miracle growing there. We talk about nurseries and names, about how to baby-proof a cabin surrounded by wilderness, about the kind of childhood we want to give this unexpected gift.

"The baby will have the best guide in Colorado," Mac murmurs against my temple as stars begin to appear in the darkening sky. "Learn the mountains from someone who knows every trail, every hazard, every hidden beauty."

"And the best protector." I lean into his warmth, feeling complete in ways I never imagined possible. "Someone who faces down wildfires without flinching."

As we sit together on the porch where this all began—where he first kissed me with desperate hunger, where he claimed me with such thorough possession—I think about the journey that brought us here. A collision on a sidewalk. Maps scattered like fallen leaves. A fire that nearly destroyed everything we love.

All of it leading to this moment. This man. This life. This promise of tomorrow growing beneath my heart.

In the distance, Scout's ears perk toward a sound only she can hear—probably wildlife moving through the recovering forest, or perhaps just the whisper of wind through new growth. She settles back down with a contented sigh, secure in the knowledge that her pack is safe, complete, and growing.

In Mac's arms, with his child growing beneath my heart and Scout keeping faithful watch, I finally understand what home really means. It's not a place—it's the people who choose to stay, to build something beautiful from whatever the mountains give them.

And sometimes, if you're very lucky, the mountains give you everything.

"I love you, Josephine Sullivan," Mac whispers against my ear, voice rough with emotion and promise.

"I love you too." I turn in his arms to meet his eyes—those impossible blue eyes that saw through every wall I built and claimed the woman hiding behind them. "Forever and always."

As if summoned by our words, a gentle breeze stirs the pines around our cabin, carrying the scent of new growth and endless possibility. The mountains sigh their approval, and Scout's tail thumps once against the porch boards.

Tomorrow will bring new challenges, new fires to fight, new trails to map. But tonight, surrounded by everything we've built together, we're exactly where we belong.

Home.

Catch up on the Angel's Peak Small Town Instalove Romance Series Featuring the TROPES you LOVE

🏔 FORCED PROXIMITY - STRANDED TOGETHER during mountain storms

🔥 Grumpy/Sunshine - Brooding ranger meets spirited photographer

💔 Wounded Hero - Haunted by tragic past, rebuilt by love

💘 Instalove - Instant attraction that deepens into forever love

🌲 Wilderness Romance - Passion ignites in pristine mountain setting

🎯 Opposites Attract - Nomadic adventurer vs. rooted protector

🐾 Alpha Hero - Dominant, protective, utterly devoted

🔥 Steamy Romance - Explosive chemistry and passionate encounters

💚 Found Family - Building home together in the wilderness

📷 Career vs Love - Choosing between dreams and destiny

🦅 Shared Purpose - Wildlife conservation brings them together

🏠 Home is Where the Heart Is - Finding belonging in unexpected places

Keep current with Ellie Masters.
CLICK HERE
Receive news of her writing and new releases.

Angel's Peak

PLEASE CONSIDER LEAVING A REVIEW

I HOPE YOU ENJOYED THIS BOOK AS MUCH AS I enjoyed writing it. If you like this book, please leave a review. I love reviews. I love reading your reviews, and they help other readers decide if this book is worth their time and money. I hope you think it is and decide to share this story with others. A sentence is all it takes. Thank you in advance!

Angel's Peak

ELLZ BELLZ

Ellie's Facebook Reader Group

If you are interested in joining the ELLZ BELLZ, Ellie's Facebook reader group, we'd love to have you.

Join Ellie's ELLZ BELLZ.
The ELLZ BELLZ Facebook Reader Group

Sign up for Ellie's Newsletter.
Elliemasters.com/newslettersignup

ALSO BY ELLIE MASTERS

The LIGHTER SIDE

Ellie Masters is the lighter side of the Jet & Ellie Masters writing duo! You will find Contemporary Romance, Military Romance, Romantic Suspense, Billionaire Romance, and Rock Star Romance in Ellie's Works.

YOU CAN FIND ELLIE'S BOOKS HERE:

ELLIEMASTERS.COM/BOOKS

Shop Ellie Masters Romantic Suspense and Steamy Contemporary Romance by series.

Angel Fire Rock Romance

Guardian HRS: Alpha Team

Guardian HRS: Bravo Team

Guardian HRS: Charlie Team

Guardian HRS: Delta Team

Cerberus Personal Security

The LaRouge Triplets

The One I Want Series

Angel's Peak Series

Billionaire Boy's Club

The Lovers

Changing Roles

SUGGESTED READING ORDER

START HERE

Rockstar Romance

The Angel Fire Rock Romance Series

EACH BOOK IN THIS SERIES CAN BE READ AS A STANDALONE AND IS ABOUT A DIFFERENT COUPLE WITH AN HEA.

IT IS RECOMMENDED THEY ARE READ IN ORDER.

Heart's Insanity

Ashes to New

Heart's Desire

Heart's Collide

Hearts Divided

Hearts Entwined

Forest's FALL

Hearts The Last Beat

CONTINUE HERE...

Military Romance

Guardian Hostage Rescue Specialists

Rescuing Melissa

(Get a FREE copy of Rescuing Melissa

when you join Ellie's Newsletter)

Alpha Team

Rescuing Zoe

Rescuing Moira

Rescuing Eve

Rescuing Lily

STANDALONES IN THE GUARDIAN HOSTAGE RESCUE SERIES YOU CAN READ ANYTIME

Military Romance

Guardian Personal Protection Specialists

Sybil's Protector

Lyra's Protector

Angel's Peak Series

Steamy Instalove Small Town

EACH BOOK IN THIS SERIES CAN BE READ AS A STANDALONE AND IS ABOUT A DIFFERENT COUPLE WITH AN HEA.

SNOWED IN WITH THE MOUNTAIN DOCTOR

Rescued by the Mountain Guide

Stranded with the Resort Owner

Matched with the Small-Town Chef

Trapped with the Forest Ranger

Snowbound with the Vineyard Owner

Reunited with the Hometown Hero

Colliding with the Coffee Shop Owner

Falling for the Firefighter

Wrecked with the Reclusive Author

Tangled with the Single Dad

Whirlwinded by the Helicopter Pilot

Sheltered by the Veterinarian

Bound by the Sheriff

The One I Want Series

(Small Town, Military Heroes)

By Jet & Ellie Masters

EACH BOOK IN THIS SERIES CAN BE READ AS A STANDALONE AND IS ABOUT A DIFFERENT COUPLE WITH AN HEA.

Saving Abby

Saving Ariel

Saving Brie

Saving Cate

Saving Dani

Saving Jen

The LaRouge Triplets

Asher

Brody

Cage

Billionaire Romance

Billionaire Boys Club

Hawke

Richard

Contemporary Romance

Cocky Captain

Romantic Suspense

EACH BOOK IS A STANDALONE NOVEL.

The Starling

The Swan

~AND~

Science Fiction

Ellie Masters writing as L.A. Warren

Vendel Rising: a Science Fiction Serialized Novel

If you enjoyed this book by Ellie Masters, the LIGHTER SIDE of the Jet & Ellie writing duo, and aren't afraid of edgier writing, you might enjoy reading BDSM themed books written by Jet, the DARKER SIDE of the Masters' Writing Team.

The DARKER SIDE

Jet Masters is the darker side of the Jet & Ellie writing duo!

Romantic Suspense

Changing Roles Series:

THIS SERIES MUST BE READ IN ORDER.

Command Me

Control Me

Collar Me

Embracing FATE

Seizing FATE

Accepting FATE

HOT READS

A STANDALONE NOVEL.

Down the Rabbit Hole

Light BDSM Romance

The Ties that Bind

EACH BOOK IN THIS SERIES CAN BE READ AS A STANDALONE AND IS ABOUT A DIFFERENT COUPLE WITH AN HEA.

Alexa

Penny

Michelle

Ivy

About the Author

Ellie Masters is a USA Today Bestselling author and Amazon Top 15 Author who writes Angsty, Steamy, Heart-Stopping, Pulse-Pounding, Can't-Stop-Reading Romantic Suspense. In addition, she's a wife, military mom, doctor, and retired Colonel. She writes romantic suspense filled with all your sexy, swoon-worthy alpha men. Her writing will tug at your heart-strings and leave your heart racing.

Born in the South, raised under the Hawaiian sun, Ellie has traveled the globe while in service to her country. The love of her life, her amazing husband, is her number one fan and biggest supporter. And yes! He's read every word she's written.

She has lived all over the United States—east, west, north, south and central—but grew up under the Hawaiian sun. She's also been privileged to have lived overseas, experiencing other cultures and making lifelong friends. Now, Ellie is proud to call herself a Southern transplant, learning to say y'all and "bless her heart" with the best of them.

Ellie's favorite way to spend an evening is curled up on a couch, laptop in place, watching a fire, drinking a good wine, and bringing forth all the characters from her mind to the page and hopefully into the hearts of her readers.

FOR MORE INFORMATION
elliemasters.com

facebook.com/elliemastersromance

x.com/Ellie__Masters

instagram.com/ellie_masters

bookbub.com/authors/ellie-masters

goodreads.com/Ellie_Masters

Connect with Ellie Masters

Website:
elliemasters.com
Purchase Direct:
elliemasters.com/shopify
Amazon Author Page:
elliemasters.com/amazon
Facebook:
elliemasters.com/Facebook
Goodreads:
elliemasters.com/Goodreads
Bookbub:
elliemasters.com/Bookbub
Instagram:
elliemasters.com/Instagram

Final Thoughts

I hope you enjoyed this book as much as I enjoyed writing it. If you enjoyed reading this story, please consider leaving a review on Amazon and Goodreads, and please let other people know. A sentence is all it takes. Friend recommendations are the strongest catalyst for readers' purchase decisions! And I'd love to be able to continue bringing the characters and stories from My-Mind-to-the-Page.

Second, call or e-mail a friend and tell them about this book. If you really want them to read it, gift it to them. If you prefer digital friends, please use the "Recommend" feature of Goodreads to spread the word.

Or visit my blog https://elliemasters.com, where you can find out more about my writing process and personal life.

Come visit The EDGE: Dark Discussions where we'll have a chance to talk about my works, their creation, and maybe what the future has in store for my writing.

Facebook Reader Group: Ellz Bellz

Thank you so much for your support!

Love,

Ellie

Dedication

This book is dedicated to you, my reader. Thank you for spending a few hours of your time with me. I wouldn't be able to write without you to cheer me on. Your wonderful words, your support, and your willingness to join me on this journey is a gift beyond measure.

Whether this is the first book of mine you've read, or if you've been with me since the very beginning, thank you for believing in me as I bring these characters 'from my mind to the page and into your hearts.'

Love,
Ellie

THE END